Also By Fred J Schneider

Last Stop Ronkonkoma

Best, [illegible] 2019

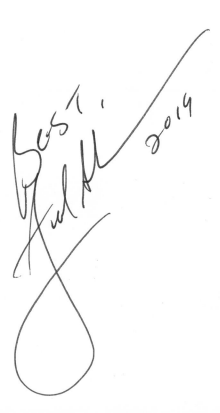

Pig In Flight

A novel of swine-size political ambition

Fred J Schneider

Glimmerglass Publishing Co

Pig in Flight is a work of historical fiction. Apart from the well-known actual people, events and locations that figure into the story, all names, characters, places, and incidents are the author's imagination, or are used fictitiously.

Pig In Flight

A novel of swine-size political ambition

ISBN: 978-1-7329518-0-8 (Hardcover)
ISBN: 978-1-7329518-1-5 (Paperback)

Glimmerglass Publishing, New York

This book is dedicated to pigs who would be President everywhere
And to those who make it possible

Chapter 1

Chicago's finest busied themselves like ants on a fallen Froot Loop, circling the park and snapping their protective face shields up and down as if they were outsized jaws. They probably didn't know it, but as they snapped, they reflected flashes from across the street where an order was trailing through the hippie revolution: "When the cops move, light your Molotov man, and watch your back: there's pigs among us sheep."

I took short breaths of the stifling August air and laughed at the battle unfolding: the Snapjaw clapping their visors with clubs to intimidate the hippies with polycarbonate percussion; the hippies responding by universally twisting their heads over their shoulders in a growing awareness of doom. The four lanes of Michigan Avenue separating the two armies released the day's dreadful heat in a wave of apparition, and I wondered if either side could be sure of what it saw through it. The street carts (Italian beef, snow cones – steaming but deserted) cowered against fire hydrants, their drooping chains and dangling locks offering but another illusion. Cops leaned on them, slammed radios on them, barked orders from them, stole some beef from them. They were there to crush the hippies, and me too if I wasn't careful.

Down Michigan, a crowd of swells gathered behind the hasty barricades, shopping bags in tow. *This*, I imagined them thinking as they pointed at the hippies, *should shut them up for a while.*

At the end of a row of swirling lights, a hiss rose from truck-sized amplifiers: "THE PARK… WILL BE CLEARED… IN THREE MINUTES… BY ANY MEANS NECESSARY!"

The Snapjaw had been doing this obnoxious public service announcement every minute on the minute from thirty and, I might add, doing it with growing condescension, annoying me because nothing really happened afterward. It was like the bell constantly going off in the ring but the fighters never leaving their stools. It was boring. But this time Snapjaw leaned and the hippies flinched, huddling against the wind to strike their matches, puffing a small sulfuric cloud into the searing air that I caught on inhale and cleared with a desiccated sneeze. It burned.

A fumbled bottle rolled between hippie feet. It spun a lit rag and exploded in a six-foot ball of fire, igniting a bush and sending the crackling hippies scattering like fragged NCOs. A singular war cry arose, and one hippie ran right through the burning bush, combusted, and tumbled on the ground to snuff out. That he knew enough to stop, drop and roll, but not enough to avoid the flames from the get-go wasn't lost on me, and I laughed. So did the swells behind the barricade, agreeing that it wouldn't be long before these breaks in primary logic snuffed out their revolution too.

Nonetheless, the Snapjaw seethed at the sight of flame, chafed against commands, but held. Not me: I spun for a clear path of exit, but there was none. In fact, wherever Snapjaw didn't block the way, the growing cabal of hippies did. Their count was growing despite the ring of Snapjaw, and I wondered if on the far side of the park, hippies weren't being allowed under the ropes just so they would catch themselves in Snapjaw glue, a sort of giant roach motel.

I leaped over the smoldering hippie, aiming for two others alone on the lawn. They jumped on benches to survey the battleground. They cast long parenthetical shadows, like their thoughts could only be completed between them. One squinted through the red and blue strobes reflecting off Snapjaw face shields and declared, "Look! Its eyes are bleeding Amerika!" Then said to no one, "Hold your cocktails until you see the Amerika in its eyes!"

Abbie Hoffman, chief spitball thrower of the '68 anti-war movement, and yin to a more conflagrate yang, jumped from the bench, snagging fingers in bouncy black hair that sprung down past his prominent nose when he hit the ground. As he approached me, his dark eyes darted and his nostrils twitched, like a horse just led into an unlit trailer. He wore cuffed gray corduroy pants with a square torn from the right knee, had bakery string twisted in many laps around one wrist, and wore a randomly punctuated t-shirt that read, "Abandon the. creeping meatball,"! Quotation marks included.

"Corman!" he spit, Boston accent hardening over the amplifiers. "What the hell are you doing up here, man? Where's Pigasus?"

"Relax," I said, sliding a bit upwind, "Sal's watching him."

The yang hit the ground next. Jerry Rubin was thin and, despite being shirtless, wore a colorful vest of many mismatched patches, one of which I deduced may have been cut from the knee of Hoffman's pants. He hardened his face into a scowl borrowed from a Che' poster, which creased the long scar on his cheek. He had not shaved for the event, nor best as I could tell, bathed either. A beaded leather cord, the kind made by enslaved camp kids each summer, pinched his frizz of hair to his forehead. Below it, eyes flamed and his nostrils flared like a horse's too, only one of the apocalypse. As he approached, his shadow grew, swallowing Hoffman's and mine in succession. He held an open palm thumb-up beneath Hoffman's chin and threw a hard fist into it. Hoffman flinched and felt stupid again.

"Goddamnit, Abbie," Rubin said as if they'd also had this conversation before. "The question's not: who's watching *Pigasus*! The question's: who's watching that guy Sal? I don't trust him. I'm getting a vibe."

A hiss rose again from the amplifiers. "THE PARK... WILL BE CLEARED... IN TWO MINUTES... BY ANY MEANS NECESSARY!"

Snapjaw cheated forward, ominous in silhouette. Hippies stampeded for cover. Out of sight, a girl screamed, then screamed again. As if coming to her rescue, helicopters appeared from the east over the roofs of low buildings, snipers dangling from their doors, red runner-lights on full glow, ready to strafe. The wind from the lake met the wind from those birds in an ear-splitting vortex that shredded swirling papers, stripped leaves, and lifted Rubin's vest, forcing him to pin it in place with his skinny elbows and to talk with funny hands.

So *this* is what "make love not war" looks like, I thought, here, in this park at the '68 Democratic Convention, just a bottle's throw from the Miracle Mile, on the eve of Nixon, in the wake of Johnson. With Rubin, Hoffman, the Yippies, the sheep, the poets, the dharma bums, the peaceniks, the pundits, the Panthers, the cops; the rumors, the threats, the mandate, *all* prone to a single spark. How I might have wished for a Zippo right then, if I believed in wishes.

"Go!" Rubin yelled over the copters, pushing me toward my post. But Hoffman snagged my arm and led me a few steps away, which made no sense because he had to scream over the copters anyway, and Rubin was right over there.

"Jerry's just a little freaked out right now," he said. "Look, Sal won't betray us. He's a little burned up, maybe. I mean, the machine got him, man. But Yippie still beats in his heart. Be his keeper, Corman. Be thy Yippie's keeper!" Hoffman paused to rub my shoulders, which I didn't like, then leaned in to make his point. "But listen… it's Pigasus first. We've got no show without the pig."

"Look," I said to both. "I don't know what you're planning with that pig, but you do know it shits everywhere, right?"

Rubin stepped close. "If you've got issues with our swine, shoot it."

"No!" Hoffman said.

"Well it sure sounds like Corman here's got issues with our pig."

"Only because when it's not shitting everywhere, it's eating it," I qualified. "And it breathes on me. And a man can only take so much stench in a day." I stepped back. "There's nothing pigs won't eat. Nothing they won't breathe back on you. I've seen it. I've smelled it. Nothing."

"Then shoot the fucking thing," Rubin growled, his voice suddenly loud as the copters pulled back. "Shoot it!"

"No!" Hoffman said. "We're not shooting it, Jerry! Corman, Corman, we're gonna run that pig for President! Pigasus for President, man!"

Rubin threw his hands at the swirling lights, then up at where the copters had been. "Can't you see it's not about games anymore, Abbie? It's about them!" He shot his chin at the Snapjaw, their face shields all lowered, black clubs all tapping. The space between their shoulders had closed, and they swayed as a colony. Rubin paced and calculated. "Oh no. This ain't our *Festival of Life* anymore!" he yelled. "It's our Tet! Yes," his voice turned jubilant, "Our very own Tet! We are about to engage the full force of the enemy, Abbie! Imagine the papers tomorrow! Above the fold!"

"THE PARK… WILL… BE… CLEARED… … IN ONE MINUTE… BY *ANY* MEANS NECESSARY!"

Hoffman stood at Rubin's side and turned his attention fully toward the Snapjaw. "If it must be war," Abbie Hoffman declared, slowly raising a fist in the air for effect, "Then I must be… Sun Tzu, the great and ancient *philosopher* of war!" He punched the sky three, four, five times. “Yes, we will honor the revolutionaries before us! We will let them show us the path to victory! We will stand on the shoulders of giants! We will embrace the tactics of Sun Tzu!” he howled to the winds. “And pretend inferiority!”

Rubin punched the sky too, but only once and only because he wished Sun Tzu were his idea. When I cleared my expression to a mere smirk, Rubin moved to put his finger in my chest, like maybe he was getting a vibe about me too, but then a tail of smoke suddenly arched over the street.

Pop.

The ground misted. Snapjaw advanced.

“They’re driving the whole machine down our throats at once,” Rubin moaned. “Get our marshals together,” he ordered Hoffman. “And you, Corman, get back to watching that pigman.” He leaped back on the bench, ducking as the helicopters returned from the east. He was the highest thing in a copter storm and he knew it, but the birds only hovered low enough to pin the tear gas in place, way shy of his head.

The gas engulfed me, my throat swelling just before my eyes stung. The backs of my hands burned, and then behind my ears where sweat coursed. Chlorine. Habanero. Napalm. Rubin fell into a coughing fit and folded off the bench, getting as flat on the ground as his vest of many patches would allow. Hoffman twirled in place, his arms stretched out like the copter blades themselves. “Don’t rub it!” he said as he spun. “It sets it in deeper. Just let the wind take it away! Twirl with me, Corman!”

I did not.

As the cloud seized the park, the revolutionaries barraged it with rocks and bottles, throwing as they ran. A doped-up kid appeared from the fog dancing wildly and playing a one-handed bongo until a Snapjaw club to the head put him down. Everywhere women held each other up, covering their ears. Everywhere, men held each other down, covering their heads.

"Run, Corman!" Hoffman shouted.

Run where? Snapjaw rumbled all around me, wielding clubs like arcade flippers to the light show of flashbulbs sparking from a hundred cameras. The park was now the Snapjaw's human pinball machine, hippies rolling this way and that, pinging off bumper-horses, tumbling through gauntlets, accelerating through shoots until well-timed club-flippers cut them off, sending them back to the bumper-horses that kicked them through the gauntlets and the shoots once again.

Finding some breath, Rubin turned his head on the ground. His expression froze then cracked. "Look!" he squeaked, motioning at a TV camera aimed his way. "The whole world is watching me! The whole fucking world is watching!" He rolled onto his back and beat his chest.

Hoffman took his lead. "Sun Tzu!" he screamed to the lenses, dropping his t-shirt to reveal his face.

"Go!" Rubin ordered, now on his knees.

When smoke rolled over the camera, I pinned my sleeve across my nose and accelerated into the rumble. From the mist, gleeful Snapjaw appeared on horseback pushing the hippies into my path. I threw a stiff-arm and sprawled into a new wave of gas that hid me long enough to scramble to the edge of a steep trench where train tracks skirted the park. To my right, a column of Snapjaw advanced. To my left, Rubin's eyes burned through the fog. Below me, a train rumbled away. I slid down to the rails where bottles shattered, sirens echoed, screams faded, and the gas above sealed out all but a faint light.

All I could see through the fire in my eyes were light shadows, but I felt the creosote railroad ties stick beneath my feet and stumbled my way one to the next until Sal grabbed my shirt and pulled me inside the large culvert that would be our foxhole until word came for him and the pig to move out. He tipped jug water on my eyes, cooling for a moment the embers there. I took the jug away, gargling and spitting the sting from my throat before bathing my eyes again. My sense of smell returned before sight, and I realized that I'd simply traded the cop's caustic gas for the pungency of the pig's. As I finally blinked some focus back, I found Sal a few feet away clutching an artist's sketchpad to his chest. Next to him, the pig basked in the ammonium of its own shit.

"What is happening up there, Corman?"

"Well, Sal, our friends are pretending inferiority."

Sal feigned understanding and ran a thumb across his face, leaving a stripe of gray through the bloom of acne that beached on his forehead. A spotty and unruly beard tangled on his face, questioning the integrity of the closely cropped, Fort Dix-style hair on his head: square at the neck, square at the ear, square at the top. This was not his only contradiction; these were bountiful. Breaded in a week of road grime, his filthy outgrown jeans hovered well above of his rolled down, lint-filled black socks, yet his shoes shone, and each night he worked incessantly to keep them that way, snapping a rag through well-positioned spit over and over and over again, as a bonus annoyance for me.

We made for one ugly platoon, I concluded, raking my chewed fingernails through the red splotches of my own beard. I dragged them up toward my cooling ears where the beard gave way to my 'fro, a 'fro that was getting too lively for its own good, beginning to move in its own direction even. Blue eyes, red hair, white skin, I was a living flag. A living recruitment poster! An *objet de cause*!

Objet de' cause? Who did I think I was? Who did this kid from monotone Delaware, fucking Ohio think he was?

Sal could not have cared less. "Where are the President's Yodels, Corman?" he snapped as I put the jug down.

"There's a wall of cops up there. The pig'll have to wait."

"Wait? The President is tired. He has requested Yodels, and I gave my word we could count on you. Need I remind you, he is about to assume the position of Commander in Chief?"

As he waited for a response I had no inclination to give, Sal stroked the pig to a snorting sleep, avoiding a hideous birthmark on its right haunch that seemed to throb and glow like the refinery skyline of New Jersey. I turned away, as I always did, but came back to notice things about the pig for the first time.

Ohio or not, I'm no judge of these things, but the pig did not appear destined for blue ribbons, let alone the presidency. Its skin was not pink like a pig's should be, but a mutant orange, like something born of kissing cousins. Curling from the top of its ass wasn't a tail exactly, but a thin wave of hair that flipped awkwardly in any breeze or flatulence. And the pig was not massive the way blue ribbon winners traditionally are, not yet anyway, though its penchant for crappy food, together with the daily consumption of its own spew, clearly had it heading that way.

And yet somehow the pig didn't stop being revolting there. A grotesque congress of flies jostled in its continuous stream of snot, suckling from it, rocking in it, dipping their big-eyed heads into it as if it were the guardian River Jordan or a molten Rosetta Stone. The flies never left. In fact, as flies are apt to do, their numbers doubled each day to drink of the snot and approach its wisdom.

And was the pig a threat? I would not trust it, but there was no jungle in *this* boar; this was a pig for the avenues that, when it bothered to stand, carried itself with an exaggerated and unwarranted swagger. I laughed at the image of it, but if they made top hats for pigs, this pig would have worn one and dipped it over one eye. True, I may have dismissed it as pig *or* President, but there was no mistaking its ambitions.

And yet I hated the pig for more than all that. I hated it for its sins of affiliation. I'd seen firsthand what pigs could do. Firsthand.

And so it wasn't long before I found myself doing math in my head estimating the pig's customary slaughter date. I just didn't realize right away how prescient that was.

As if hearing my very thought, the pig snorted and rose to its feet, just as the last hints of daylight abandoned the trench.

"The president cannot sleep. He is too hungry," Sal whined. "He's slumping his head now, Corman, and that makes him look weak. And he can't really get elected if his head slumps, can he? Americans hate a slumping head. We must lift his head. And for that we need Yodels!"

Sal shined a flashlight on his face, highlighting both his anguish and a dull spot in his eyes, a spot I'd seen in men before, a spot that confirmed Sal, like me. had been in-country, 'Nam, fought the fight.

Above us now the battle churned, rolling a wave of glowing cinders into the trench. I slid deeper into the culvert, expecting Sal to do the same, but the battle noise jigged him forward, sketchpad in hand, until he staggered onto the tracks. The pig followed, but at a speed suggesting it absolutely would rather not. So when a flare lit the trench in blinding red, blowing Sal backward on the bank, setting him scrambling to slide the sketchpad behind him the way villagers shield children, the pig was understandably pissed.

What was in that pad, I wondered, for Sal to shield it that way, for his first impulse to be its protection? Just that morning, I'd awoken at dawn to the annoying scratching of his pencil on paper, woke to his hissing and harrumphing, woke to the all-too-frequent grating of the pencil against the pitted metal of the culvert to free some lead. I watched him work, rubbing the page as if rubbing that dull spot from his own real eyes, scrubbing, ripping, revising, harrumphing, hissing, and, finally, *finally*, quitting as I stirred.

When a second flare ignited, the pig hollered and bucked. I made my way to the tracks to shut it up and pull Sal back into the culvert, but he shook me off just as the sky spat glass. A bottle shattered at the feet of the pig, launching shrapnel and sending the pig into a fateful cry that rang along the rails until it tuned down the tracks into something familiar. I fell back. And the ground softened beneath me.

"The president has been shot!" Sal screamed, trembling with his flashlight. The pig jounced its head as blood coursed from its ear. The flies smelled it and left the stream of knowledge to cover the blood like a buzzing scab, making the pig more hideous than ever. I turned away, but Sal stopped me, crying.

"Corman!"

No.

"Corman! Now is the time for all good men to come to the aid of their country, Corman!"

"What?"

"The president's been shot! Help him!"

The noise of the two of them was too damn much. I groped in the dark for quiet, but found only mud. I held out a handful, saying nothing, expecting Sal to slap it away. But instead he pulled my hand and the mud to the pig's ear. I felt the flies take wing to settle again on the snot. Sal pressed my hand and the mud on the wound, but the pig would not suffer it. Wrestling free, it ran its head against the corrugated steel of the culvert, sounding like a stick against a picket fence, scraping the mud clear. Sal scrambled to collect more but stopped, eyes wide, spooked. "Look," he gasped, steadying the flashlight. "You healed it!"

"The mud's just clogged the blood, that's all. Now get it quiet!"

"No, Corman," Sal said, "his wound; it's gone! You healed the President!"

"It's a pig, Sal. And I've never healed anything."

Chapter 2

Sal would not let it go, staring at me through the flashlight as he might a schoolgirl from Fatima, even as he stroked the pig's dirt-caked ear, even as he flicked the muddy facts from his fingers. "You healed it," he mumbled.

How strange for me to be called a healer, and how equally unwelcome. If I'd wanted to carry the weight of expectations, I would have done it without the pig. I'm not sure where it's written, but it is; you cannot reenter the world as a healer after a full tour in country. Well, you can, only...

Down the tracks, a scream moved away. But another scream, closer, plunged us further into the culvert, dragging a frantic pig. "I took an oath, Corman. And now is the time for all good men to come to the aid of their country."

"That's not an oath."

"We pledged it."

"It's not an oath."

A beam swept the tracks in front of us. Sal looked to me and we pushed to the rear culvert opening, ready to make a break for it, but a second beam caught us from behind, shining first on Sal, then the pig.

"What the hell is that? And what's that smell?" a rear Snapjaw sneered, drawing his gun. "Shit, it's a pig! And hippies!"

"Yeah, but which one is the pig?" a front Snapjaw wheezed, doubling over at the waist "Out of there! All of you!" he managed. "And keep your hands and hooves where I can see them! Now!"

I held. It seemed the smarter move, but Sal stepped mechanically toward the front light, empty hand raised, the other clutching the sketchpad to his chest. When he turned back to call the pig, a rear Snapjaw leveled his gun.

"Get that other hand up!" He spit stringy phlegm. It dangled from his lip and he snapped it off with a twist of his gun barrel. Brave, but not too bright. But isn't that always the way?

"Geneva," Sal said.

"Get it up, or I'll shoot!"

"Geneva!" Sal raised the pad. But the Snapjaw were prancing now, like they had worries of their own.

"Drop it!" one said.

"The Convention!" Sal called.

"Last time, freak! I said drop it!"

I moved as Sal got drilled to the tracks. I don't fully recall which direction, but when the gun cocked behind me, it didn't matter.

"No!" Sal cried into the mud, pulling at the sketchpad buried by a grinding boot, letting go only when the other boot collided with his ribs.

"Hey look, he puffs smoke when you kick him. Watch this!" Sal groaned and folded around his wound as the sketchpad slipped away. The pig circled his convulsive body before fleeing like a dodger down the tracks, its swarm of dependent flies in pursuit. There is no conduct unbecoming *this* Commander in Chief, I thought.

"Cor-man," Sal managed. "Get the Pres-i-dent!"

The Snapjaw's face lit. Sal's fingers twitched in the dirt.

"Get the *President*? Get the fucking *President*?" the cop laughed, beating Sal even as he went cold, even as the sketchpad swelled in a crimson puddle, even as I stepped forward and identified myself.

Here I was, just a few days in, this kid from monotone Columbus, Ohio loathing both sides and breaking the clearest rule of my contract, which was to *stay* undercover. I told them I wasn't ready. Perfect, they said.

"Informant, huh?" a front Snapjaw said, sucking more air and wiping the sweat from his face with a fat hand sporting two rings. "Show me your shield."

"We don't get shields," I chided, brushing past him to turn Sal's face out of the muck.

"So you got no shield? No identification?"

I stepped close. "I told you, I'm…"

His double-ringed fist drove my lips back through the gaps in my teeth, and when I splashed beside Sal the sand beneath me oozed. The rings followed me down.

"You're what? A Fed? – Uh huh."

The rings hit like ordinance.

"Co-what? Never heard of it, hippie Fed."

My night folded in, silent but for the fading splash of soles and a distant groan from Sal.

***

I awoke to the annoyance of sirens blaring. Sal, the sketchpad, and the pig were gone. Around me, footprints stamped the mud as if a platoon had marched through while I was out, leaving me for dead. I pulled myself up, thoughts rattling like a bag of recovered bones: Sal, Rubin, Hoffman, my cover. Shit, my cover. What did I say? What did Sal hear, that I wasn't fucking Yippie? That I wasn't there to protect the pig?

And how much did I spill to stop the fists? That the Fed planted me as an informant for COINTELPRO, its secret unit charged with snuffing the anti-war protests? Jesus, had I become the pussy on the playground?

I told them I wasn't ready.

Perfect, they said.

Hunched in the bloody mud, tuning my alibi, I was little prepared for the mass of sheep stampeding down the tracks, sucking me to my feet, pushing me, elbows and heads bouncing, all of us squeezing through a narrow gully cut by a recent storm. Hippies fell where the ground ramped steeply, one or two bouncing beneath my feet like thin planks. I was walking the hippie plank!

I stumbled and fell near an 'el' where a dozen Snapjaw and TV cameras held ground while hippies took their beating. A girl, a woman, sat down on the street, legs folded, hands in her lap, eyes blank and locked like a doused monk poised with a match. "The whole world is watching!" she chanted. And the Snapjaw came, shields down, clubs up. She fell there, in place. Most of the hippies covered their heads with their arms and fled up the hill with awkward balance to the presumed shelter of darkness. But the remaining fifty seized a Snapjaw by his chin strap—maybe the one who swung, maybe not—and dragged him, mob-like, to the open-air vestibule of an apartment building. The lights there flickered, projecting the bludgeoning as if every other frame of the film were missing. Second-flank Snapjaw fired guns in the air, but who could hear over the screams bouncing among the brick facades? A hippie cheer rose and the helmet appeared, severed, aloft, like the head of Lord Hastings. A first-flank Snapjaw swung at the air wildly and blindly. Moths took to the streetlamps. Cars with swirling lights slid around the corner, tires smoking. The remaining hippies scrambled uphill to the dark before launching the helmet back into the yellow light. It tumbled downhill like a fake leg. A medic attended to the beaten one. Snapjaw spread out, and all grew quiet.

In that yellow light, I held once again. It was an acquired instinct, if there is such a thing. Maybe I was still drunk from my own beating, or Sal's, or hers, or the Snapjaw's; I didn't know. Still, the ground softened and I fell to my knees.

But I was the weak now, separated from the herd. TV cameras were trained on me. I felt eyes: cop eyes, Rubin's eyes, TV eyes, eyes from behind shades, eyes from an Italian ice vendor, eyes from a pimp, all lining the street… all pinned on me and assessing my allegiance. But allegiance to what? To what was I allegiant? To the Bureau that shiv-ed me into this deal? To Sal, who wanted to make me some kind of pig healer? To Rubin? To Sun Tzu? To the Snapjaw because of the hippies? To the hippies because of the Snapjaw? How the hell did I end up here, on my knees, asking reflective questions? I hated to kneel, and I hated to reflect.

And the Snapjaw hated me. They circled. Cameras whirred. I sprung.

***

In the metallic blackness and rank of the riot truck, I sifted through odors and moans for Sal.

I didn't find him at lock-up either, not in the cells lining the thick-painted hall and not in the cuffed human chain clogging the vestibule of which I was a link, a link needing air. The body odors and the endless chatter… Jesus Christ, shut the fuck up! I needed out, I needed air. I needed out like I needed air. I locked on every passing cop, signaling, darting my eyes to where a badge gets pinned, scratching and tapping my chest, gritting the consonants in *informant,* "n…f…m…n…t."

I needed out. I needed air. What was my next move? Get a car. How? Wander streets peeping into windshields until I find one with the keys in it? With a tank full of gas? Maybe a nice piney air freshener?

With a map that says with a few big red arrows, "You are here, you need to get there?" Jesus.

Do I even get out? After the deal I cut with the Fed, do I ever? How could a guy from Columbus who knew so little, somehow know too much? I knew. I dropped my head to my chest to remember my Fed briefing of a week before, where I learned all the rumored Yippie plots.

1. NYPD reports the Yippies are traveling with a pig and publicly pledging to flow LSD through Chicago's water supply, turning on the entire city in a giant acid trip. (This was everyone's favorite call to action; their best chance at being heroes. There were high-fives of solidarity.)

2. Acting on another rumor, the munitions experts at the Bureau confirm that a rigged pig could deliver an explosive large enough to take out the convention hall or, worse, disembowel enough Southern delegates to hand the presidency to McCarthy. (There was nodding of many heads, as if to say, "We can absolutely see that happening.")

3. Chicago PD was chasing reports that a wired pig – also rumored to be greased – will be released by the Yippies to breach security and deliver an explosive to take out Mayor Richard Daley. (Someone joked, pointing at me, "You've got this one, rookie." Everyone shared an unbecoming chortle.)

On the call at the time, Daley scoffed at the notion of being killed, let alone by a pig but, Herod-like, proposed the slaughter of every swine in the city, just to be proactive. But to Daley's great annoyance, the Bureau pulled rank. There would be no preemptive extermination, they ordered. A live pig with a live plot was the best chance to achieve the mission: get Rubin and Hoffman for life. That's what everyone wanted, Rubin and Hoffman taken out forever, and with them their insipid anti-war campaign. But no martyrs, goddamnit… goddamnit! Taken alive but taken out forever, not a year, not a decade… forever; that, everyone wanted, everyone said.

What I wanted, sitting on that precinct linoleum, cuffed to pungent sheep on either side, was not to be touched, not to have my hand yanked each time they swiped hair from their mouths or crust from their eyes. And I wanted earplugs. I had to get out, and I would have killed them all just to pay my way. "Shut the fuck up!" I screamed.

Locking eyes with a fresh cop (a rookie, by the crease in his pants) I scratched furiously at my phantom badge. He stopped, kneeled, and cocked his head. I scratched again while furiously blinking a code for "undercover" that I made up as I went. But just as I thought he was decyphering, the barging in of indignant suit guys spun him away. The suits slid behind opaque glass, leaving a wet trail like snails.

"If it's Dellinger, we'll be out of here soon," someone said. "He's all about the peace."

A voluminous enthusiasm grew among the sheep that it was indeed Dellinger, one of the anti-war leaders come to set them free. Someone started singing a folk song. A few others joined.

"Stop! It's not Dellinger!" I screamed. "Do any of them even look like Dellinger?" I didn't now what Dellinger looked like, but it turned out neither did they, and they grew sullen and quiet, and that's what really mattered.

The rookie cop took notice of my leadership. He nodded before moving down the line aiming his finger at each individual sheep. "I'd give you, and you, and you, and each and every filthy one of you a dime from my very own pocket to call your daddy for bail if I thought for one second I could flush you out of my city that way. But you're not exactly the kind parents pay a ransom for, now are you?"

He had a solid argument, and I shot a supportive snort. Cops heard it and nodded. They were beginning to realize: I was just an ugly dolphin trapped in a tuna net.

In a few minutes, the door with opaque glass flew open. Suits stomped out, and the creased cop knelt to face me again. "Now, where were we?" he asked, scratching his badge. "You were saying something to me. What was it?" He scratched his badge again.

"Dolphin," I said, confident we understood each other. But when two more uniforms swaggered to his side and escorted me behind the privacy of the opaque glass, they didn't release me gently overboard so much as threw me face first down a flight of stairs.

***

I tripped onto an empty street where I could not clear my nostrils nor stay my own voices quickly enough. But, stair plummet or not, I was thankful the cops released me for good behavior, and *not* because I was trying to tell them I was an informant. The latter would have required they debrief me. And what could I tell them, that I was the worst in my field? That the Bureau was a lousy judge of talent? That I sucked at gathering information, which – as an informant – is pretty fatal? That it wasn't my fault no one ever taught me how to ask probing questions, or that no one taught me culvert psychology? That they just plucked me out of the court-martial queue like they were casting for "The Dirty Dozen" and put me on the front line here, even when I told them I wasn't ready?

They'd ask about Sal, but what did I know? Last name? No. Middle name? No. Hometown? No. All I knew was he thought his high-school typing exercise was a fucking oath. And, oh yeah, he actually believed the pig would be president, and that he had been chosen to protect it, Secret Service-style. I could only imagine the beatings those tidbits would have earned me.

I told the redeemers I wasn't ready.

"Perfect," they said.

You'd say that too, Lieut, remember? Please god, you said, please Pentagon, please send me more fucking new guys like this, more babies like this who cry they're not ready to step into the fight, because I'd rather spend my days over here throwing these schoolyard pussies into the pool than winning this fucking war anyway!

Perfect.

Chapter 3

I stumbled on a dark sidewalk, where nearby the sounds of night turned a corner and slashed through an unseen puddle. High above windows slammed in contempt of air conditioner buzz. I brushed at my sweat and the gnats drawn to the salt. Beneath my feet, the ground softened again.

It would have been a good time to pause, to rewind my way back through the jungle with its whistling odds to its recruitment of sinners like me for the fight back home. But I wasn't sure I could stop in time before rewinding all the way to the slate-flat plains of central Ohio, where buckeyes littered the street, football nuts every place else, and where I ran those hashmarked fields to seek the love, if not the breasts, of a certain cheerleader with a smoky voice and auburn hair.

But this is how things go: with my crimson 'fro and matching freckles, we were, she declared, "Just too red together." So I took the deal with my Uncle Sam, who got me the hell out. What's an *objet de cause* to do, anyway?

So I didn't rewind anything, and it was just as well. As the ground firmed, so did my thoughts. I needed to restore my cover. I needed to find Sal. I did some math in my head. Even busted up as he was, if he found the pig, he'd be out looking for its food.

***

"Huh?" the doped-up night clerk coughed, stuffing fingers into a penny roll like it was a Chinese finger trap.

"Yodels," I repeated, "little cakes, chocolate-covered, something like cream in the middle?"

"HoHos?"

"No. Yodels."

"Sounds just like HoHos, man."

"Okay. Jesus, HoHos. Got any?"

"Nah. But we got pink marshmallow balls on that rack."

"Anyone else in here tonight asking for Yodels, maybe with a pig?" I headed him off with a raised palm. "Yeah, a real pig?"

"You mean like *oink, oink* real?"

"Oink."

"A real pig... with a jones... for Yodels?" he giggled. "Not yet, man, but the night's young!" He called to my back, "Anything can happen on a night like this!"

Empty-handed (even shit-eating pigs refuse those marshmallow things) I wandered the echoing streets pinging from newsstand to bodega (Mexican!). Chicago brimmed with stoned-out night clerks rolling and smoking their minimum wage, poised for a draft notice, one eye cast toward the Canadian side of the big big lake and its offer of refuge for the objectors.

"See a guy in here tonight looking for Yodels?" I asked a few blocks away.

"No," he said, pointing at the wound on my head. "But did you see the cop truck with the barbed-wire wings? It was like Dobermans coming at you. *Huge* wings of barbed wire! Did you see it? It was like that German wall, man, on wheels; like the seven signs of Armageddon. No, no Yodels. No, no pig."

I crossed against the light.

"Looking for a guy might of come in here asking for Yodels?" I asked another.

The clerk closed one eye as if drawing a conclusion.

"Canada, man."

"Huh?"

"McCarthy's finished, man, the war will rage. I've got to get north, got to make it across the lake, across the border." He gestured north with a rolling flourish of his hand, down Adams towards Lake Michigan.

"That's a long swim," I acknowledged. "But you should try it."

"Yeah, maybe, man, maybe. The border's pretty tight now. But they say there're still trails if you're willing to go the hard way. Just follow the dipping gourd, you know."

He laughed awkwardly and cracked his fingers.

"Four days. That's all I got left. On five they come looking for me. But, okay, I think, there's trails I heard, trails from Georgia to Maine. You hide in the woods the whole way. Nothing but woods filled with snakes, and bears and wild pigs—you know, boars with tusks!"

"Yeah, I know bores."

"Appalachian Trail, man, the AT! I heard fifty a day are crossing on it. Doesn't really end in Canada, but real close. Fifty a day and I bet another ten thousand more are on their way now that McCarthy's finished. Say, you're not heading that way, are you?"

"Not likely. Anyplace around here have Yodels?"

"Let me think." He tilted his head like he was really trying. But in the end he was captured by a flickering florescent light, and it was all he could do to resume droning on about how the vote was supposed to end the draft, stop the war, bring boys home, heal the wounds, plant a seed, grow a beard, milk the cow, flip a coin, bang a drum, bang a blond, make it snow, and every other three-word cliché he could summon.

"Yodels," I reminded him.

He put his face back to the light and came back with something about how weird Thanksgiving would be when he was in Toronto because, "Canada never even had Indians, man."

"Yo-dels!"

"Let me think."

"Jesus. Never mind!"

"Remember," he called to me, "If you need it, the AT is the trail that sets you free! We've got to help each other."

"Yeah," I mumbled from the street, "that's not likely either."

***

As if a switch were thrown, the voltage of the night now spun squad car lights on every corner. Sidewalks emptied. Shops killed their neon and rolled their metal grills down. Sal could never nudge a pig through these streets, I thought. No. A guy would need a hole to stuff a pig in on a night like this. I went back to the park to get back to the culvert, but a dozen cops, heavy in armor, squeaking like drawbridges, paced the entry gate. One blew a smoke ring and with a pronouncement to his buddies, thrust his finger into its hole. "See? Everything gets fucked," he declared to their amusement.

I could never bust such an un-oiled blockade, I thought, and neither could Sal, not to get out, not to get in. If he were in, he'd have to stay for now. If he were out, well, I could have debated where to look for him next, but I had to move on. What was left of my cover was a fragile thing. Hoffman and Rubin must be wondering where I was, my absence screaming suspicion. Sal and the pig would have to wait. I needed to get back in Rubin and Hoffman's sight.

***

With an objectivity modeled on Pravda, *The Chicago Seed*, a radical two-page tabloid with a single-digit circulation, slathered its print space with smudged hyperbole and globby black fists. Its office smelled like darkroom chemicals, pot, and the affronting piquancy of hippies huddled together.

Bruised, swelled and winded, I crossed the congested production floor, appearing more leprous than most, despite their many heads wrapped in gauze. The room clanked with the manual cranking of a mimeograph machines. Hoffman stood beside one, staring at my head.

"Nice dent, Corman. Pigs do that?" He scanned the room. "Where's Sal? Is he here? Pigasus?"

"Cops were out of control, beat us pretty bad," I said, restoring my cover and rubbing my dent. "But when I came to, Sal and the pig were gone."

Hoffman fumbled a stack of handbills, passing the mess to a red-haired girl sucking a lollypop. She looked at me and nodded. I knew damn well what she was thinking.

"Pigasus busted?" Hoffman gasped. "Sal too? We got no show?"

"Cops wouldn't beat Sal so bad if they were hauling him in. Too much blood to answer for."

I said it with too much authority. Hoffman cocked his head. I thought fast, adding, "Never cuffed me after kicking my ass, either."

"True enough, man." Something drew his eyes down. "Shit!" He swiped at a streak of mimeograph ink on his red t-shirt, one with an upside-down American flag.

"Anyway," I said, "I'm guessing Sal and the Pres are still holed up in the park somewhere. But it's crawling with cops so they're just laying low, someplace where it's dark."

"But the nomination's all set! The parade is queued! Get the hula-hoop dancers, man! Get the kazoo band! The children of war are coming home to roost, Corman, and they want a parade! A Yippie parade! Now, to the park! Go find Pigasus! We've got no show without him!"

"The park's just a hunch."

"Hunch? Well, Jerry's got a hunch, too, man, and he swears Sal's a narc."

"What?"

"Look, I can't see Sal on the dark side either, Yippie lives inside him. But Jerry's like a dowser and he's getting clear Fed vibes. You want to prove Sal's clean? Bring him to Jerry, but first find Pigasus, and hurry! The trouble begins at ten!"

"I thought it wasn't about Pigasus anymore," I challenged, asking a question meant to probe, meant to reveal more important info. I was training myself! "Jerry said so, remember?"

"Yeah, but he's just on this bad trip right now. He thinks he wants a real war, but that ain't Yippie! Believe me," he lowered his voice, poking his head toward the open office door where Rubin sat, back toward us, tilting in a chair. "Black ink pumps in his veins, man. His brain's just this giant newsreel. When the bulbs pop and cameras roll, he'll be there. He's in there with the press right now."

Hoffman took the straightened handbills back from the stick-sucking redhead and held them up on an inverted palm like a serving tray. "Calling Uncle Walter! Calling Uncle Walter!" He mistook my dismissal for ignorance. "Cronkite, baby! One little piggy nominated for president on Uncle Walter's show kicks the shit out of Mayberry. He knows it and we know it. We both need a media spike, man, a Pulitzer moment!"

"Sun Tzu again?" I asked.

"McLuhan, man! We need images, Corman, images!"

Images like the press clippings handed around the informant briefing, I figured; pictures of Hoffman and Rubin on the Stock Exchange balcony showering ass-rich brokers with dollar bills so the cameras could catch them clamoring over each other to catch a single shitty dollar, one hundred pennies, big fat guys with houses on stilts in the Hamptons, maids maybe, imported gardeners, prettier wives than they deserved, white patent leather shoes, tumbling, ripping their pants to reveal odd underwear, tearing each other apart for a floating buck. Even in the briefing, we had to admit it was funny. Ended up on the cover of *Time*.

I rejoined Hoffman, who was always talking. "…And the press will catch everything!" he said. "Even the looks on their faces. *That's* Yippie! That's what we came here to do." He grew pensive, rubbing at an eyebrow. "But Jerry forgets. He thinks we need a little blood spilled."

"Last night spilled a little," I said, wishing I'd phrased it differently, more open-ended to continue the probe. But I was remembering the sitting girl, and the cameras rolling, and the be-helmeted cop. I was thinking about *those* images. And, oh yeah, Sal too.

I refined my approach. "Listen. Sal and I are down in that trench with no communication at all. If the plan is to escalate, I need to know it now."

"Escalation ain't me. And blood ain't me, and it ain't Yippie either. Yippie is keeping them dancing on Broadway, that's what *we* do!" He twirled the stick-sucking girl, singing, "They say there's always teargas in the air…

"And," he motioned at Rubin, who was still holding court with the press, "We need Pigasus for that."

Leaning back in a metal chair, toes pushing against a wall, Rubin gestured emphatically at two underground reporters, one of whom fumbled with a legal pad, the other puberty. Rubin saw me and motioned to wait, but the reporters grew bored and stopped scribing: same hippie shit, different hippie day. Being a dowser, Rubin naturally picked up the vibe and dropped his feet to the floor with a loud annoyance. "Well?" he demanded of me, waving the kids out, "Does the guy with the pig check out? Is he clean?"

"The cops are everywhere, okay?" I was annoyed I had to go back through this litany.

"No shit. That's the point. Your boy's probably sipping tea with them right now. What about our pig?"

"My – guess – would – be," I said slowly, as if each word were separated by a dash. He wasn't really listening anyway.

"Abbie's got quite a crowd showing up in a few hours for that pig."

"So I heard."

He ignored me. "Screw it. We're almost out of time. How can we get another one?" He circled his chair, keeping one hand on its back all the time like he thought the music was going to stop.

"Another?" I asked.

"Yes, another! One pig's as good as the next, right?"

In the doorway, Hoffman choked.

"Right?" Rubin asked him. "One pig's as good as the next? If we can't find our pig, we'll just replace it."

"Pigasus, replaceable? Never!" Hoffman challenged.

"Abbie, this town's the hog butcher to the world! Don't get hung up on any one pig!"

"No, Jerry, stay authentic. That's Yippie."

"Well, maybe we need a new Yippie! We're in a war and Sun Tzu does not concern himself with authentic! Any pig will do."

"People will know, Jerry. Pigasus all the way! Pigasus has an aura!"

No, I thought, what the pig *has* is a birthmark that fucking glows.

"Damn it, Abbie, we're wasting time. Chicago's overrun with stand-ins," Rubin insisted.

"Stay with the original, the one and only pig that would be president, Pigasus!" Hoffman's diction was not good. Too many P's, maybe.

Rubin stopped circling his chair and pointed at Hoffman. Maybe he was dizzy (his finger did draw wild W's in the air) but some light switched on somewhere in his head and a dim smile made it to his lips. "You're right, Abbie. You're right; stick with the original, be authentic!

Pigasus it is! And I just cooked up a little surprise." He laughed at his inside joke. "Remember, every army moves on its stomach…"

Hoffman clenched his teeth and inhaled loudly.

"Relax, Abbie. We're just going to throw a little roast, a little barbeque, that's all, for an army of press."

"Jerry -" Hoffman threw himself into Rubin's stiff-arm.

"Abbie, you said it yourself, *be authentic.* You and I know that no other pig fits but Pigasus, the only pig that would ever be president! But in their Amerika with a K, Abbie, the politicians devour the people. In Yippie-America, people consume the *politicians* - it's justice, Yippie style! And you're right Abbie, *not* stand-ins, but the real thing! Pulled pork, ribs, cracklins – the whole works! First we nominate Pigasus, then we serve him at a banquet! It's perfect!"

Hoffman clenched his teeth again. "Jerry, this is a coup d'etat of our *own*!"

"War has casualties, Abbie. I am Sun Tzu!"

"McLuhan," I corrected, struggling for his identity.

Remember when I thought I shot a charging boar, Lieut? Remember how I shot it blind through those fronds and how moonless the night was? How I waited before squeezing off a string with you screaming in my ear? "A boar," I said, "Only boars charge like that." And how you said, "Boars don't cry that way, Boot. Or this long. But it don't matter anyway. It's all just squirrels here, new guy. Everything is. This thing ain't nothin' different than hittin' a squirrel with your car. There's just one less, is all. Just one less squirrel in this fucking Swellsville."

And remember how I wanted to go see, to be sure, maybe fire one more round to get some quiet, but how you pulled rank and pushed me back and said, "Welcome to the fight. That's one less thing to get you. Whatever tips the scales, Boot," you said, adding, "That's all you gotta know, the law of war numbers."

I pulled myself back to Rubin. But before I could ally with him to strengthen my cover, the pubescent scribe was back in the room, breathless, handing a note to Hoffman. "The cops just killed one of ours, a kid from South Dakota!"

Rubin fell into his chair, narrowed his eyes, then jumped to his feet again, circling the room in a kind of jig. "I told you this was our Tet! Now we have our martyr! And now their authority is nothing. Stop the presses out there!" he ordered through the door. "Abbie, get the fliers up!" Rubin faced me, a bubble of spit resting on his chin. "And Corman, go find our banquet's guest of honor."

"How's this going to work?" I asked. "The pig has to be alive when you nominate it, right?"

"Yes, but as soon as the press leaves, slit its throat." Rubin pulled a long knife from his drawer and drew it slowly along his neck. Studying the clean blade, he added, "You might want to put an edge on this."

I surely did.

"I don't like your new Yippie, Jerry," Hoffman bemoaned. "This is not *me*."

With the knife in my pocket, I made my way to the park. There was training I lacked, but this wasn't it.

What is it you preached, Lieut? Squeeze hard, lean in, and lean up?

Chapter 4

At the entrance to the park, the Snapjaw patrol squeaked in its armor among a swarm of rising gnats. Behind them, the sun wedged through early gray and cast the sky in an ugly jagged purple, like a scalloped beet. I'd seen a sky this color before.

But here and now, the cops squawked about delayed replacements. They cited the Constitution. They cited collective bargaining. They worked themselves into a collective huff. They hopped around like they had to pee. And when one left, forcing the rest to gather like a raft of ducks, I sprinted through the gap across Lakeshore, crunching glass beneath my feet. A Marlboro box tumbled by me, cart-wheeling over the revolutionaries asleep against the park's statues.

Deep in the park, I shimmied down the ravine, careful to avoid the refuse from the night's melee: torn shirts, charred rags, splintered bench slats, and to my glee a set of bongos, skins punched in. Below, the rails were a steeplechase of rumble shit—the bigger stuff that could roll all the way down, stuff like the skeletons of benches, dented garbage cans, and a burned-out bucket seat from a foreign car. It was as if a giant civic broom had just swept the night away.

I was sidestepping this chaff when I heard a voice down the tracks grow louder, then frantic, then quiet and finally still, like it never happened. From the culvert, Sal craned his neck to see what all the silence was about. Long streakes of dried blood blazed his shirt. Behind him, the pig balled up, smeared with mud, snout twisting from the dirt. Sal stumbled to comfort it, careful not to kneel on the curling sketchpad, it too streaked with mud.

"I tried, Corman," Sal cried. "I tried to heal him, but the mud won't work for me."

Knife in my pocket, I stooped beside the pig, not to smear mud, but to study its throat. My exit was becoming clear, if not messy: Deliver the pig alive to the parade and gain the confidence of Hoffman. Kill the pig because it was, well, a pig, deliver it to the barbeque, and gain Rubin. Use my new probing skills to play them against each other to tip their hands. Then, deliver them to the Fed and gain my release from COINTELPRO. Listen to me making plans – a quadruple jump, no less! Who did I think I was?

The pig shivered. Blood pinked its drool.

"Please, Corman?"

I fingered the revolting folds of the pig's neck, finding a weak pulse in the artery I planned to sever. But that was later. I had to keep it alive first, achieve the mission, *then* I could kill it. I slid my hands over the lumps trailing down its back, the way you might first embrace a corpulent date. "He's busted up good," I said.

Scraping mud from the slick, Sal spoke in sharp notes. "America hates weakness, Corman. He must not be seen this way. Here, take it. Now is the time. You are a healer."

A healer of pigs? Me, with a knife in my pocket? Me, who blindly shot through jungle that way? "How'd it make it back here?" I said, stalling, probing.

Sal turned his head away. "I carried him."

"From where?"

"From where he fell." Sal tucked more mud in my hand. "You didn't say anything last time, Corman. You didn't do anything. Just hold the mud there."

"Stop this!" I flung the mud against the steel.

"Corman, there's no time!"

The pig moaned.

Sal stroked its snout. "Shhh. Shhh..."

"Are you humming a song to it?"

"I'm doing everything I can, Corman. What about you? Are you just sitting and watching the President die?"

"I never healed anything in my life," I said for the twenty-second time. But Sal read something new in it.

"But that was once-upon-a-time, Corman..."

"Sal..."

"The President is going to be very hungry after this. We'll need to get out of here, quick, and find his Yodels before his speech. He'll need all his strength today."

You cannot fight conviction like Sal's. It is a riptide. You can only swim across its current or hope a shark takes you quickly. I let him take my hand and rake it through the mud. I rubbed it between my fingers like he wanted me to, feeling its grit but nothing else. I might as well have been rubbing the shine off a baseball. No amulet, no magic. I kept rubbing it. Kept shaking my head, but Sal looked up and nodded, "Now is the time," anyway.

"Hear that?" he said to the pig. "Corman's -"

The pig shuddered again and belched a long whine as the artery in its neck swelled. The brain was calling every ounce of blood in one final charge, as if death was just one last hill to take. And I guess that was right. I reached for the knife. When the blood is all in one place, the bleeding is easy. They teach you that.

"Corman, rub it like this!"

I pulled my hand away. But Sal took it again and steered it in loosening circles. The pig's breath rattled beneath, eyes cellophane, drifting, flickering, closing. I turned away fearing death, *not* of the pig, but of my quadruple jump plan.

"Look, he's, he's watching you, Corman," Sal said. "The President knows the Shaman! Feel, his nose is wet. That's a good sign, right?"

I pulled my hands away again at the sign of life in the pig's eye, but Sal pressed them back.

"Not yet," he implored. "Let's count to a hundred."

By the time he hit eleven, his counting was as obnoxious as the Snapjaw announcements from the big speakers. I needed a distraction. I needed to probe. "Got a last name, Sal?"

"Not any more. Families choose to forget too, Corman. Yours?"

It was a firm place to draw a hard line on the informant code. "None that I remember."

"You mean none you want to share, because Corman is nothing but secrets."

Why I didn't just make up a name wasn't clear, except I was wholly unprepared to be an informant! Once again, a little damn training and this stuff would come as second nature, a reflex. Instead, I could not conceal what should be concealed, and I could not prompt others to reveal! I had no skills at all. At best I was an informant on myself!

"Nothing but secrets," Sal bemoaned.

"Hodges," I sighed, inexplicably telling him my real last name when McNamara would have done just as nicely.

"It's a good name, Hodges. Strong."

I looked to change the subject, to get something revealed. "Got a girl?"

"Are you counting things I no longer have, Corman Hodges? Is that your big medicine? I cannot count forward for the President (thirty-one) and backward for you at the same time. Working on one."

"A girl?"

Sal grew agitated, ordering me to look at the pig's eyes, but I just kept probing him until the pig squirmed. As I leaned back, the knife stabbed through my pocket.

"That's it!" Sal cried. "That's it, Mr. President! Just a few seconds more... ninety-eight, ninety-nine, one hundred. Easy now. Easy, that's it. Corman, you stay here. I'm going to walk away and try to get the President to follow. No! Keep your hands on him!"

The pig made the long low moan of a burdened coal train and twisted its head to understand Sal's growing distance. A stench arose.

At the end of the culvert, Sal slapped his thigh. The pig shook off my hand, shook off his flies, and juggled to its feet. Sal slapped again and it stumbled forward.

"Pigasus is going to be President!" he sang. "Hang on, Mr. President, and you shall be elected!"

The pig stumbled toward Sal, throwing up pink as it neared. Sal winced as he pulled his dripping shirt from his skin. Beneath, his broken ribs glimmered blue-green. The Snapjaw boots had taken their toll.

Chapter 5

Sal and the pig navigated the tracks like victims of a derailment, the pig hobbling, stumbling, reviving and spitting occasional blood, Sal clutching the pad to hold his ribs in place.

"What time is it?" Sal called back.

"Almost nine."

"We've only got an hour to the nomination, and the President needs Yodels first, Corman!"

Yodels. I recalled my search for Yodels the night before, the medicated deli clerks, the buzzing streets, and shook my head in astonishment. How did I end up here? Who did I think I was?

Sal let the lame pig lead the way. Every piece of rumble-shit required it do a three point turn. You haven't suffered until you've watched a busted-up pig choreograph twelve-step, three-point turns one after another. I seethed at the pace; not that I had a better place to go, but with no speed and no distance between us, and me in the rear, the pig's flatulence was pervasive. I thought to slide up front, grab the lead, quicken the pace, but my cover with Sal hinged on him being the General, so I held back. Besides, Sal's steps were growing hesitant, as if all of a sudden he was unsure of the plan. And who could blame him? There was no cakewalk up top. We'd be in open the whole way. They'd have a clear shot if they chose to take it, at me or Sal or, most likely, the pig. I was sure Sal's hesitation was not about taking a bullet for the pig, but whether he'd get the chance to. I was rooting for him.

"What's Abbie's plan?" I probed.

"That's closely guarded, Corman. By them. Your orders will come. My only orders are to meet in front of the Ulysses statue, then it's on to Chicago and let's win there. But I must keep the President safe. After all, now is the time for all good men to come to the aid of their country."

Not the "all good men" thing again, I thought. Now I wanted to take the bullet, and not for the pig, for me! I fought for position.

"Okay," I said, "Let me go up first, alone to plan the safest route."

Covering my pocket to shield the knife from his view, I scrambled up the embankment to where the park waved in the heat. In the west, priests-for-peace gathered like a murder of crows beneath the wilted maples. A tent city sprung up near the statues. To the east, a dharma monk chimed baby cymbals, winning over hippies by stroking a wild beard. Shiny lines of Clean-for-Gene kids marched by chanting McCarthy for President! Snapjaw pursued them on horseback, clomping, backs covered by snipers perched on surrounding rooftops. When the horses split a flock of agitated sheep, I followed freely in their wake until I was grabbed from behind and spun around to face the filth of a hippy making peace signs with both hands.

"We've been waiting for you, Hodges," he said, flicking one peace sign toward the latrine, a brick structure with yellowing glass and a mossy roof. "Report now. Third stall." As he fell back into the fold, he repeated, "*Now.*"

The latrine blistered in ninety-degree heat, releasing like a fog the festering spirits of piss over-spray. A cut padlock dangled. As I lifted it, a shadow slipped by the murky window and the third stall slammed.

"Lock the door, Hodges," scratched an unfamiliar voice. Beneath the stall door, a pair of black high-top sneakers crossed. Whoever it was wasn't in uniform. Whoever it was didn't find me funny.

"I'm going to tell you this once," he said. "Do not fuck with me, Hodges. This place is an oven, and I hate you. You broke cover. You've put the men in this unit *and* the Bureau in harm's way, risking lives, lives that matter, unlike your own. By all rights, I should put a bullet in your head."

There was a lot of that going around, I thought.

"You've got a history of screwing the pooch, don't you?" he continued. "Couldn't even take out your lieutenant without fucking it up. Isn't that right? Let's see, it was a knife, wasn't it, just north of Khe Sanh?"

"Not exactly."

"You put a knife in your lieutenant, and you didn't even think to pull it back out. Left there, prints and all, right in his fucking ribs. What a shmuck."

"That's not how it happened."

"You put a knife–"

"We promised each–"

"I don't care."

"He was dying. Half of him was gone. That was our deal."

"Save it. I don't give a shit anyway. This is about *our* deal, now. You're the one who decided to roll the dice on this little mission of ours rather than man-up to your twenty to life. But how we end up with a guy too stupid to take the knife with him is marvel of fucking engineering. You know what happens next, don't you?"

I heard a gun click. On a hunch, I slid to the left. "I go back to work," I guessed.

"We have no reason to think you can be successful at that."

"What do you mean? I've got all the moves planned; a quadruple jump and I'm one jump in! Brillante`! Italian!"

"What?"

"I mean, I'm just about to put all my great training to work! I've been pretending inferiority! I have encouraged their arrogance!"

"Jesus, I want to shoot you so bad right now. But we all have our orders, so I'm giving you a shot at redemption."

Christ! Just what I needed, one more redeemer, one more blind shot through the dripping fronds. The Fed was throwing good redemption after bad, and I sensed we both knew it.

A thick envelope came to an abrupt stop along the multi-cracked floor. He grunted, disturbed by how little it slid.

"What's that?" I asked.

"Your new deal. I'd take it if I were you."

"What kind of deal?"

"The kind of deal we had to make to kill that PD record of you exposing COINTELPRO to a couple of motherfucking Blues, that's what!"

So it was in the report, I surmised. Chairass just didn't read far enough. I feigned innocence. The guy in the stall bought none of it. "Bullshit. How else would they know? Of course, their misspelling was priceless. Colonpro. But never mind that. Luckily, the Blues want the same thing we do, and you're the one that gets it for us. Pick it up. This is how you deliver Rubin and Hoffman. Just get it in their hands. We'll take care of the rest."

"What is it?"

"*Their* twenty to life," he laughed, "the magic powder way. Just get it in their hands."

"No way," I said, not because I revered the rule of law, but because I sensed a set-up.

"It's them or you."

"If I pick up that envelope, I'm in possession of that envelope," I said.

"You think we're setting *you* up, Hodges? You think we have time for that? Give us a little credit. When we get rid of you, we'll get rid of you. "

"One less squirrel in Swellsville?"

"Good God, how I wish I could shoot you right now! I'm losing patience. Pick it up."

"So I plant it. Then what?"

"Then we put them away. What part of this aren't you getting?" Beneath the door, his sneaker toed the envelope further along the floor.

"The part that happens afterward," I said, "to me."

"If I were you, I'd play this one move at a time, Hodges. The only thing for sure is that if you don't pick that envelope up, you don't walk out of here. I'm the guy they've sent to clean up your mess, one way or another."

I picked it up. It was heavier than I expected and folded over my palm. The back was taped. A gummy end of it rolled up beneath my thumb.

"That's it, one play at a time," he said. "Smart."

I weighed the envelope in my hand. "There's enough smack here to put the whole city away."

"Fifty grand worth. Possession is just five to ten. Intent to sell is life. Now your orders are to take that to the Seed office. I understand you met with them there this morning, so you know where Rubin's desk is. Place it in the middle drawer. We'll discover it at eight o'clock tonight."

"So I plant it and I go, right? I'm done? Skip right out of Chicago and never look back?"

"You're done when we tell you. That's the deal. You're to maintain whatever's left of your cover until we tell you otherwise."

I was finished, I thought. There'd be two bullets waiting for me after the plant, no matter what: one for breaking black ops silence, and the other as a firsthand witness to the Bureau falsifying evidence against Hoffman and Rubin. I curled the envelope again and took a step toward the door.

"Now you're thinking, Hodges."

Yes, I was thinking. I was thinking about how I was fucked. I backed up against the panic bar of the door. In my hand weighed the government's real conspiracy against Hoffman and Rubin; in my back pocket (the knife) the surreal plot of Hoffman and Rubin to shame the government. I wanted no part in either. As the tape rolled some beneath my finger, I imagined hurling the envelope, crashing it against the ceiling, filling the third stall with a white storm. I imagined him coughing and fumbling for the stall door latch, yelling, "I'm going to fucking kill you! I signed this shit out!" before puffing from the stall covered in the magic powder, a smack specter. And I named him that: Smackspecter.

"How do I get this out of here?" I said. "I can't walk through those hippies with this in my hand. They'll be on me like flies on that pig."

"We thought of that. Use this." He threw an ACE bandage over the door. "Wrap the envelope to your chest."

I peered down into the trench where Sal paced, looking up in pain, awaiting my return. I slid down.

"It's worse than I figured," I said. "Cops have doubled, and this heat's not helping anyone's mood."

"The President is not afraid, Corman."

"Maybe he should be, Sal. It's all going to explode up there."

"You appear to have lost your nerve, Corman."

The knife was still in my pocket. "No."

"Then why do you keep rubbing your chest as if to comfort yourself? We have to go. Pigasus knows he can't lead the country from down here, that he can't make America great again by being absent. The whole world will be watching. He must look them in the eye, Corman. He must stroke their souls! What time is it?"

"Late. Let's get this all over with."

Sal clutched his sketchpad and ushered the moaning pig up the hill. They trailed through the park behind me and I had to keep stopping to make sure I didn't lose them. Like Hoffman, I had no show without the pig. I urged them forward, but the pig would not walk a straight line, distracted as it was by burger wrappers and shiny things. And Sal weaved behind it, matching the zigs, matching the zags, maddening me with the delay. I rubbed my chest and reminded myself that at eight o'clock that night it would all be over: no more pig, or Sal, or Yippies, or sheep. We plowed a sinuous swath through the loitering revolution, often losing sight of the statue for long periods of time, but the snipers never lost us in theirs. I squinted through the sun at their rooftop silhouettes to regain my bearings, studying them for any hint of alarm.

And right there the irony caught me: I was now just like the stoned-out night clerks. They were never getting out, and if the Fed had its way, neither was I. Smackspecter's assertion that COINTELPRO didn't have time to worry about the likes of me (even as they were in the *middle* of worrying about me) rang somewhat hollow. Plus, I was only one cop altercation, one pat-down away from taking the fall for the dope. I still had a triple jump remaining, but I had to get it to the *Seed*, to the middle drawer right after I butchered the pig, then assess my chances from there, knowing full well that sometimes the best you can hope for is to get shot in the back. Right, Lieut?

As we crossed an open patch of the large littered lawn in the direction of the rising Ulysses statue, throngs of pig devotees fell in behind us. Some twirled. Most screamed the tired mantra of the night, "The whole world is watching!" until competing choruses emerged.

"The whole world is watching!"

"Pigasus for President!"

"Pork Power!"

"Vote Pig!"

"Winning again! Winning again!"

I paused to stare back up at the snipers, conveying my blessing should they choose this as their moment to open random fire. Nothing. What kind of war was this?

As we neared the statue, this first seep of Hoffman's parade took over and its greasy multitude meandered with the pig, cartwheeling, dancing, clapping, chanting, and tripling in number as we flowed toward the exit on Michigan Avenue. In fringed rawhide vests and smudged crinoline blouses, they crowded the pig, jolting it into anxiety. It pranced in painful circles in the direction of its tail, mirroring their own spinning, snorting, squealing, charging and farting to protect itself from being touched. The crowd closed. The frantic pig spun in tighter circles, moaning, butting, stumbling and falling on its side, spending what little was likely left of its life before the pain from its beating staked it to the ground. Sal screamed, throwing a wild, arching, aimless punch, clutching his ribs. A hippie charged him. I threw a forearm. I needed that pig alive for another hour. In my best hippie accent with my best hippie logic, I tried to focus the crowd.

"If we miss the press," I declared, "We miss the score, man! And we came to score, did we not?"

The crowd *oinked* on behalf of the pig.

"Pigasus the Immortal has got to make the show, man, or he joins Martin and Bobby as victims of all things ugly!"

The crowd chanted, "Pig–a-sus! Pig-a-sus!"

"To be late for the cameras is for him and the movement to die man! And…" I waved at the advancing cops, "…some have come to keep him away!"

"Noooo!"

"Do you believe?"

"Yes!"

Sal smiled big.

"Will you clear the way for him?"

"Yes! Pigasus! Pigasus! Vote the pig! Pigasus!"

Sal looked at me with a pride that gave me the creeps, although I was privately celebrating my oratory skills. Only the damn hippies didn't clear the way, closing in again instead! I fought them back while Sal eased the pig to its feet, pulling it close. I called out to the crowd again and, with some additional direction they finally got the gist, parting to form two facing lines. We ran the channel between them. Cops pushed, but the lines held long enough.

At the end of the lines near the Ulysses statue, a gray wood-grained station wagon smoked. Rubin stared anxiously above a half-dropped window as a Snapjaw swung in from the east. Sal pointed at a gap in the crowd and we sliced through it, tucking the squealing pig beneath our arms. We zigged through revolutionaries in pig masks and zagged around a girl flashing her breasts at the would-be President. The pig threw a hoof her way.

In the car, Rubin bristled at our delay, his voice raspy from the exhaust fumes filling the cab. Choking next to him, Hoffman breathed through a paper napkin. In the far back, on top of the cavity for the spare tire, the pubescent scribe giggled.

"Your only saving grace," Rubin sneered, putting the car in gear, "is that without us, the press has nothing, so they'll wait."

Hoffman pulled his napkin away to wheeze, "We are their ghost-writers! We are ghostwriters of history!"

"And we are here to feed it back to the people," the reporter laughed. "Isn't that right, Jerry?"

Hoffman shook his head with a broken resolve.

Rubin filled the pause. "*That* is the theme of the day!" He tilted the rearview mirror, catching my eyes. "Feeding it back to the people. Isn't that so, Corman?"

Hoffman was still shaking his head.

"That's the plan," I mumbled, nodding slightly to the mirror before slanting my eyes toward Sal. He was absorbed in soothing the pig. I looked back in the mirror. "Donde`?" (Spanish!)

"The alley next to the civic center," Rubin said. "Immediately after. Our boy in the back will help you wrap it." I turned to the back where the reporter crinkled a large white plastic bag.

"This ain't Yippie," Hoffman brooded under his breath. "This was never the plan."

"It always was, Abbie. This is the building of the myth! It's shock and awe time! No revolution ever succeeded playing it down the center. There was a time for shits and giggles, but we're long past that now."

"Images," I said.

"Exactly! Right, Abbie? Right." Rubin turned back to the reporter. "Write it down; the second rule of a revolutionary is to eschew complexity!"

"Sun Tzu?" the reporter asked.

"McLuhan," Hoffman answered. "We fuel the revolution on images, simple soul-ripping images, man! Until our best vets smuggled back Polaroids, no one believed what was happening over there. Nobody stays fooled once they see a picture of the prom king's head on a Punji stick. But they've *got to see it,* that's where the power is. And they've got to see it on page one, above the fold! I just never thought it would be us shedding the blood."

"Is there a first rule of a revolutionary?" I asked, unfulfilled. "Something I can take away from this, maybe, to be a better citizen?"

"Take this away: Myths don't write themselves," Ruben said. "We need an h-bomb moment, and that's your job, Corman. Our own Little Boy or Fat Man is snorting right beside you." He climbed over the seat. "Anybody else need help in seeing the kiloton muscle of people eating the flesh of their own candidate, and being caught on film doing it?"

"What?" Sal asked, piecing some things together. "Pigasus is still going to be President, right?"

"Sure pigman, President." Rubin laughed. "Shock and awe! I am Sun Tzu!"

Sal pinned his back against the door, pulling the anxious pig near him. "Corman, What's happening?"

I turned away.

"What's happening, Abbie?"

Hoffman stared straight ahead.

In the growing exhaust, Pigasus sneezed, bringing the pain of its wounds back to life and with them the coal train moan.

Rubin peered in the mirror. "Listen to it. Too bad you don't have a knife or something, Corman."

***

A wheel of the station wagon scraped the corner of West Washington Street where a five-story twisted steel sculpture hulked above a jostling mob. At the sculpture's base, cops tightened around a knot of reporters.

"Look at all these cameras!" Rubin declared. "We own this day! Nothing can stop us. Nothing!"

The wagon slowed again for jaywalkers. Rubin hit the horn. "This is what's wrong with Amerika; everyone doing whatever the fuck they want! Like motor homes in the left lane doing fifty miles an hour, man. *That's* what's wrong with Amerika! These things are the establishment slowing down the revolution, that's all they are, holding everyone back in their upholstered status quo. You can't have a revolution as long as the beasts of oppression are allowed to roam free on the highways, to do whatever speed they want! This wagon *is* the revolution, and it wants to go east and it wants to go fast, but these fat plutocrats wont let it go!"

"So the revolution is about minimum speed?" I asked.

"It's a metaphor."

"Well, someone needs to tell the people that this is a *metaphorical* revolution before they start beating their plowshares into swords, and all that."

"This isn't a metaphorical revolution!"

Hoffman stirred. "It's an enlightenment, man!" he said "It's just a little blurry right now because everyone has their own thing going, their own groove, and we're not being Yippie."

"So it's a blurry enlightenment?" I asked.

Rubin once again took to the mirror to stare me down. That move of his was getting old. I may have rolled my eyes. Who did I think I was? "What kind of psychological warfare is this?" he asked. "You a cop? A narc?"

"Jerry's a dowser, man!" Hoffman sang. "I told you!"

"You think I don't know these tricks?" Rubin continued. "I studied with the masters! Kesey! Leary! Spock!"

I waved both hands. "I'm only trying to learn from the best too," I said, gesturing between them.

Everyone relaxed except Sal, who had been pinned to the door for some time, and as the smoking wagon begrudgingly held for cross-walkers, he reached slowly for the door's handle. But it didn't matter anyway; he was too late. And as the car accelerated, he placed his hand back on the pig.

The hulking sculpture was upon us now. "Some guy named Picasso did this," the *Seed* reporter said. "Weird shit. Some say it's supposed to be Mrs. O'Leary's cow, the one that smoked the city. Others think this Picasso was, like, pissing on America, like it's a falcon or some killer bird representing America eating, you know, the rest of the world."

Rubin leaned over the steering wheel, looking at it high through the windshield. "They're all wrong. It's Circe."

"Huh?"

"Jesus doesn't anybody read? C-i-r-c-e, daughter of Perseis? Turned men into swine? And how fitting, huh? Look at them!" He motioned at the press, leaned back, laughing. "But one man emerged to save them, Odysseus! Wait! I get it now, you're Odysseus, Abbie! You're Odysseus saving swine!"

Hoffman squirmed in the front seat. "I am not Odysseus. I am Sun Tzu!"

But Rubin wasn't done.

"Yes, you *are* Odysseus, and your myth is born! But this is war Abbie, and I am the warrior, so *I* must be Sun Tzu! If we are to surprise the enemy, we must be subtle to the edge of formlessness, mysterious to the edge of soundlessness!"

The station wagon exploded in backfire, spitting a mushroom cloud. The press swallowed us, cameras popping against the glass, rocking us with hands against the doors. Sal reached for the handle again, but the press of flesh outside pinned it shut. Rubin egged them on with a drum roll on the dashboard, but the press soon yielded for a hula-hooping kick line dancing in the formation of a pilcrow, or a pitchfork, I wasn't sure which. They smashed against the car to sing a round of, "He's a grand 'ol pig..." Behind them, two sheep jumped on Pogo sticks while stretching a banner that read, "Trip with the Pres!" Their timing grew off and they fell, yielding the street to a giant papier-mache pig's head on a shouldered platform. Rubin was punching the dashboard in disgust now. Hoffman turned to us and beamed as if to say, this is my finest moment.

The giant pig's head bobbed toward the civic center and Rubin grew anxious again, like the parade was taking the myth with it, which it obviously was. Equally anxious, Hoffman threw himself out of the car and folded into the crowd. Sal reached to do the same, but Rubin interfered.

"Hand me up the pig!" he ordered.

Sal froze.

"Now, Pigman! This is what we came here for!"

The *Seed* reporter reached forward and leveraged the pig free.

Pig in arms, Rubin kicked his door open, car still running. "Alley," he said to me.

The reporter followed. Sal fought his way into their wake, reaching out and quieting the pig as Rubin elbowed his way toward the podium. But the current of hippies proved too much. Sal fell hopelessly back and soon walked alone to the stage. I killed the ignition, pocketed the keys, and followed.

At the microphone, Rubin wrestled with the pig and its flashbulb phobia. "What's that, Pigasus?" Rubin asked into the mike, holding his ear to the pig's snout. "I, Pigasus, hereby seek and will absolutely accept the nomination of my party, the Youth International Party, as your candidate for President of Amerika with a k!"

Rubin paused for applause, but none came. He looked stunned, as if that joke had never failed to kill 'em at Grossinger's. He stared at the pig to blame it, and sought to fight off his failure with additional volume, screaming: "If elected, our pig will run the country on the same principles that have always guided our government's existence. It will drop napalm on Vietnamese children! It will waste money while many starve!"

The crowd turned their backs. Behind them, Hoffman entered the square walking on his hands, kazoo band right behind him. He fell to his feet at the podium, hushed the kazoos with a flourish, and took the mike.

"The Democratic Party will most likely nominate a pig for president, and a pig for vice president too, but don't be fooled by them! Be fooled by the pig of the Yippie party!"

"Let's get fooled! Let's get fooled!" chanted the sheep.

Rubin ripped the mike back and screamed louder, his words more feedback from the amps than discernable syllables. "Our campaign slogan is…"

"Let's get fooled! Let's get fooled!"

Hoffman stepped in front. "You've been denied your half of the hog! Others have come to take it from you! Why take half the hog when you can get the whole hog? Claim your right to the trough!" he prodded, shrugging off Rubin's glare.

The crowd nodded, indicating it was a very good point Hoffman made and that they were ready to believe anything. They joined in. "Pigasus! Pigasus!"

It was Rubin's turn. He stepped forward, thrusting a fist in the air. "The Democrats and Republicans have been offering us inarticulate pigs for years."

Hoffman: "Our pig will continue to make a stupid mess of things!"

"Mess of things! Mess of things!"

I had made my way to the podium for the hand-off of the pig. Sal stood to my right, as devastated as Dorothy when the mutt pulled back the curtain.

Rubin tried again, pig aloft. "Our pig will make no false promises!"

Sal swiped at his eyes. The pig had wilted from the heat and the pain. It lay still, maybe dead. He moved to touch it. Rubin spun away, livid at all the intrusions, barking now into the microphone.

"If elected, there will be American boys sent overseas, there will be chaos, and finally, finally the American people will rise up!"

"No, we won't! No, we won't!"

Sal's hands were reaching, eyes darting, horrified. I moved up the platform steps for the handoff just as Rubin held the limp pig aloft, shaking it for a sign of life.

"Make it dance!" someone called.

"Make it dance! Make it dance!"

Rubin tilted his head with a bewilderment matching Sal's.

Hoffman joined in. "Make it dance!"

The pig bounced in the air. The laughter delighted Rubin, energized him even. He was back on the beam. He twisted the pig to flail its legs. The laughter swelled. He twisted it again and the pig, urged by mounting pain, revived, squealing, kicking its own legs about, New Jersey flickering, and jolting me to take a strange inventory. I felt my pocket, the knife still there; felt my chest, the smack still there; and felt Sal clutch my arm. I didn't want to turn, but his tug demanded otherwise. With welled eyes and shaking hands and lips pursed on a word he couldn't find, there, amidst this fucking circus, Sal's heart broke.

"And now," Rubin said, lowering the pig, "our candidate will feed the people!"

"Feed! Feed! Feed the people!"

I reached. Sal reached. But from stage left two stealth cops lunged, sending Rubin sprawling into the crowd. The pig fell free. Sal dived, but the pig squirmed like half a worm, found a hole between the sheep and staggered down the alley of its planned execution, cops in full pursuit.

"I am Odysseus!" Hoffman screamed. "Savior of swine!"

"Odysseus! Odysseus!"

And there, as if I gave a shit, amidst the victorium (Latin!) celebrating Hoffman, Rubin's heart broke too, just as other cops plowed through the crowd, rounding up the usual suspects. I dropped the knife behind me and would have ditched the smack too, but there were too many eyes.

"Ho!" Hoffman wheezed a moment later, a cop under each arm. "We are the ghostwriters of history, Corman! Did we not get a show? Did I not save the pig, and you, and Yippie?" He looked toward Sal and smiled, but Sal was sliding down the alley after the pig.

Rubin emerged from the chaos, cuffed, despondent, eyes cast away from the crowd. "Was the whole world watching?" he groaned.

"Pretty much," I said.

"Narc!"

The cop pushed him forward, spitting on the back of his head and throwing him prostrate across a car hood. When the crowd parted again, it was Sal being dragged out.

"Corman!" Sal clutched his side.

"This schmuck with you?" the cop barked. It was the freshly creased rookie from the precinct. "Then get him out of here before he gets himself hurt. And remember this act of kindness from your friends, the police. Next time I see either of you, bang!"

I caught Sal before he hit the ground. He winced as I walked him away.

"They have Pigasus," he said.

"Who?"

"The police! Will they kill him?"

I thought about Mayor Daley wanting the pig as much as he wanted Rubin. I thought about the plans they'd made to see it dead.

"I don't think so," I lied.

Sal let my answer fall. "We've got to save him."

No, I thought. I'm done with pigs. They're horrifying.

"Hey, Blue!" Rubin called from his car-hood face-plant. "I'll be out by morning. Let's have tea!"

"Yeah, tea!" Hoffman added from another hood.

"Don't count on that, dirtbags. You're under arrest for inciting a riot. That's federal, and only a federal judge can spring you. Seeing how it's Saturday, and them being union and all… Then there's that bail thing, could take a couple more at least!" Rubin's head collided with the jam of the back door. "And who knows, maybe something happens along the way that gets you laid up for a while. So I wouldn't make too many hippie plans."

The other cop pushed Hoffman's face through the wax, deep into the blue paint. "Now let's get this over with. Everything you say (and everything you don't say) will be used against you."

Two, three, five days? I rubbed my chest, worrying as the cops sped Rubin and Hoffman away. "Wait! Where do I put the smack now?"

Sal grabbed his side and doubled over. I reached for him. Again I didn't want to, but again his tug demanded otherwise. "I'll make it," he said. "But we've got to find Pigasus."

Chapter 6

But Sal couldn't make it. No sooner had we hit a stretch of sidewalk where the crowd thinned than he doubled over again and stayed there awhile. I thought he was just gasping for air, but when he couldn't get it I leaned in to evaluate.

"Pigasus," he whispered, trying desperately not to exhale and move the ribs. "And Geneva." Sweat rolled off his ashen face, darkening the collar of his red shirt. A clock in one of the nearby towers was ringing a lot of frigging times. "Geneva," Sal said over the chimes. "Left her in the car. If she's gone, Corman, and Pigasus is gone, then…"

Drifting off while Sal talked was rapidly becoming a survival reflex, but through my drift a thought came, and I smiled that smile that confirms to yourself, "You're an idiot." I pulled the key to the wood-grained wagon from my pocket and held it up. Sal nodded. Until something sprung Rubin and Hoffman, their confinement meant the wagon was mine for the taking. That could buy me three or four days, or longer if they searched the impound lots before reporting her missing. A block away from where the wagon was parked, Sal managed through short breaths, "We will not come to the aid of Jerry and Abbie."

Come to the aid of Rubin and Hoffman? Not likely. In fact, I was not disposed to come to anyone's or *anything's* aid except my own. I knew how Sal felt about that pig, and yes, in some way (to someone else) it was some kind of fucked-up beautiful thing, I guess, but I did not share that assessment or Sal's pig adoration either. Besides, that pig was as good as dead; I saw it up on the stage, lifeless in Rubin's arms, eyes checked out. I was sure if it was living at all, it was only in the vivisected earthworm sense that I saw it last, cut in half and wriggling, not alive so much as propelled by an involuntary response to pain. I'd seen guys do that after the blow, counting the pieces of themselves, dead but for their final and involuntary inventory.

What is it you said, Lieut? Don't leave them here, Hodges. Don't leave my pieces here for the pigs to eat.

The noon sun reflected the wagon's metallic wood-grained side panels into a pool of freshly leaked oil, enraging someone enough to graffiti the car's hood with, "Save our forests, asshole!" While the wood grain looked more like a fading photo of stretch marks than lumber, to be sure it wasn't my perspective that was distorting I rapped on the faux (French!) wood.

The cops had been busy too. Six summonses flapped beneath a shredded windshield wiper: Plates expired 1966! Tires, bald! Taillights, missing! Parking, wrong side! Parking, curb! Parking, hydrant! Judging from their unequal penmanship, it appeared three cops took turns citing the wagon. But as I studied them closer, I realized it was just one cop getting angrier with each ticket (having to write so much in the summer heat, and all) squeezing the pen harder with each slip, stopping to shake blood back into his hand and sweat from his brow before turning his g's to e's and drooping the loops of his h's. The pen even pressed through the paper in a number of spots, pulling carbon to the front.

As I read, Sal spotted his sketchpad in the back seat where he'd left it. Relieved, he lifted it out of the car bending from the knees, not the waist, like it was very heavy and he didn't want to slip a disc. With a moan reminiscent of the pig, he thumbed methodically through the pad until content it was all there.

I threw the tickets in the glove compartment. Sal tucked the pad into his lap.

"Perhaps things are returning to normal, Corman."

I thought he was talking about the cops. "Maybe, but can you imagine doing that for a living, walking around looking for bald tires all day? Screwing up people's days that way?"

"They are the keepers of the peace, Corman!"

I dropped it, but silently imagined the dinner conversation our angry ticket cop would have that night.

"Daddy, how many people did you save today? Was it ten? Was it twenty?"

"Son, we may never know."

Well, I had a pretty good idea.

The car turned over with a momentous clatter.

"What is our plan, Corman?" Sal said. "We have to find Pigasus."

First, I didn't have any plan. What I had was a no-gaskets, bone-dry, blue smog, clear-cutting station wagon with "Save our forests, asshole!" tattooed on the hood, and half a kilo of smack strapped to my chest that I had to get rid of.

Second, I didn't have any "we" or "our".

But even devoid of the plural, I couldn't leave Sal doubled over in pain every time we thumped over a sewer cover. He needed a hospital, and he'd never go with the pig unaccounted for. And just like that, damn it, I had a plan and a "we". But only for a moment, I promised myself. I would take Sal to the hospital and get him to stay there by promising to go look for a pig I knew was already dead. Meantime, drop the smack at *The Seed*, load up on 10W40, then get the hell out of Chicago. An honest day's work by any standard.

Sal was not happy with the plan, but because he had a tragic habit of woefully misplacing his trust, I convinced him.

As I clattered away from the curb, I reread the hood, drawing an acronym from the tattoo. Save our forests, asshole. "SOFA," I said to no one while cleverly naming the wagon. That's the other thing I liked to do, name things. Collect foreign words and name things. Helps me stomach the rest.

A hundred lab coats darted through Mercy General like leukocytes on their way to an abscess. The peaceful revolution had left the city in stitches, or needing them anyway.

A triage nurse came into the waiting room.

"Blood over broken!" she yelled. "Blood on this side, broken on that side. What? What if you have both? Listen up! If you've got something broken *and* something bleeding, and I mean really bleeding, not like this," she pointed down at a girl with a dried gash above her eyebrow. The girl turned her head to reveal a fresh flow of blood over her ear. "Yes, like that," corrected the nurse. "Line up here in the middle. I'm not saying we're gonna fix them both, just that we'll get you in first available," adding under her breath, "Though that's not saying much today."

She stopped on her way out. "What did I just say? Broken is this side, bleeding is over there. Broken," she motioned with both hands, "Bleeding. You get that?" she asked Sal, who stood silently in the corner, protecting his ribs from the jostling sheep. "Broken," she started to repeat. Sal raised his shirt, exposing his blue-green torso. "Oh, lord. Follow me."

In the lobby, three acid freaks sat in a circle, pressing fingers into their faces. EMTs wrestled a fourth to a gurney, cinching two straps at a time. Some revolution, I thought, but it got me focused. I rubbed my chest as Sal fell into a wheelchair, wincing. An orderly steered him sharply through a maze of drawn privacy curtains, pulling me to follow against my will. He was a black man of significant size squeezed into a lazy white uniform, and Sal seemed to take to him immediately, mostly, I assumed, because his clothes didn't fit either. The orderly's head was huge and shaved, and his smile was constant, and when he found an open chamber, he locked the wheels.

"Stanley," he said, tapping his nametag, stooping over and peering into Sal's eyes. "You been in country."

"Yes."

"You too?" he asked, leaning toward me.

"Yes," I said.

"Then how's it you get all tied up in this thing, all busted up in this? This ain't no place for you. This is their fight, ain't that so?"

Sal looked at me. "Long story," I said.

"Well, makes no difference." He touched Sal on the shoulder. "Stanley's gonna take real good care of you. But you," he said, poking me, "can't stay in here. The doc is only goin' to throw you out or worse, just keep walkin' to the next patient, and we gotta get our man here fixed, so..." he pointed me to the hallway, "go back up and have a seat. I'll wheel him out when he's done."

"How long?" I asked, despite having no intention of hanging around.

"Dunno. What's broken?"

"Rib."

Sal harrumphed and shook Stanley's hand off his shoulder. "What am I for, Corman? I can answer for myself. Ribs." Sal lifted his shirt.

"Whoa. Well, hate to tell you but nothing gets done for that 'cept wrappin' you up and gettin' you somethin' to take the sting out. Won't be long once we get it goin', but it's the x-ray gonna take some time; got chairs stacked six deep down there already, and if you ain't spittin' blood you're gonna be here a while. Maybe tonight, maybe tomorrow."

"Stanley," I feigned to keep Sal's trust. "Anything you can do to get a vet to the front?"

I looked at Sal and nodded.

"Vets don't make no difference to them. These docs got their own rules. Can you lift your shirt?"

Stanley pressed in four places. Sal groaned at each. Stanley assessed that one rib was broken, maybe two, and that Sal was going to get his gallbladder stabbed if he walked out of here like that.

That was my cue.

I looked at Sal with a finality I didn't want to convey. But this was it. I was done. I was dropping the envelope at the *Seed* before they released Rubin and Hoffman, then hitting the road. Alone. In SOFA. If COINTELPRO still wanted me, they'd have to come find me.

"You're in good hands with Stanley here."

Sal's eyes sharpened.

I softened. "I'm going to look for the pig. That's what you want, isn't it?"

Sal handed me his sketchpad.

"What are you doing?"

He said. "I can't keep her safe here."

But I didn't take it because I knew damn well what he was doing, testing, and it wasn't going to work. I waved it off. "I can't do both."

And with that, I left Sal.

Chapter 7

I parked SOFA among the hijacked shopping carts on an abandoned street three blocks from the *Seed*. It would blend in as forsaken there, plus no one from the *Seed* or the remaining revolution would see me pull up to know I had it.

Climbing the stairs, I heard nothing. No groans, no murmurs, no diatribes, no mimeograph machines; nothing except an enamel clicking. And with good reason: no one was there. The *Seed* office was empty except for the red-haired girl sucking a lollypop, clacking it against her teeth. She was packing a box. She'd been packing them all morning. Five piles of boxes listed in the corner. She hummed with boredom, more of a drone, lips closing around the white stick.

"It's over," she blurted, as if she'd finally hummed her way to the only lyrics in the song she knew. She tapped papers into a neat pile, corners aligned, before slapping them into a box. "They snagged Jerry and everybody, but Dellinger, what's he do? Sends a courier to wake me up! 'There's going to be lots of trials!' his memo says, 'Pack the papers! We'll send someone to move them.'"

"When? To where?" I asked, my new probing skills taking over naturally.

She shrugged. "Watch them stiff me on this! If I didn't need this two dollars-an-hour for bus fare home to Wichita…"

I looked over to the rubble on Rubin's desk, diverting her attention.

"You supposed to pack that too?"

"Soon as I get to it. Just the papers. The desk stays. Something wrong with you?"

"Why?"

"You keep rubbing your chest like you're – look, I'm telling you right now, I'm not reviving you. I'm not pumping your chest and I'm sure as hell not blowing into your mouth. I'm just going to pack around your body, that's all, wherever you fall. I've got no time for dead men."

No time for dead men? And with that lollypop clacking against her molars? Could she be any more beautiful? What the hell do I do now? If I drop the envelope in the drawer then she'll find it, and *she'll* be in possession of it. Desperate to bust somebody, *anybody*, the cops could bust her, and she wouldn't see the light of Kansas until, well, I couldn't do that to her. Not this Midwestern redhead with the lollypop in her mouth. Not with nineteen-year-old bangs like those, and nipples dotting her blouse. Not with butterflies stitched into the calves of her bell-bottom jeans, just above the telltale fraying of her cuffs where threads trailed like kite strings. I couldn't do that to her, even if she *did* think we'd be too red together, which I could only assume.

What the hell was I doing? Who did I think I was, letting my mind wander to the future? There were snipers still, and a large amount of smack right over my heart. And I was leaving. No, what I had to do now was come back after she was gone and after the pick up of the boxes, but before eight (as Smackspecter ordered) to get this smack off me. Was there ever a city harder to break out of?

"Did you hear about Pigasus?" she asked without looking up.

"Dead?" I forced a sad furrowed brow she never saw.

"I don't know. I don't think so. The pig squad caught it right after the nomination and took it out to the Hormel plant."

"Hormel? Like in Spam?"

"Keyed can, jelly, yep."

Keyed can? Jelly? God, she was gorgeous! But the Hormel plant? They were putting it right into the food supply after all their fears of the pig being laced with acid and explosives? No, they'd have to test it first, some kind of dissection to check for these things, maybe fly in some rubber-gloved guy from the USDA.

"I can't believe it still might be alive," I murmured. "Pigs die hard."

"Yeah, well, it's a little sad, though. He was kind of cute. Did you see this?" She flung a *Tribune* at me. "Jerry and Pigasus made the front page." Below the fold was a grainy picture of Rubin on the podium holding the limp pig. Even in print, the birthmark glowed.

She ran her hands through her red hair and said something about the pig being pink like us. I offered that it was mostly orange, and disgusting, in as much as it ate its own shit and all. But she got on this soapbox (way up high, where her beauty began to fade, really fade!) about me not having a heart and the pig not knowing any better.

But all I really wanted to know now: was the pig dead?

"We'll know when Andy calls," she said.

Andy was on Pigasus duty at the Hormel plant. She told me he sneaks to the phone on his breaks to let the Wichita girl know what's what. Turns out Andy's from Wichita also. That seemed believable. When I asked if Andy was pink too, she flared her teeth and ripped off a foot of packing tape. She was stunning! "Meatpacking left Wichita," she said as if I should read the *Wichita Intermittent News* to keep abreast of such things. "Now he's with Hormel, but sympathetic to the larger picture. I mean, who knows what they'll do to it?"

Precisely, I thought. Who knew? Because even if the chief concern of the federales' (Spanglish!) wasn't for the consumptive safety of everyone's pork by-products, they'd still see this as their new and best opportunity to set up Rubin and Hoffman, now tucked in jail and unable to be in possession of the smack on my chest, or, later, in their drawer. It wasn't a very far ethical leap from planting heroin to lacing a pig with fistfuls of acid. They were going to "find" acid in the pig one way or another.

And that would be fine by me. Why should I care as long as they didn't order me to do it? Except that lacing the pig as evidence would implicate Sal, and me too. Sal had been the caretaker of Pigasus and I the caretaker of Sal, de facto (Latin!)! Who else better to blame than the caretakers? I did some math in my head: the Bureau would see this as *their* long-prophesied quadruple jump to clean up the whole Chicago mess. Jump 1) Kill the pig; 2) "Discover" the LSD Rubin and Hoffman promised to poison the water supply with; 3) Lock away Rubin and Hoffman for good; 4) Clean up the rest, namely Sal for being Chief Caretaker and me for being CBOCP of the revolution (I like to name things!) Chief Breaker of COINTELPRO Protocol. Four jumps! Count them! King them! And fuck me, I thought, realizing I'd been set up from the beginning. They were always going to clean me up too. They never intended to let me go, to keep up their end. I told them I wasn't ready. Perfect, they said. I told them, Train me. No training is preferred, they said. I was always their tool to plant the heroin, and their tool to be erased.

"I just wish I could save him somehow," she added, screwing with my clarity of thought.

Who did I think I was? I looked closely at the way her eyebrows feathered. I wanted to run a finger over them to see if I could feel. When she snapped her head back, I pulled my hand, asking, "So why don't you? Why don't you save it?"

I wasn't urging the saving of any fucking pig, I reasoned. I am the killer of pigs. No, I was urging the saving of me, a slightly different thing. Who did I think I was? But if there was a way to substitute a penned pig for *the* pig, then maybe I could hold some of the cards, so that when it was announced that massive doses of LSD were recovered, proving the Yippies' intent to poison the city's water, I could expose the government by bringing forth the real pig just before their hunt for me began.

It was a bad plan full of holes on account of there being snipers and a pig, but it was the only one I could think of. I had nothing left.

"How well do you know this Andy guy? Would he help you?" I asked.

"I don't know. He's got a promotion coming."

"But he's sympathetic to the cause, right? And sympathetic to a certain girl from Wichita, I presume?" I was getting very good at the probing thing.

"So what? What's he going to do?"

"Couldn't he get another pig as a stand-in? One that's already good as dead?"

"Either way a pig dies, right?"

God, she was beautiful.

The phone rang. She put her hand on the receiver and looked at me as if to say, "Do you believe this?"

"Hello? Hi, Andy. Hi. Okay. Good. Say, I've been talking to some people over here about maybe trying to save Pigasus. Well, I guess they're wondering if you couldn't just, you know, swap it out for another pig. You know, for the cause. I know, I know, foreman. But you said you were looking for a way to help. What time is that?"

She put her hand over the mouthpiece. "They're doing some kind of test on him at eight," she whispered.

"You're confusing pronouns," I said. "Andy or the pig?"

She rolled her eyes, ratcheting her beauty downward. "Pig-a-sus. A test on Pig-a-sus. I'm guessing you don't have a girlfriend, do you? Eight o'clock."

What the hell is it with this city and eight o'clock? I wondered.

"That should give him plenty of time to swap it out," I whispered for no reason.

"That should give you plenty of time," she said into the phone. "I don't know. Let me find out." She put her hand back over the mouthpiece. "He wants to know, 'Then what'?"

"How do I know? Let's play this one move at a time. Ask him what time I should come get the pig."

"He clocks out at four," she relayed. "He can do it then, but he says Pigasus is in bad shape. That he thinks it's going to die anyway."

"If it was going to die," I snarled, "it would have done it already. Four o'clock," I acknowledged. But who did I think I was? Could I really save myself by *rescuing* a pig? Was it worth the risk? I had a car of sorts, and a wide-open field to run it through, west/north/east/south. I could be in any state's Bumfuck before the Bureau knew I was gone, change my name to Ralph, tile bathrooms or sell whole life insurance, and build a new identity as an honest church usher before you could say, "Pigasus who?"

When she hung up the phone with Andy from Wichita, I sat in Rubin's chair, watching her, rubbing my chest. "All right if I just hang here for a few hours?"

"You do know the plant isn't in Chicago, right?" she said.

"What?"

"That Hormel plant is west of here, almost to the Iowa line. Maybe two hours?"

I pushed myself out of the chair, doubtful that SOFA's ungreased wheels could get me that far. I waved the *Tribune* at her. "Can I keep this to be sure Andy gives me the right pig?"

She gestured back, palm down, fingers flicking, up as if to say, "Take it, but go." I opened the door, looked back where she was tapping papers, aligning corners, gorgeous, and thought we would have been too red together anyway.

"Way too red," she said, head down.

***

The Hormel plant rose from tall grass about fifty miles east of Davenport, where the prairie rolled gently up and gently down. My eyes drooped with the monotony, and I fought it off by conjuring a list of the reasons cars are better than women, including cars are colorblind and stop chattering when you feed them oil. I caught myself caressing the headrest on the passenger side and made myself stop, twice.

A haphazard campus of old brick and new steel rimmed a hole that might once have been a pond. To the north of the hole, feedlots stretched to the horizon. Thousands of pigs fed at mechanical troughs. I searched for a station on SOFA's radio to drown out acres of pig snorting, and fumbled for a fan speed to cut the stench, only to find radio preachers snorting even worse and the stench inescapable. A water tower and a smokestack cast long afternoon shadows into the parking lots lining the plant. White smoke puffed from the stack and tumbled south. Either a pig was being charred or a pope had been elected.

It was 3:15. SOFA had done well to get me there forty-five minutes early on, just three more quarts of oil and a top off of the radiator. But like so many missions, the trick wasn't getting there, it was getting back.

I had time to kill, and sitting in SOFA in the August heat was insufferable. I parked in one of the visitor lots, where a guard pointed at the graffiti on the hood and asked, "Fucking hippies do that?"

To escape the sun, I took a tour of the pig disassembly plant. Thick, tubed, battleship-gray railings were the only things separating me and a tour group from Memphis from a wide series of bubbling yellow vats below. Women kept to the far side, pulling their dresses close to their legs, as if the vats of pigs had eyes. Men leaned over for views of the poached meat.

We shuffled above gelling cooling tanks via a see-through steel walkway. It steered the tour single file around a sharp corner, bringing us face-to-snout with a chorus of pig carcasses dangling from chrome hooks, swinging to an ethereal Bossa nova (Brazilian!), gutted, silent and cleaned.

When the tour group began to ask questions about hotdogs, putting my rendezvous (French!) time in jeopardy, I reversed course and exited from whence I came. Listen to me! "Whence"!

I circled back to SOFA and eased her to the meeting spot Andy described to the Wichita redhead, a wide ally between the newer steel buildings. I paced with one eye on my watch, the other on the handful of metal doors lining the pathway. In silent moments, I fashioned myself on a soundstage, waiting for Ann-Margret to emerge, but I don't know why and I didn't think much about it because through the creak of a half-opened door the pig rasped and stuttered toward me. Not out of recognition, I thought. Certainly not out of affection, I hoped. But I was the only one in the alley, and it was hurting. The door slammed behind it, forcing the pig to try to turn back. But it would have turned for no reason; Andy never showed his face. Now it was just the crippled pig and me. Only the worst dreams come true.

The pig put its orange-haired chin on the sill of the back door and stood there, doing nothing, not trying, not pretending to try, not looking back. Just stood there. I coaxed it, saying things like, "There you go!" and "Up now!' and "I swear to God I will fucking kill you if you don't get in," but pigs don't care about any of that. They are fat. They are disgusting in their appetite. They are lazy, until they charge. They are all the same. I looked down the alley and remembered that I'd already debated this plan. I knew it wasn't a good one.

Chapter 8

The trip back to Chicago was uneventful unless you count the endless moaning in the back seat, or the thirteen trooper cars we passed all lit up and (thankfully) already ruining someone's day. They sent me into a panic nonetheless, not only because of the stolen government witness in the back or the smack taped to my chest, but because SOFA (with its spray-painted tree-hugging manifesto) was anything but inconspicuous. It screamed hippie! It screamed beat up the driver! Fortunately, the graffiti on its hood blurred at sixty miles an hour, so the trick was to not get pulled over, and not to let a trooper pull up alongside me. Not so easy.

Ahead, a trooper pulled off the shoulder back onto the highway. I decelerated, falling back to keep the manifesto out of sight of his rearview; easy enough. But the highway was teeming with them and it made for exhausting driving. And the pig was moaning. And the lights of an occupied trooper appeared up ahead. I rubbed my chest. The pig moaned in agony, and I thought about the Saigon cure. Right, Lieut? The Saigon cure, the little plasticine envelopes every grunt but the new guys kept tucked in their helmet. Not to shoot up, not to snort, not to escape to survive, but to swallow if needed because, as every fucking new guy needs to know, when swallowed the smack metabolizes in the stomach as morphine. It's a pharmaceutical fact! No high, but no pain. And you never could count on the medics to spend one of their golden syrettes if they didn't think you were going to make it because the body will go into shock soon enough (for them!) and shut down its own pain. What is it you said: "You'd better know the rules of letting go, Hodges. You'd better know your own two-minute drill, because there won't be time to think. I've got mine." You gestured at the envelopes in your helmet, remember Lieut? 'The first play, Hodges, is these to stop the screams. Just pour them down my throat, all of them. It takes a lot. Don't think, just pour! You've got to stop the screams first. They follow the screams, Hodges. The pigs follow the screams. The second play? Well, we'll save that until you see a few things over here. Just keep an edge on your knife."

The pig in the back seat moaned at a higher pitch now, like a pennywhistle, only more annoying, as unfathomable as that may seem. I rubbed my chest and imagined pouring the whole envelope down the pig's throat while screaming, "Metabolize this, you fuck!" But the Fed would know to the gram how much was in that envelope, and I didn't need to set *myself* up for a fall; the Bureau was already handling that. No need to duplicate the effort. What I did need was to be rid of them: pig and smack.

It was past seven when we pulled into Chicago. The late August sun was setting and taking with it some of the heat. A cool breeze rolled in fits from the lake, swirling papers in alcoves and forcing bums to switch sides, losing the remaining sun. The pig moaned to raise its snout. It noted something familiar. Pigeons turned their backs to the eerie and empty streets. It was if the circus just left town, as if the revolution folded its big top and caught the 6:30 train to Peoria.

At 7:40 I parked SOFA in my customary spot near the hijacked shopping carts, and set out for the *Seed* office, exultant to soon be rid of the smack. But as I turned the corner, I was greeted by a colony of Snapjaw. They had the building surrounded.

"Eight o'clock, you said!" I snarled to myself. "You impatient bastards!"

Why I ever thought I could trust them to keep time was beyond me. They must have realized that with Hoffman and Rubin behind bars, the smack was just going to sit there in the drawer, waiting for some hippie to hit pay dirt. I crossed the street pretending to be window-shopping, hoping for some sight of Smackspecter's sneakers, to tie a face to the voice. I needed to see the man I was running from. But at 8:30, with the Fed still inside, the streets fell dark. I'd have to get a whole lot closer to see shoes, and I wasn't taking that chance. I was already taking a big enough one leaving the pig in the car, moaning, where anyone passing by would hear it. What choice did I have? The place was crawling—no, that would indicate movement. The Snapjaw and snipers stood frozen like pickets of a stockade. The only thing that moved was my hand to my chest again. I did quick math in my head. There was no planting the smack now. It was mine to mail back. It was mine to ditch. It was mine to sprinkle on a precinct's powdered donuts. I needed a better plan.

I slid around the corner, back scraping against bricks. Now that there was no clear path to hand it back, no night deposit box, the smack seemed heavier, like it was pulling on the bandage, pulling on me. I didn't need the additional weight, but like the pig, the smack was proof of the Fed's plot, and as long as I held both, I might manage a negotiated release. He'd need a deal if I held all the loose ends, the smack *and* the pig. I jumped a cab near the Marriott and headed back to the hospital. If the pig were to play a prominent role in the swap for my freedom, it would have to stay alive. For that, the pig would need an unassuming caretaker.

***

I found Sal in the exit queue of radiology, where they either assign you a toe tag or cut your wristband off for release. Behind the little privacy curtain, Stanley was wielding a set of scissors.

"Corman?"

"Yes, I found him, Sal. He's waiting for you."

Sal smiled like he knew it all the time, then tried to launch himself from his wheelchair, only to fall back wincing.

"How many?" I asked Stanley.

"Three ribs, and in a row. That was one big foot that got him! But he's gonna be just fine in a few weeks."

"I'm fine *now*," Sal argued.

"He jus' needs to take it easy, stay all wrapped up."

A voice filled the far end of the hall. Sal spun at its volume, Stanley at its rage, me at its recall. I halted Stanley with my hand. The voice came again, closer, approaching with the abrupt drawing of curtains. Someone was looking for somebody. And I knew them both. The hunt for me was on already.

"Let go!" I motioned, grabbing Sal's chair.

Stanley threw up his hands and stepped aside. I shoved Sal through a curtain overlap and into a broad hallway, the center of which contained an unbroken train of gurneys, most dangling feet. Doors lined the near side of the hall, curtains the far, and someone was jerking them all open in our direction, one after another, to the protests and screams of those inside.

Preferring the bullet-slowing properties of wood to those of wool (unless still on the sheep) I pulled each doorknob. Locked, locked, and goddamnit, locked. The slamming and ripping drew nearer, and Sal stood to take up position, but Stanley eased him back down. "Best hang on for this ride," he said, assuming captainship of the chair again. "Stanley will get you out of here. We done our fightin'!"

Then, in a gap between a curtain's hem and the floor appeared a pair of black high-top sneakers.

Smackspecter.

"What the..." a nurse inside gasped.

"Shut up. You, turn around!" he ordered the patient. "I said turn around!"

The nurse protested. "What right do you have busting in here? Get your hands off of him! He's in shock!"

"I don't care if he's *dead*," Smackspecter growled. "I said to step aside."

There was a grunt.

"Jesus, he's a specimen, huh? *Huh*? No wonder America's losing."

Stanley moved quickly, like he'd outrun a thing or two in his day. I motioned us behind a curtain two away from Smackspecter, then slid into the one between. He was heading Smackspecter off.

"Who are you?" Smackspecter demanded.

"Stanley."

"Well, Stanley, who's in that next room?"

Stanley backed up to our curtain. "Lady."

"What lady?"

"Lady you ain't gonna walk in on."

"I'm only going to tell you this once. I'm with the FBI. Do not fuck with me."

"FBI don't make a difference to the lady if she's not ready to be seen."

"You don't want me coming back for you."

"How you gonna come back if I ain't lettin' you leave?"

A body crashed into an examination table.

"I ain't lettin' you leave."

"Corman, what's happening?" Sal whispered.

I gestured with a chop of my hand. Not now, Sal. Good God, not now.

"I ain't lettin' you leave and I ain't lettin' you move that curtain." Stanley warned, "I aim to protect the lady with your life."

Sal nodded at a parallel commitment.

"You're killing American boys, Stanley!" Smackspecter managed. I envisioned him in a full nelson.

"That be the gov'ment, sir," Stanley corrected.

The heels of black sneakers appeared beneath the hem then rose and dangled from the floor. I waved Sal into complete silence, and then, except for the flapping of a gurney wheel down the hall, everything was quiet.

That didn't last long.

"Corman?"

"That man has come to take back your pig, Sal," I lied somewhat, rubbing my chest. "Let's go!"

Stanley's voice rang from the hallway. "Now would be a good time to run through billin' is all I'm sayin' to all you. Billin' will be clear for about an hour, so get your bills paid and get on your way, everybody. This place will be busy as a hive soon."

Sal and I crashed through the billing office and onto the avenue. Our pace was all his ribs would allow, but in the backstreets where the sirens wailed, we hailed another cab. Before we slid in, I held my finger to my lips as a warning to Sal. It was a plea not to speak. (Spies were everywhere.) It was not a plea to let me pay for the damn cab. Sal read it as both. I pulled my bankroll out and counted under the dome light: three hundred and seventy two dollars. Half my discharge money was already gone. Working for the government was expensive.

Two Snapjaw remained outside the *Seed* office, securing its entrance. "Had this whole block locked down an hour ago," the driver said. "They don't give a fuck what they do to traffic! I get no money standing still." At the curb, I handed him three dollars for the two-eighty fare. "I get no money moving, either."

Down the abandoned street, newly hijacked shopping carts surrounded SOFA like a gang. What light flashed down the alley lit their vertical chrome like wet blades. I was relieved to find the pig still there, wheezing.

Sal opened the rear door. If it were a dog, the pig would have wagged its tail or licked a face. But it was a pig, and it didn't. Sal lay down next to it, petting its head, gently running his hand over the pig's lumpy spine. They groaned together.

"Just like it was, Corman," Sal said.

Yes, I thought, reading the dipstick in the moonlight then pouring two quarts into SOFA, including the price on my head.

Chapter 9

The ramp to I-80 swarmed with refugees seeking a ride to safety: some held thumbs, some held signs, some held hands to create a chain across the road only to scatter as the clacking of SOFA swiftly came upon them.

"There's so many," Sal said with a predictive kindness.

"No," I said, heading him off. "Stop for one and we'll get ambushed."

Where the ramp split west or east, I slowed with indecision. But when the hippies crowded the west, I went east, and soon as the highway hummed beneath us, the pig and Sal were both asleep. With the exception of their wheezing, there was a fifty-mile radius of silence. I welcomed the time to talk aloud to myself, to sort things out, to do some more math in my head about SOFA and me.

SOFA was displaying her insatiable appetites again, just as she had on our trip to Hormel, gulping a gallon of petrol (British!) every ten miles, a quart of oil every fifty (if I kept moving), and cool water to slake intermittent hot flashes. Gas at forty-five cents, plus oil at sixty, plus tolls, carry the two, add some pig food and… I put my hand on my lap and rubbed my bankroll. A diminished bulge told a woeful story; my relationship with SOFA was simply not sustainable. I'd be flat before I hit the coast. More disturbing, she did not have a long lifeline, not the way she smoked and rattled and slouched in recline, not the way transfusions hardly made a difference anymore. I was losing her, and she was spitting her charm out right underneath me. So the question was, where could we spend our last thousand miles together getting to what would buy me more time for my escape from the Fed – a *lot* more time?

And how could I get there before the morning shift of cops everywhere got briefed on the wanted man (me) and, separately, the missing car (SOFA) before they put the two together and set out to ruin my day?

I sat up in my seat as if watching a quiz show. More math! Word problem! How far could a car go between 9pm and breakfast (i.e., ten hours) if it went an inconspicuous five miles over the speed limit on I-80 heading toward the sunrise? Answer: I didn't know. I wrote a big question mark on my mental card and flashed it with a camera-ready smile. But I concluded I'd use our pit stops to study a map, sharpen some numbers, and take a fortuitous guess.

Until then, drive through the night, keep us on the pavement without sleep for ten hours. But where do I part from SOFA? A train station, and board with a pig? A bus terminal and board with a pig? Plus, those routes were so predictable they were likely sealed already, and by people with training. I wouldn't make it through my first Mrs. Wagner pie before they dragged me off.

"Sal, I'm lost," I said twice, although I knew he was sleeping. "There's Snapjaw and hippies and smack, plus my past!"

The cool night through the windows vented the fumes enough to keep me alert. As we skimmed over marsh along the top of Indiana, moths streaked the windshield in alarming numbers, but I got it. SOFA did not. She swerved and Sal awoke.

"Pigasus is hungry," he said.

"Do you see anything out here?" I challenged. "We'll stop to oil up in another half hour. The pig'll have to wait."

Sal grimaced but did not object. He was busy looping his rib bandage around the pig.

"You need that," I said.

"Not as much."

I ran the wagon near Gary, Indiana and its smokestacked horizon before finding a rest area on the eastern side. The lot was empty but for a rumbling tractor-trailer and a few sedans. I pulled back into an unlit corner, then admonished myself for not assimilating. The first thing a patrolling cop would do is go to the single car in the unlit corner. I repositioned SOFA nose first into a lit spot between the sedans, front bumper against a grassy median, graffiti shielded from uniformed eyes. I fed her two quarts of oil without reading her dipstick. I just knew her that well now.

"Five minutes," I warned through Sal's window, like a father on vacation. "Get the pig out to do its thing. We've got no time. I'm running in to see what they have to eat. But stay close to the car and get inside if any lights come at all. Here, I'll leave the keys. If it's a cop, pull away slowly. You can circle back to get me."

I sneaked into the building for no reason, hiding in the shadows until a passing minute proved its vacancy. A vending machine full of frosted snacks stood next to a photo booth and a contraption that, for a dollar, would roll your penny between out-sized gears, flatten it and stamp it with "Gary, Indiana." A sign above urged me to collect all thirty Indiana cities. "It's fun!" it said. Not everyone thought so. Some Canadian vandal had jammed one of their nickels into its coin slot, disabling it and the snack machine too, for the pig and me.

"Nothing," I said, showing Sal my empty hands. "Let's get fifty more miles behind us."

SOFA was reluctant, slowly shuddering up to speed with a revived guttural knocking. And just when I assumed she was done and I eased off the gas, she backfired in the entrance lane. I forgave her, but it wasn't pretty. We were getting too comfortable with each other. I was beginning to sense her every mood, her flexing, her weakening, and her short-lived hopeful resurgences. More and more, it was like studying a monitor in ICU. "She never said goodbye," someone in my imagined ICU said. "True, but she never said we were too red together either," I argued.

Sal was focused elsewhere. "Corman, I don't know where we're going. And I don't know why we're going there."

"I told you, they are coming to take your pig away, and they won't be kind to it if they do."

What should I tell him, that his trust was once again misplaced, this time in Rubin and Hoffman, yet to trust me? Should I say the Yippies were using him, even as I was using him? Should I break his heart, revealing Hoffman and Rubin's duplicity even as I put a sharp little edge on my own?

Yes.

"Sal, I know it's not like you, but your trust in Rubin and Hoffman was misplaced. They never wanted the pig to be President."

"In the beginning..."

"In the beginning, Sal, they threatened to poison the water of Chicago by stuffing your pig with acid, then drowning it in the lake."

"They would never really hurt him."

"No? You heard them in the car this morning! They were planning on killing the pig and barbequing it, literally feeding it to the press. Sal, every plan they had for the pig ended with it dying!"

Stunned, Sal rocked in the back seat, as if these thoughts were too heavy to even move his head.

"But I saved it," I added, eyes moving to the guardrail where SOFA's weakening headlights diffused prematurely. What was I doing? Who did I think I was?

Sal grew solemn. "Where did you find him?"

"I got a tip they sent it to Hormel for processing. I found it there. No, that's not true. It was more like he found me, Sal. There were hundreds of pigs in the pen, and they all sort of parted, and here comes Pigasus right at me, like he knew me."

"He does know you, Corman! You're his healer!" Sal's faith rebounded, momentarily.

"But now they think you're the one who took him, the one who stole him from the plant. The one tampering with state evidence! And Sal, listen to me, the man in the hospital, the one Stanley contained, the one in the sneakers, was hunting for you!"

"They think I saved the President?"

"Yes."

Sal smiled. "Where are we going, Corman?"

"As far as the wagon will take us."

Another smile, then, "We need a plan. We need to find a place to set the President free."

I muttered another string of consonants. There would be no setting the pig free. I needed the pig contained, alive and ready for exchange, not free-range and eating its own shit someplace. "What do you mean?" I asked.

"The President needs to be with his own kind," Sal said. "And he needs to be where he can't be found."

No, I thought, what the pig needs is to be with you to keep it alive until the swap is made. But Sal's thoughts were provocative. Something in the way he said "President" and "with his own kind" started a preposterous new word problem in my mind: "How many votes would a pig running for president get in Iowa, if …" but I couldn't breach the sheer implausibility of the first part to concoct a second part. I just kept inserting "if Iowa could chuck wood", which didn't really work, as I wasn't sure if Iowa even had trees. I let the problem go. Self-training!

"He can't be set free. He's all busted up," I said.

"Yes, but you can heal him. More."

Jesus.

I thought quickly, impressing myself as I did. "A true healer only clears the way for the body to heal itself," I said, revealing a heretofore-unknown trade secret. "We take the screams away, then the body takes over."

Sal bought it. Of course he did.

For two guys and a pig trying to outrun execution, we made horrible time. I cajoled SOFA through three more oil stops in Indiana. At each, Sal unwrapped and rewrapped the pig, and the pig let him. Just over the Ohio state line, the Buckeye Welcome Center rose on the dimly lit horizon. I shook my head in defiance. Don't stop, I thought. But SOFA had her own needs and she wanted them tended to. Gauges began moving in portending directions: amperes dipping, pressure plummeting, temperature ascending! All the signs were there, and I knew it; SOFA and I were clearly parting ways, but were not yet ready for the big tell. We were codependent. She had no miles ahead without me, and I none without her and so, she had her way. We stopped again.

The rest area was a clone of the ones in Indiana, same photo-booth, same penny masher imploring you to collect all cities in Ohio. I ran my finger down the alphabetical choices: Akron, Cincinnati, Cleveland, Columbus, and there it was, Delaware. How strange to read it and feel that tug of home. Delaware: Battling Bishops, Brown Jugs and a haze in the wind when the corn silked up. Why did I think I was getting homesick after all these years? I ran a penny through the gears and stuffed it in my pocket.

Near the penny masher hung a map of Ohio. I calculated two hundred and twenty miles standing between the Pennsylvania border and me. One topped-off tank of gas should do it. Check. Five more quarts of oil? Check.

Beside the map a vending machine squatted in its own yellow light, coin slot clear and, as if the god of pigs himself had intervened, three sleeves of knockoff Yodels called "Klappy Kakes" dangled in the third row.

The pig ate and perked up. By 12:30 he was spewing gas like a refinery. By 1:30 he was ready to shit and re-eat.

Maybe it was the miles I'd put between Chicago and me, maybe I was just tired, but as we pulled over to allow for the pig's disgusting digestive system just west of Cleveland, I did not panic at the sight of numerous cars at the rest area. Condensation on windows hinted that many were sleeping.

The pig rooted in the grass bordering the parking lot, looking for roughage, I assumed, to complement the chocolate soup it just lapped up. Even in the dark, cars slowed to watch it. Where the hell all these people were going at 1:30 in the morning, I had no idea. Parents woke kids who leaned bleary-eyed from finger-streaked windows. Tourists gathered, gawking, cranking wind-up cameras and giggling like they'd seen a unicorn. The pig and Sal grew anxious at the attention, both pulling against the leash, both groaning in their pain. Someone's flashlight illuminated the pig's hideous glowing New Jersey. The crowd pulled the children away.

"How far are we going to get?" Sal asked as he ushered the pig to SOFA.

Under the influence of fresh air, it was a solid question: how long would it take for word to spread about two guys traveling east with a pig in a car sporting "Save our forests, asshole" on its hood. I needed a stronger plan. I needed a map. I went back to the vending area and returned with an atlas stuffed in my pants. Under the faint dome light, I placed my finger on Ohio and traced east along I-90, the New York Thruway, running south of Buffalo and Rochester, north of the Finger Lakes and through the salted guts of Syracuse and Utica. I paused at Albany, where I traced I-87 south to Manhattan, then north to the Canadian line where the map changed from a pulmonary web of red-and-blue roadway to the expansive green of the Adirondack Mountains, and I wondered if that wasn't a hospitable home for a pig and two vets. All that open land, wild water and the huge cover of forest. I showed it to Sal.

"I lived here," he said, pointing to Long Island. "Ronkonkoma."

"We can't be safe there," I said.

"No," he agreed. "And families need to forget."

"But a man could hide here," I said, drawing my finger north to the Adirondacks, to the center of the green at a small town called Saranac Lake. "Make his living from the woods carving ducks or something."

Sal balked. "We need someplace to set him free, Corman, somewhere he won't freeze."

"Sal, allow me to refresh your memory on the pig here; it eats Yodels and eggs. Unless you set it free in a 7-11, it has no chance! We, um, can't, Sal. We can't set it free. Not yet. Not at least until it heals and learns to eat right."

Not until I swapped it for my freedom.

I paused for Sal's reaction, but he was winding the bandage around the pig again. I turned my attention back to the map, pushing my finger south, sliding it east. And there, black among the red-and-blue roadway lines, I found what I was looking for. "When you need it, man," the stoned night clerk had prophesied, "it's the trail that sets you free!" I ran my finger from Pennsylvania, then to Maryland, Virginia, and Tennessee, and I knew how I might find the exit. And it seemed to work, this plan to take flight on the trail. It seemed to check all the boxes: Forested? Check. Directional? Check. Concealed? Check. Elusive? Check. But when I looked down from high atop my imaginary ascended mountains, I saw a busted-up vet with a stumbling pig too injured to endure the climb. How could Sal and the pig possibly hike the trail when they could barely walk on blacktop? I let my head fall back against the rest and squeezed my bloodshot eyes shut as if the answer were *that* close. And it was. I rubbed my chest, then smiled and coaxed SOFA back onto the highway. Who did I think I was? Would that even work, I wondered? Was Lieut even right? Did it work for him?

At the next oil stop, I studied the map in silence, flipping pages back and forth, using my index finger to scale the distance while mentally hiking south. The trail would take us about two hundred miles through Pennsylvania, a couple of dozen in Maryland, then touch West Virginia before starting the longest stretch, about five hundred, through Virginia to Tennessee and the great Smoky Mountains. It was there in the Smokies, I determined, I'd find the open land, wild water, and huge cover of forest I needed to hide until the heat cooled down or a swap was made. And it was there, I would convince Sal, that feral pigs flourished better than rats in Cancun. There that the pig could finally be with its own kind. There in the Smokies, eight hundred miles by foot, up and over mountains… in summer. Brilliant.

"Am I insane?" I asked aloud unintentionally, optimism fleeing.

"No," I heard Sal say. "Now shhh." Without looking, I knew he was rewrapping the pig.

We made a piss, oil and sandwich run at a gas station off the highway, then bolted for the Pennsylvania border.

"What's the plan, Corman?" Sal asked again.

Weariness of that question was only dwarfed by my lack of confidence in the answer. And both showed in my tone, but there was no sense telling him the truth yet. There'd be too many annoying questions.

"Everything's a little complicated, Sal, don't you think? You need to keep the pig safe; I need to keep you safe; someone needs to keep me safe, and there's no keeping this wagon safe. How do we do all that, Sal? Got any ideas? No? I didn't think so. So I'm still working on it. All I know is when that sun comes up, cops will be looking for us on every road between here and the borders. The further we are from Chicago when that happens, the better."

We cut through Youngstown in a blur and crossed the Pennsylvania border with no words from Sal. I thought of cutting south through Pittsburgh, then east on I-70 to meet the trail closer to Tennessee and reduce the hike, but I had no faith SOFA would stick with me that long, and each mile of gas and oil reduced my pathetic bankroll for this expedition. We'd need supplies.

As Sal and the pig slept through stops in Grove City, Dubois, and Milton, a Plan B formed in my head; more of a Plan A+ actually. I needed proof that I had *the* pig and still carried their conjured evidence against Rubin and Hoffman, the smack, and I needed to get that proof, that first round of negotiation, to the Bureau so they would know the strength of my position and call off any dogs. In Hazelton, in the final moments of that night's blackness, I pulled SOFA along the curb outside the glass rest building. From there I could see the lobby and its vending area.

"What are we doing, Corman?"

"Just trust me and stay in the car."

As in the other rest areas, a photo booth sat next to a penny crusher. I waited until the room was empty, then jumped from the car and inside the booth before anyone could see me. I pulled the envelope from my wrap, held open the flap, and dropped a quarter in the machine. The flash caught me with the white powder in various sinister poses, trying to arch an eyebrow to add to my position. When I heard no one in the lobby, I drew the curtain and went back for the pig, throwing open SOFA's back door and grabbing it to an unholy squeal (Sal's or its). I dragged the pig to the booth, pinned it to my lap with its hideous New Jersey exposed, and dropped another quarter. The succession of flashes in the dark sent the pig reeling back through the lobby to Sal's waiting arms.

Back on the highway, Sal rewrapped the pig's ribs and stressed the need for me to have more respect for the President's health. I explained my Plan A+ (I like to name things!), or at least the part I wanted him to believe, that the pictures were his protection should anything happen to him or the pig. It was full of holes, but it filled some gaps. Sal seemed satisfied.

With each mile east, SOFA's clacking grew more ominous. I read the odometer and did math in my head, counting down the remaining sixty-five miles or so, urging her "Don't stop, don't stop" until we sputtered into the waking town of Delaware Water Gap just as the sun rose fully above the horizon. A rustling in the back seat prompted me to lay out the rest of A+ to Sal, but like the incessant crow of a damn rooster, the maddening scratch of his pencil on the sketchpad shut me down.

I made a left onto the moonscape driveway of the local diner. Hitting a pothole, SOFA rose high on her springs, then bottomed with a denting of floorboards, jarring Sal's pencil and ribs and setting the pig to grunting. She bounced to a stop behind the propane tank where I squeezed her key between my fingers, halting my cut of her ignition for fear that this was the end of our beautiful codependence. She knew it. She shook and heaved and trembled and fought, but casting my eyes aside, I turned the key. Her lights faded, her gauges settled, and she let go. She was done with me. It was a great run, the best ever, but I could not have pleased her another mile. It was the big tell. They always end the same.

"Okay?" Sal asked, sensing my loss.

"It was a good run," was all I said.

In wake of SOFA's quiet came the screech of the diner's exhaust fans. The potato and onion smell of grilling home fries roused the pig. Bacon wafted. Perfect, I thought.

"The President needs eggs so bad I can smell them," Sal said, folding his pad. It was time to tell him about Plan A+.

"I have a plan, Sal. Just beyond that bridge over there is the entrance to a long trail, the Appalachian Trail, that'll take us along these mountains as far south as we want, even to the Smoky Mountains."

"I don't like the woods, Corman. Everything is wet."

"I don't like them much either, Sal, but the wagon's finished and they'll be closing the distance, so we've got to keep moving. They want that pig, but I don't think they'll follow us there."

"But the President is not strong right now, Corman. How could he…"

I rubbed my chest. "I think maybe I can heal him some more, Sal. And in the Smokies there're lots of wild pigs."

"Can we set him free there?"

"I think so."

"Then lots of eggs today, Corman. It's a celebration! I had a celebration with eggs once too, back home in Ronkonkoma. It was a diner too, nine eggs, Corman. Nine! Ethel and the waitresses and Sammy the cook, they all knew I was getting called up to the army even before I did. The draft board ate lunch there every day, and they would tell the girls who got chosen, so the girls could call us to celebrate. And when I won, they called the house and promised my brother, "Anything he wants". Those waitresses and Ethel, they made like my girl, Corman, fussing all over me. I sat in the big booth that night, the one they always kept for the guys leaving or coming back. And when they slid in beside me and touched my hair, I ate everything they brought out. And you should have seen them, Corman. You should have heard Ethel and the girls whooping and hollering when I ordered even more, whooping like the Mets won something! And them taking turns sitting on my lap, making me promise to come back and marry them all? That's why I like that the President likes eggs, so now we can celebrate like when I got home. You should have seen them, Corman. You should have seen them."

"I bet that was something," I said, wishing I hadn't. That errant moment of warmth was only me coping with the loss of SOFA.

Chapter 10

The gravy-stained door swung open, and a fat man wiping one hand on his apron limped through with a large smile, filling coffee cups for the truckers at the counter.

"Gonna be a hot one," one of the drivers said.

"What do you mean, gonna?" He flashed his smile again and ran his fingers inside his paper hat, alluding to the sweat.

I studied the menu board. Time to fatten the pig.

"Six?" he asked incredulously.

"Yeah," I said, "promised to bring some back to the guys on the trail. Save them a trip up, you know?"

"I hope they're not the same guys who did that to your face," a driver at the counter said into his cup. I pressed my split lip. I'd all but forgotten it.

"Say," I said to the cook, "Can I buy an envelope and a stamp from you? I'm a little late getting word home that I'm okay."

"Trail don't look like the only thing beating on you," said the driver. "You running, boy?"

But the cook shut it down. "He bought six," he said. "I can help him out."

In a corner booth, I tore the clearest birthmark snapshot and the most sinister smack pic from the strips, writing on both, "I have everything. Let's make a deal." Then, along with the *Tribune's* picture of Pigasus at the podium where I'd circled his birthmark so they didn't have to think too much, and sealed them into the envelope.

When the cook read the address, "COINTELPRO, c/o FBI, Langley, Virginia," he nodded as if we shared a secret and respect. I winked to confirm, but cleared up any misunderstanding. "COINTELPRO's my last name," I said. He slid it atop his other outgoing mail.

The eggs sizzled quickly. I slathered the rolls with ketchup, stuck a plastic spoon in the bag, and headed toward the men's room with the egg sandwiches tucked under my arm like a *Washington Post.*

"You know, you can leave them on the counter here while you're in there," the cook called. "It ain't the cleanest." I pretended not to hear. I was good at that. Self-training!

Behind the stall door like Smackspecter, I unwrapped my chest and squeezed the envelope in my hand, smirking at how my most important work happened in latrines. I did not know how much smack to sprinkle on the eggs. It wasn't like salt. And they weren't like Lieut, where all that mattered was to quiet the screams. Too much and the pig or Sal would die, and hiding their bodies could set me back hours. Too little and the obstacles of their pain would ruin my plan, not to mention their whining ruining my day. I couldn't afford either of those, and I couldn't afford making them sleepy, or getting them stoned either. But what did I know about dosing? What training did I get except a look at the cellophane envelopes in Lieut's helmet? It takes a lot, right, Lieut? Don't think, just pour, you said. I dipped the plastic spoon in the envelope. It looked like a lot. It takes a lot. I dusted the ketchup, swirling it with the spoon until orange. "Agent Orange," I declared. I liked to name things, but I didn't like that one. I duplicated the dose on six rolls, and would dole out the sandwiches to Sal and the pig one at a time, depending on their effect. I put the spoon back in the bag. Using a consistent measurement would allow me to approximate the missing volume later on.

Who did I think I was, a pharmacist? An alchemist?

On the way out, I ordered one more sandwich. Mine.

"My God, you didn't eat one in there, did you?" the cook asked, cracking the egg.

The driver spit something into his cup.

I left the diner just as a delivery van tossed out a stack of morning papers. I slid one through the bailing wire. Headline: Hippie Pig Euthanized! Massive Narcotics in System!

Perfect, I said, tossing the paper back on the pile. The rest was just details.

Back in SOFA, the smell of eggs sent the pig into spasms. I threw a foiled sandwich through the window, and it dove from the backdoor with an alacrity and strength it should not have had. I questioned if it was hurt at all, and wondered if it hadn't just been playing possum, a rare species-on-species play. How else to explain its vigor? Was I being gaslighted by a shit-eating pig?

But the pig soon cleared up any doubts about its injuries when it fell to its side next to the eggs and couldn't get up. Stroking its snout, Sal said, "He's waiting for more healing, Corman. He's waiting for your hands."

"He needs to eat," I said, sticking the sandwich in its face.

"He's waiting."

I wiped my hands on my pants for no apparent reason, then placed them on the pig's bumpy back. And waited. Sal placed his hands on top of mine. And waited. The pig just flicked its eyes and waited, until finally, like a carny medium, I said, "I feel a force emerging. I feel the warmth of healing. We must allow the body to take over now. Get it to eat, Sal."

Sal wiped sand from the egg and held it to the pig. The pig pulled back at the ketchup before saying what pigs everywhere say when presented with unidentified shit to eat: "Fuck it." It inhaled the whole sandwich except for a dab of dosed ketchup that clung to its nostril, which the pig went at it with everything it had, frenzied, like it was a junkie already, running its bottom teeth out along the bottom of its tongue to push it to its maximum. And when that fell short, its tongue flicking out of its mouth with ever-growing acceleration, in hopes of snapping whatever was holding it back. In the end, Sal swiped the dab on his finger and fed it to the pig.

"The President is getting better, Corman! He will be strong!"

I held out another sandwich. The pig got to its feet. With a scrape of its snout, it rolled the prescription on its back where the first crispy white edge of egg flapped out. The sandwich, the foil, the air above, the dirt below, and the weeds and rocks to the side all disappeared in a pig gulp.

Sal looked down at his own eggs pulling at the fried edge.

"You need your strength too," I urged. He ate the fringe, then bit the sandwich.

"I like eggs," he said.

"I know, Sal. That's good." I shook the bag. "I've got more for later. Right now, we need gear and to get ourselves on the trail before the sun gets much higher. What's your shoe size? We need boots."

"I'm done wearing boots, Corman. I like these." He leaned on the edge of his polished shoes.

I looked at him sternly.

"Eleven, but make them squishy."

I found an outfitter down the hill. The room above his store flickered in the blue of early morning reruns. He answered my knock as if anticipating it.

Streetlight crept through the small shop's blinds, illuminating dust that stirred when the door opened. It settled back on the narrow shelves of dehydrated food, backpacks, boots, and rain gear, mounds of rain gear. I browsed as if I would know what I needed when I saw it. I did not. The outfitter followed, plank floor bouncing. He was yawning, bony and balding. And he asked too many questions.

"What? You forgot to pack your gear? And you just noticed it now? Sorry, just wondering. You sure you want such a big pack for a just weekend trip? You'll what? Maybe just keep going? To where? I mean, who makes a decision like that? Who's the other pack for, and sleeping bag? Spares? Who carries spares? You don't know anything about this trail, do you? Sorry, I'm just trying to help, is all. Let me tell you something, son, I don't feel good about selling this stuff to you. It ain't a walk in some park, you know. This is the Appalachian Trail. It's got its own ways, plenty of danger, and it has to be planned! Yes, of course I'm going to sell it to ya. This is America, right? I mean if a guy wants to get himself killed by the elements and stupidity, that's his right, right? It's just I don't feel good about it, is all. But there are some things you have to know. Here, read this book and learn them in an hour or so. It's a guide for people just like you, who don't know. For a few bucks it gives you a step-by-step, you know, where the shelters are, where to find water. Almost forgot! Suppose you'll need a 'spare' one of these, too? Of course you cross streams in places, but not mostly. And the next twenty-five miles south are dry as a bone. Not much better north. Trail rides the ridge, up there." He pointed out the window. "Too high for springs, too low for rain. If you don't carry, you'll end up scrambling down a blue-blaze– maybe all the way to the river this time of year."

A truck with loud mufflers rolled by, pausing for a moment his interminable caveats (Latin again!). But he continued as soon as he thought I could hear. I pretended not to be listening. He didn't care.

Like an algebra teacher, he insisted I know more than I would ever use, and so he went on about it being late summer and that springs would have dried up by now. And how blue-blaze trails veer off the white-blaze trails to idiot-proof finding shelter or water. And how they were different from white blazes, because, "they're blue and the white blaze *is* the AT, son! All right, look, you gotta promise me you'll only go out for a few days and stay in this section. It's harder to get killed right around here, unless you're aiming to. Sorry, but you, son, are not ready for the big trip yet."

Turns out, the white blaze marked the AT and I needed to keep them in my sight, because they have a tendency to hide or something, causing you to wander off. And it can happen to the best, which he wanted me to know emphatically was not me. I rolled my eyes and rolled my right hand to get him to ring the stuff up.

"You lose a fight or something?" he asked, leaning in. "Sorry. All told, with the boots, food, and your spares, this comes to $82.19. Let's call it $83 even."

"You round up?"

"Just a one-man shop, son. $83."

"I got a dog," I said. "I almost forgot."

He winced. "Good God, don't hike with a dog, not unless it carries its own water, anyway. You might think about these pet panniers over here. They're expensive, but..."

"How expensive?"

"Lists for $7.99."

"Your price?"

"Nine, but they're worth it. Water's heavy, son. Every ounce matters." He ripped the covers from the book. "So, you can throw this out now or use it for your fire tonight. Do the same with all your food wrappers."

"Rations have no wrappers."

"No, but these aren't rations, see? Wait. Is that what this is all about? You back from 'Nam or something? You okay, son? Look, you don't have to worry about getting judged in *my* place. Hell, I figured right off you weren't dodging, but I didn't go the other way, truth be told. I didn't see any 'Nam signs in you until just now, so I didn't figure. But now the "spares" make sense, I guess. I hear of other vets out there, but I don't ever see them. Plenty of dodgers, but no vets. All told, it's $92. Listen, I'm going to worry about you. You'd think a guy with 'Nam time would know more than you do about woods, is all I'm saying. Tell you what, I'm throwing in this whistle, on me. If you get yourself in some trouble, blow this whistle. Somebody's going the hear it and help you. Okay? That's the best I can do. Now, only *after* you read that book, go over that bridge." He motioned to where a shadow grew on the window. "And on the backside of the Route 80 sign is a double white blaze. You'll turn left, over the highway on the other side. Got it?"

"No shrapnel here," I said, drumming my fingertips on my head. "Got flashlights?"

"You mean for finding the outhouse?"

"Or maybe I hike at night. Got anything for that, hiking at night?"

"God, do *not* hike at night! You don't know what you're doing up there! It ain't paved! There's big pointy rocks, and you gotta hop from one to another!"

"Still, got any lights that clip to a cap or something, in case I want to read this book you gave me?"

"Now you're thinking! Sure, here, like miners wear."

Chapter 11

I clambered up the hill with packs slung over each shoulder, boots swinging from their frames, sleeping bags grasped in each hand, and dropped it all behind the sign with the blaze. Near the propane tank, I found the pig chasing Sal around SOFA. Sal was laughing like a kid at recess. Pigs don't laugh. Clearly the "cure" was having some effect. Sal stopped when he saw me. The stupid pig kept going for two more spins. When it stopped, I escorted both down the hill to the gear.

Out of breath, but in a much lower voice, Sal said, "You are a healer, Corman. And we are thankful. But we require knowing what the mission is."

I leaned in to examine his pupils with no clue what I was looking for. "You all right?"

"Yes, I'm all right, Corman. As you have healed the President, so the President has healed me! It is from his strength that I too am strong now. His overcoming his pain has erased my own. Now what is our mission?"

Sal was standing tall and urgent. Lower voice? Standing tall? Urgent? Had the "cure" ejected Sal from some prolonged adolescence?

Had his balls just dropped? And was this the under-the-influence Sal I should expect from now on? Who did he think he was?

"The mission, Corman!" he demanded.

"The mission, Sal," I said, sliding into my pack, "is for you not to get seen. That is our mission!" I ground my teeth on the word. "If word spreads that there are two guys hiking the Appalachian Trail with a pig, somebody is going to do math in their head and add a few things together. And if that's them doing the math, Sal, they'll strafe these mountains bald long before we reach the Smokies."

The pack sat stiff on my hips, and I turned awkwardly in time to see Sal hoisting his. He grimaced suddenly when synching its belt. The "cure" was wearing off. I stepped to help. "I'm fine," he said, belt dangling on either hip. "Then what is our objective?"

"I just told you, the pig can be with other pigs in the Smokies."

"The Smokies are far away. Have you considered that?"

Of course I considered that! Of course eight hundred miles was far, seven hundred and ninety too far, and we would only get as far as the gods and smack allowed, maybe ten, maybe fifty. But that just might be enough, I calculated, if the deal could go down. They already killed the wrong pig, and in two days the brains at COINTELPRO would get my pictures. In three days they'd be strategizing for a nice clean exit. In four, they'd get word to me somehow. It's not like I wasn't leaving enough damn clues where I was. By noon today, the cook at the diner would report an abandoned car in his lot. They'd trace the plates back to Hoffman or Rubin and impound it. Maybe they'd dust for prints and pig hair and maybe they wouldn't, but when they got my pictures it would come with a post office origin that all but put them on the trail. They'd talk to the round-up outfitter and learn of the guy with an unseen dog, hiking with spares. They'd do math in their head. So yes, Sal, it is far. But I need time, and you need something to focus on, so for you it's the Smokies. Just keep going until I tell you to stop. Meantime, I stop when I get word. And yes my plan is full of holes, but as long as the smack and gods hold up, I've got a chance. But we've got to keep the pig alive.

Pivoting to the data book, I said, "Look, I don't know how much we can do today. Sun'll be high in about an hour, and we can't take the chance of being seen. So, if we hold up until night, maybe here," I tapped on the book, "at Winona Cliff or if we move fast enough, here, Kirkridge Shelter."

"What mission is this requiring we move under the cover of night? You said they wouldn't follow us here."

I missed the old Sal already, the one prone to blind trust, and made a mental note to reduce his dosage.

"Well, we're not going to outrun anybody standing still, are we? We've got to get in deeper, away from roads… like this one."

I laid out a strategy Sal was sure to accept. I would hike fifty paces ahead of him and use the whistle to alert him if I saw anyone hiking out. Sal would then dive into the woods, keep the pig quiet, and stay there until I blew it again.

Sal had his own concerns. "Who's giving the orders here?"

"Here, eat half of this and give the rest to the pig. Keep your strength up."

"Once again, who's giving the orders?"

"Okay, Sal, then what are *my* orders?"

"Don't let them hear you blow the whistle or they will get suspicious."

"It's a whistle."

"Yes, and so you will need to be stealthy in its application. One more thing, Corman, Pigasus does not like his saddle."

"That's a pannier for carrying water."

"The President was injured, Corman. I will carry what he needs."

This was a tough call, because a live pig was more valuable to my plan than Sal now, but I knew the pig could never survive without him, or Sal maybe without the pig, even with a heavy dose of smack.

They were a lot like SOFA and I in that regard, codependent. "Let's just agree that in this platoon, every man carries his own gear. The pig'll adjust. Now let's move out. Count to fifty, okay?"

I hit twenty strides before looking over my shoulder. Wrapped in elastic bandage, the pig bristled against the leash, shaking to eject the panniers, bucking toward the highway, spinning, tying up Sal's legs in a cloud of dust. When it settled, Sal was still counting, and the intrinsic futility of my plan grew pronounced. I doubled back.

"Let the pig off the leash," I said. "Count to fifty again, then bring up the rear. It'll follow as soon as you're out of sight."

I moved out across the undulating ground, covering two hundred strides before pausing at a double blaze and a sharp turn in the trail. Sal arrived a minute later, pigless and frantic.

"I need to go back for him!"

"Wait," I said, anxious myself until I heard it snorting. The pig burned two more minutes of prized sunrise, but finally came charging up the trail grunting, plunging its way through the narrow run. Chest heaving, it fell to a stop at our feet. Sal dropped to his knees to tighten the flesh-toned bandage, wrapping around the pig like bacon around a roulade. The cure was still working. Neither the pig nor Sal showed signs of pain.

"It's straight up from here," I said, shaking my head. "Count to fifty, keep the distance, but keep the pig in sight too. I won't be stopping anymore, so if you hear this whistle..."

"How is it I'm not equipped with a whistle, Corman?"

"You can just call me."

The trail rose steeply on scree, forcing me to fix my eyes on the ground sliding beneath me. I turned sideways, skinning my way up hill on the sole edge of my boots while sending a small avalanche down on Sal. The barrage spooked a plague of beetles that rose to collide with my head. I flailed. I slid. I covered. The beetles regrouped and moved down the mountain. Through the trees below, the pig bucked in bewilderment. Sal swung wildly.

Intent on keeping our distance, I increased my pace, but the scree and steepness sapped me and I soon pulled up out of breath. I did some math in my head and carved the ascent into achievable rushes of twenty-five strides each. Ten rushes – two hundred and fifty strides – and I'd stand at the top. I drew a short pull from a canteen and started up. After fifteen strides the rush of blood to my brain trapped sounds in my head, annoying sounds like the creaking of my pack frame, the sloshing of canteen water, the scratching of my bedroll against the damn bottle of stove fuel. I pretended not to listen, but it didn't work.

At twenty-five strides I stopped, let the blood drain, counted with deep breaths to twenty-five, then resumed. "It's only the damn Poconos," I admonished, forcing myself to let go of a tree. So began my campaign of mountain management: twenty-five, stop, twenty-five, go. What the hell was I doing?

But it worked. I staggered to the ridge near a cairn named Council Rock. To the southeast rose Kittatinny Mountain, its tree line stalling at the thin edge of dawn. Below, beneath the reach of early light, the roar of truck tires rolled uphill. I dropped my pack and waited for Sal, wet shirt cooling in the breeze. I heard him way down the mountain, chattering again. I should have given him the whistle, I thought, and invited him to blow it at will; it would have been less alerting than his constant theatrical pleading.

"You must believe. Yes, it hurts, but what is it worth for you to be who you were before? You must believe… and climb."

I was not certain who he was speaking to, the pig, himself, or me, but when he emerged from the trail and saw me, his jaw stiffened. "Was this the plan we made, Corman, for us to rendezvous here? So soon?"

"Just checking on the pig, sir, making sure he's not hungry."

"Your loyalty is never taken for granted, Corman, but the President is fine, thanks to you. Now go!"

"And yours?" I stalled, gesturing at Sal's ribs.

"Our concern is for the President only. It is from his strength that I remain strong."

Pine needles carpeted the flat trail along the ridge, but the data book warned of miserable terrain ahead. I wobbled into it when the trail became a sadistic pavement of jutting rock shards, as if the Roman infantry had been buried in place with pikes aloft. Fighting the shifting weight of my pack and all its damn noises, I teetered over the spearheads point-to-point, grasping limbs and boughs to steady myself, feeling pretty strongly that nature sucks. I was one wrong step from a snapped ankle. I surveyed for each step the nuance of rock, the slicks of mud, even the intermittent tufts of grass.

What is it you said, Lieut? You better see the blades of that grass, new guy! It's not one big field; it's a million blades, and how they lie tells the story. When one is out of place, we have got ourselves a Betty, and if she jumps then one of us ain't walking out of here. So keep your damn eyes on the ground! Remember, two wires, twisting up like this, around each other. Got it? But Boot, listen, listen to me now - stand and listen! If Betty does blow, if I lose them, you've got to promise to stop the screams, then take me out. I got a boy, and he's got better things to do than wheel his stump of an old man around. Okay? We good? Just keep your eyes down and those fucking voices out of your head, and maybe we got a chance to walk out of this hole.

I was beginning to wish I could get Lieut's voice out of my head! Instead, it was like I'd swallowed his screams. Now they rattled and creaked and scratched in my head just like the shit in my pack. No good deed ever goes unpunished. Ever. Ever!

"What a mess I am," I mumbled, rubbing my chest. "And what a broken-ass platoon."

"Yes," Sal said.

I hadn't noticed him standing by, the pig at his feet.

"And that will be to our advantage, Corman," he said, handing me the canteen. "Very much to our advantage. We will outwit them because they cannot think like us! What reveals itself to us will remain hidden to them. Now, on your feet. We have the advantage and a mission to conduct. Correct? Where are we to rendezvous next?"

Reading hesitation my eyes, he lifted the data book from my pocket. "Here, Kirkridge Shelter, and not before, Corman. You will never outrun anything if you keep pulling up to wait. They can never outwit us, so we have nothing to fear. In the end, the President is in no danger. In the end, we will be better." He read my eyes again. "Once upon a times don't last forever. That's the thing about them. Now move out, Corman."

The next three hours clung to the ridge and should have allowed for a rapid and unencumbered gait. Instead, their monotony invited Lieut's voice to echo. It wouldn't stop. I thought I'd heard the last of him many weeks before, but now there was no escape, and soon I was doing fearful math in my head, the addition by my own subtraction. I thought I'd left that behind too.

I came to Winona Cliff squeezing my head between my hands. I dropped my pack. Sweat behind its straps had striped my shirt. I pulled the envelope from my chest to confirm its dryness. No, that's not true. I wanted to weigh it to know if I still had enough to quiet one last scream. I was imagining that scream was mine, when a breeze puffed from the trees behind me, nudging me forward to where the cliff fell into the dark, two thousand feet below. I braced against the breeze at first as if it weren't entirely my idea, but then let it nudge me until I toed the cliff's edge with a scuff of each foot, just over the end where my toes stretched free from the ground. My neck cooled. The numbness in my bruised face eased, allowing me to feel my smile. Lieut laughed.

Confused, I looked out to where the remaining porch lights met the lingering stars, then looked back to see myself as a winged hawk, as a celebrant, an infant, weightless. I imagined my shadow riding the thermals below. I held my arms out crucifixion style and filled my lungs for the scream. Lieut laughed again.

The valley below stretched taut like a giant quilt, feigning to catch me. I wondered what the first nineteen hundred feet would sound like, would feel like. Would the scream follow? Would I arch my back in joy? Would I take you with me, Lieut, shedding your weight in the fall? Or would it just bury me deeper?

And then… the light unassailable notion to step back, the ironic truth that at that moment, when a slide of sand or the roll of a pebble might have won the day, the ground firmed.

Who did I think I was? Besides, I had a plan, and splattering on some rock below, while romantic enough, was not part of it. The time to splatter had long passed, so shut the fuck up, Lieut.

Chapter 12

The miles between the cliff and the spring crammed my head with a new voice: my own.

You put your arms out, I said.

Yes.

And you might easily have leaned forward.

Yes.

But you didn't.

No. I didn't.

Which one of us didn't?

Does it matter?

I think it might.

The sun was high now, and the switchbacks of the dramatic ascent replaced my voices with my breathless counting, which was worse. Heaving for oxygen, I tried to remember when I last enjoyed my own damn company, and came up empty. I had become the chief bore in my tedious life. Maybe this was the point: I counted twenty-five, stop; twenty-five, stop; twenty-five stop – until finally even *I* couldn't take the repetition anymore! And only then did I seek relief, counting *down* from twenty-five, until one-stop! This was all the verve I could add to my own life, doing math forward, then when bored, doing math backward. Jesus, what a mess!

Counting done, I found myself on a ridge kept dark and moist by a heavy canopy of pine. And that dank, moss concealed the blazes, forcing me to feel my way forward. I proceeded down a gulch, sliding on faith and pebbles. But like a comma lazing on its back, the scooped bottom of the gulch brought only a brief pause before the trail cut back up through steep pink rhododendron - twenty-five, stop. I read my watch and did math in my head. My pace was a sputtering two miles an hour. It didn't get any faster when the white blazes resumed, snaking me to the next ridge.

Twenty-five and stop. Drink. One and stop. Drink. I was parched and waterless when I finally reached the blue-blazed to the spring. As I stuffed my pack in the underbrush, it did not escape me that at one moment I was toeing the abyss with arms stretched, and the next answering the instinctive urge for water. Did men not call for water on their deathbeds? What a mess.

It had been three hours since I'd seen Sal or the pig. Their pain would be crippling when the smack wore off. "Maybe wait for them here," I said to myself. "Dose and keep them going!"

I found the wooden sign to the spring torn from its tree and discarded in a bush. It read 1/4 mile, but a number of hikers had called this into question, etching "bullshit" with knives and gouging out the backsplash between the one and the four to make it look more like a slanted plus sign. The data book simply read, "Vertical killer." My peek down the side confirmed it, but I had no choice and began my prolonged and spastic fall. I might have tumbled right past the spring if not for a glimpse of what I thought was a large figure flashing in the woods. The curl of smoke spiraling from the ground told me I might have been right.

I moved toward the smoke, scanning the woods for any movement. At the woodline, a torn blue tarp stretched between skeletal trees.

A canvas bag dangled from a branch. Where the smoke curled, the gutted carcass of a small skinned animal glistened on a rock (maybe squirrel, maybe not), but as I poked at it with a stick, the woods moved, and something yelped. I put my hands up and backpedaled, tripping over a nub of terracotta pipe protruding from the hillside. It dripped. Canteens filled slowly. The woods stayed still.

The scramble up from the spring parched me again, and I would have stopped at the top and drained a quart had I not heard the clacking of loose rocks and Sal's voice urging the pig forward. I hung a full canteen on a branch, tucked the last of the egg and opioid sandwiches (still warm in their foil) beneath it, then moved just down the trail out of sight. It was stupid, but I was honoring the rendezvous agreement Sal had forced upon me while satisfying myself they ate the eggs. Sal recognized them in the tree and rested, spilling water into a cupped hand for the prostrate pig. I stayed until it groaned to its feet and both devoured the eggs. Sal and the pig were cured for another three hours, more than enough for the remaining miles to Kirkridge Shelter where I would wait for my deal to find me. I reassumed the lead, ready to whistle warnings of any oncoming hikers. It did not take long.

Where the trail entered a rabbit hole of tree boughs, two sweaty hikers shuffled up the trail, heads down, towels draped on their necks to protect from bugs. They were not enjoying themselves any more than I was, looking nearly dead on their feet. I blew the whistle, startling them. One did all the talking. The other kept his back to me.

"Sorry," I said, "There's a gal down by the spring, you know, washing up. I told her I'd send a little warning if I ran into anyone up here. Just trying to protect the lady." I forced a smile. "Many behind you?"

"Six that I know of. Sleeping when we left."

I rolled my eyes; the universal sign of disdain for the sheer number of people that always seem to be somewhere you wish they weren't. And I meant it. These kinds of crowds were not in my calculations.

They brushed past. After they cleared, Sal and the pig hobbled up the trail. Sal slapped his hands to convey my failure at this rendezvous thing. "I can tell you, Corman, that the President did not appreciate that whistle drill, at all!"

"It worked."

"Yes, but for how long, Corman? How many times will we have to dive into the woods? There're webs in there, Corman, and I saw ass tissue. Outwitting does not mean diving into the woods. That's cowardice, not wit." He clutched his elbow to his ribs.

"You okay?" I asked.

"It comes and goes, just like the President's. Now, remind us of our mission."

"Our mission is to protect the pig and go undetected. And that means we use the whistle, especially when we know others are coming. There're six more up ahead according to those guys, and who knows how many more after them. We're like a country of refugees, so be prepared. We may need to set up camp away from the shelter to stay out of sight."

"Again, Corman? Dodging into woods? Staying out of sight? A lifelong game of hide-and-go-seek? I have very bad memories of not being found, of no one coming to look for me. I don't want a life like that where no one looks for me, Corman. You're afraid someone will find us. I'm afraid no one will. We are not the same that way."

The eggs should kick in soon, I thought.

The ridge stretched for two miles without any debilitating change in elevation, and the rocks cut me enough of a break to allow a brisk pace of three miles or better for a few hours. I felt like I was running. I was in control, center of gravity squarely beneath me, commanding the trail for the first time.

Fearful of outpacing Sal and the pig, I held up a half-mile from the shelter. They appeared a minute later. Amazing smack.

"We're not far. I need to scout it out," I said. "Slide out of sight until I come back. Yeah, I know, hide and seek."

Through the trees, a handful of hikers at the shelter broke camp at hangover speed. I slunk past them and surveyed the mountain where it folded away into a series of gray terraces with mammoth rocks. I had a premonition the boulders were just beginning. But it didn't matter, not if I could coerce Sal. I located a secluded ledge for our tent then rubbed my chest. I was stalling. I needed to convince Sal now to stay put, to not push toward the Smokies and the pig's promised emancipation. And I needed to do it knowing full well that when my deal came, the Bureau would take that pig, and that Sal might not survive that. I should have hit a moral bottom here (how low can you go?) except for what came next. If I could be the healer and mask their pain to keep them moving by dosing smack, I could also be the infirmity. I could withhold smack, let them rediscover agony, and keep them stationary.

Hitting bottom was more comfortable than I expected, hardly a splatter.

The pig did not take to the tent. It preferred instead to lounge with its head through the door flap so flies could have their way with its snot.

"He's trying to tell us something, Corman. The President senses danger here." The higher pitch of Sal's voice and narrowness of his logic told me his dose was beginning to wear off. I nodded to hold off on more discussion. But the male voices now climbing the mountain below us vindicated him. Who would be climbing where there was no trail?

Motioning for Sal to zip the tent and muzzle the pig, I crouched behind a larger rock and listened carefully, considering the possibility that the swap was going down this soon. It made no sense unless they were smarter than I thought and had been on us the whole time. I crawled to a more concealing rock farther away from Sal, where maybe a discussion could be had without being overheard.

When the saplings parted, two longhaired kids emerged from the woods. They were twins, identical, eighteen or nineteen, accents giving them away as Long Islanders. They wore blue golf shirts and looks of despair. It didn't take a genius to know where they were heading, although collectively they could have made good use of one.

"C'mon," one urged, seeing no one at the tent. "Let's go. It can't be too friggin' far from here. We're at the top already, for Christ's sake."

Emerging from the rock, I shocked them. "Another fifty yards. Canada is left."

"Thanks, Gus." (Gus?) "Anything we should know, you know, about up ahead?"

"Rocky," Sal called from the tent as the zipper whirred. He squeezed out, pushing the pig back. But the pig saw daylight and darted between Sal's legs, running wildly around the campsite until Sal corralled it, grimacing and holding his ribs.

"Holy Christ!" one the twins exclaimed, "Pigs are taking over the world! Did you see that riot in Chicago? They were trying to run a pig for President."

"Not the same," I snarled. "Canada's left."

"I know that," the twin scoffed. "They iced that pig yesterday. It was all over the papers."

Sal let the pig go and glared at me. I could see him doing math in his head.

I walked the dodgers away from Sal. "Look, Gus," I said. "You can see that we're dealing with a few things, right?" I nodded toward Sal. "So, we don't need people looking for 'the crazy vet with the pig'. I'd hate to be forced to interrupt your little hike north. Get me?"

"Who's there to tell?" the twin said, waving at the emptiness. "It's the end of the friggin' world up here!"

Back near the tent, Sal sat on the ledge with one knee cocked, staring rather dramatically into the distance. The pig wandered behind him. I had hoped the dose had worn completely off, so I could maintain his misplaced trust, but not yet.

"You knew, didn't you, Corman? You knew another died in the President's place."

"It changes nothing. Let's stick to the plan, Sal."

Sal grew tense. "We can no longer stick to our plan, Corman, because our plan was to outwit the enemy, and there is none! They think the President is dead. Why would they come? No one is hunting us, are they? We cannot outwit enemies that don't exist. Have we not learned that before, Corman, once upon a time?"

Sal's rambling gave me time to think. "That was just for the press, Sal. They claimed to have slaughtered your pig for the press, to show they were back in charge. But they know better."

I drew his attention to the pig's New Jersey. "Don't you think they know about this? Don't you think they know the pig they killed wasn't the original? Think they'll take the chance that the original will show up? They're coming. Remember the hospital? Remember the black sneakers? They were coming then, and they're coming again. They know he's still out here."

It was a provocative and flawless argument. I almost convinced myself. Sal, however, saw it a different way and, grimacing, stood to object. But with the dose waning, his thoughts escaped him. I took the liberty to fill the gap.

"You want to set it free, don't you?" I challenged. "If word spreads we're out here, we'll never make it to the Smokies."

Sal was buying none of it. "There is no enemy here, Corman."

"There will be."

"Enough riddles!"

"Sal, listen…"

"I demand your full report, Corman! I cannot assess this situation with you withholding facts. Am I clear? If the President is not in danger, then he and I are hiking out tomorrow. There are faster ways to freedom than this!" He waved at the woods.

Damn smack! It had nine lives!

"I just need you to trust me, Sal."

"Trust *you*? Apparently, it is I who has yet to earn *your* trust, Corman."

I circled my confession, orbiting the facts.

"Think back, Sal, when we were driving to the pig's nomination and Rubin insisted I was a cop. He was wrong. I'm not a cop. But I am with – that is, I *was* with - the FBI as an informant."

"Stop the riddles, Corman!"

"There's no riddle. I was an informant for a covert operation named COINTELPRO. And I was directed to put heroin in Rubin and Hoffman's office so they could be busted, locking them up for twenty years and cleaning up the whole mess."

"Nobody was busted," Sal challenged.

"I know, because I wouldn't do it, Sal. Not because Rubin isn't dangerous, but because…"

"You didn't do it?"

I rubbed my chest. "That's what I'm telling you. But what I did do puts me in great danger. I was so angry at what they wanted me to do – it just wasn't right, Sal! - I threw the envelope of heroin at the Fed who gave me the order, a superior officer, and it opened all over him. He was a coughing cloud."

Sal shook his head. "You ruined his day?"

"Yes. But now I have their secrets, and they'll need to make sure they die with me."

The smack was giving up the ghost on its eighth life now and Sal's misplaced trust returned.

"So they're looking for us both, Corman? We're both being hunted, like outlaws?"

"That's right, Sal, like outlaws. And I'm pretty sure the same man is hunting both of us now."

"The one who fought with Stanley?"

"Yes. The Fed I threw the heroin on."

"You saw him?"

"No, but I knew his voice and I saw his shoes, black high-top sneakers. The agent with the heroin wore the same. I know, sounds ridiculous, black high-top sneakers, but this whole thing is ridiculous, and Sal, he was at the hospital for one reason only."

There was a long silence as the smack came back for number nine. Sal paced to figure something out, like a timeline.

"At the tunnel, when I got beaten, did you help them?"

"No. Look at my busted face, Sal."

"And Geneva?"

"I tried to save her, Sal. I tried to pull her out of the puddle! And I didn't have anything to do with the pig being beaten either."

"I know that much, Corman. You are a healer."

***

The shelter was empty, and for an hour we sat beneath the lean-to watching the pig lap at a dripping faucet as its pain resumed. Sal grew anxious in his own agony as well.

"We are reverting," he said, rubbing his side. "Perhaps you can…"

"The body must take over," I answered. "We'll hold up here until you're both ready to go."

In the rustic siding of the shelter, hikers had carved their trail names, dates they passed through, and really clever snippets like "Katahdin or bust!" or "Beware the WOLF!"

"Are there wolves here, Corman?"

"No."

In the corner sat a pitted galvanized box, the type our uniformed milkman once filled before knocking up Mrs. Buckstein. On its lid someone with a marker had scribbled, "Donations to the cause." Sal lifted it and pulled out a poncho, some kind of geode, a can of soup, an antler, a candle, and a tattered paperback.

High off the floor and wrapped in a plastic bag, a marbled notebook swung on a nail. Sal took it down and brought it to where I was sitting. The cover read, *Thru-hiker Log, Kirkridge Shelter, 1968.*

Inside the log beat the droning, scratching, and misbegotten reflections of every stoned, frightened, and drafted hiker that stumbled through the shelter. I read a few aloud: bitching, waxing, wondering, worrying, cursing, and lamenting – rocks, splendor, weather, mountains, snorers, scarcity, girls, and water. "Drink at each spring until you pee three times," someone named Toaster advised.

The final entry, dated that day, simply read, "No deal, Hodges."

I dropped the log.

Chapter 13

I immediately imagined Smackspecter hunching over the hood of his car, map spread, orienting, thinking something like this: "We know from the outfitter that Hodges got on at the Water Gap about 7am, probably heading south. Even with these hills, he's running at three, maybe three-and-a-half-miles an hour. That puts him here at this shelter around noon."

I imagined the specter slamming his trunk for effect when his math was done, then clawing up the mountain so confidently, bushwhacking (straight line/quickest distance) only to find his targeted shelter full of hangovers.

And I imagined him hiding in waiting for a while, doubts creeping in, wondering if he chose wrong, wondering if his math was wrong, wondering if this was going to be yet another long division mistake in a career racked by them.

And, while it served me to do so, I could almost hear him recalculating. "I bet that stupid fuck went north," then certainly turning up the trail to chase me.

These things I could imagine fully through six drafts and in living color, but somehow I hadn't been able to imagine that Smackspecter was on my trail the entire trip out of Chicago, ten, twenty, a hundred cars behind me, but keeping me in sight the whole way.

I also hadn't imagined that he would intercept the mail at the diner before it got picked up. How else could he know I was offering a deal?

But most fatefully, it never occurred to me that a pig-swap could never compete with the delight Smackspecter would feel hunting me dead. When he said he wanted to kill me in the latrine, he really meant it! Here again, my lack of training was biting me in the ass, but I still sensed that Smackspecter had headed north from the shelter... for the time being.

Sal nudged me with the open notebook.

"What's going on, Corman?"

"He's here. The hunt is on, outlaw." I motioned to the entry.

"Who's Hodges?"

"My informant name." I didn't know why I lied, but mostly I didn't know why Sal believed me. What an enabler he was!

But he understood the situation, immediately breaking camp, inhaling pain as he ripped the tent stakes from the ground.

"We need to eat first," I said, rubbing my chest. "We'll need energy. We may be running until nightfall. You pack up and get the pig set, and I'll boil something from the outfitter."

"There's no time for food, Corman."

"There will be," I said, but this was a fading decree because time is finite and the small shitty stove I bought with its whisper-blue flame (as if that were an important feature in the woods) required the help of a sun twice the size of Earth's just to soften butter. I was trying to boil water at three thousand feet above sea level, so the stove naturally mocked me. I rammed twigs between it and the pot, frantically scattering the small puff of smoke. The water slowly warmed, and the noodles slowly coagulated into some kind of hive. With Sal occupied, I released the envelope of smack from my chest wrap. It would be five hours before the safety of nightfall, at full run. I swallowed my share of the noodles and double-dosed theirs.

Double dose? Who did I think I was? And yet, I was so reassured. As I thought about it, if I could elude Smackspecter long enough, he would have to tire and see the folly in his ways, see that a deal was best, that I was holding the whole package – the original pig with its throbbing New Jersey and the envelope of government issued narcotic. Smackspecter might not know it yet, but he'd get to take the pig (if it didn't die from the double dose) and what was left of the smack triumphantly back to Chicago, like Caesar! Who did he think he was?

I counted the holes in the new plan: same number as the old plan.

"I don't like these chewy noodles, Corman." Sal was feeding them to the pig.

"No!" I screamed, ripping the bowl from his hands. "No, Sal, no. You… no you need to eat them. We've got a tough stretch ahead. Just swallow them. There. Now, make sure the pig's panniers have water and let's go. Same drill, same whistle. We've got to make it all the way here." I pointed to the data book. "Wind Gap."

The maddening slosh of newly filled canteens afflicted what little peace the shards of rock left me. I stubbed and tripped repeatedly, and flogged myself to lift my feet higher to clear the stone points. As a result, I must have looked ridiculous, like one of those stupid prancing horses from Europe.

What Sal witnessed, I don't know, but he held the rear, keeping pace. He was not chattering, but I would not have heard him anyway through the unmistakable roar of tires on a highway that now rolled up the mountain. I thumbed the data book. We were about to cross PA 191. And once we crossed it, the book warned, we'd be heading straight back uphill into the dreaded Wolf Rocks.

Sal came up behind me.

"Fox Gap," I said, waving the data book. "Straight up. Through Wolf Rocks." I did not tell him about the boulders, but Sal sensed we were about to understand what was meant by, "Fear the wolf!" We waited for a long break in traffic then ushered the pig out of the woods and across the road.

Our early steps up the mountain were tenuous, anticipating the rocks just around the bend. But it wasn't until we reached the first shoulder that we met the wolf, where the pines stopped abruptly and boulders stretched across the landscape like a Sisyphian scrap heap. Some stood alone rifle high, some stood on the shoulders of others. Some wobbled in their roundness, others glistened in slippery moss. All demanded acrobatic leaps across broad rifts, one boulder to another.

I leaped and lunged twenty-five paces, sweating out my water. The double-dosed pig floundered. The double-dosed Sal urged him forward.

"Beware the wolf, " Sal said to the pig, I assumed. "We must outwit him."

The trail steepened and the rocks grew in number, crowding out trees and orphaning the directional white blazes to the tops of boulders. The blazes zippered up a merciless series of switchbacks, and I imagined them as a series of dashes among the giant dots of rock – dashes and dots, a cipher – and laughed when I broke the code. "Send the fucking pig to a farm upstate," it counseled. Who did I think I was?

I negotiated the full length of each switchback one at a time before pausing, whether it was twenty-five strides or not. In this way, the tempo became the mountain's and not mine. I smiled at the thought of yielding control and felt my pace accelerate. Soon Sal and the pig were nowhere in sight.

Two more switchbacks up, I forced a longer pause and waited for a sign of them. When none came, I imagined the double dose had had its way. I dropped my pack and bounded down the trail boulder-to-boulder to see. It was a strange reaction for someone needing to go quickly forward, but I didn't think much about that. Sal had half the food, and I would need it.

I found Sal four switchbacks down standing high atop an egg-shaped rock, backlit, swinging a gnarled tree limb the length of a broom stick and calling encouragement to the pig.

"What's that?" I asked of the tree limb.

"Know you nothing of history, Corman? This is Excalibur, and I have freed it from the rocks! The knights were great warriors, Corman, with a noble cause. I am a knight."

As I saw him now, the double dose seemed a sweet spot. Sal had no pain, but his misplaced trust remained abundant. Swashbuckling, he closed the distance between us, moving nimbly along the rocks, wooden staff swishing, poking for voids and vaulting him forward. Half way, he pulled up abruptly and freed from a crevice a second dead limb and, stripping it of leaves and twigs, vaulted to present it to me.

"This, Corman, will help you outwit the wolf. I declare you a knight. And as a knight, you must walk like a knight. Two steps forward," he said, hopping forward, "then one to the side. Two forward, one to the side. In this way, the trail has revealed its secret to me."

Sal continued hopping up a switchback with the pig scampering behind him. It was ludicrous, and I watched him with an open mouth. But as I began my own ascent, I soon found the rocks *did* lay out that way, two forward, one over, and with far less effort we put some trail behind us. As evening set in we lit our headlamps. Their light cast flat shadows across the rocks.

"How long do these go on?" Sal asked.

"I'm not sure they stop."

"Good. We've seized their advantage, their secret knight-walk of passage. In this way, we will outwit, Corman."

We continued in the dark for the better part of an hour up to the ridge where the moon sat bright enough to turn our headlamps off. But soon the trail turned back beneath the darkening canopy, and there we were met by an insistent wind. At first it refreshed, cooling the sweat in my hair, lifting my step, chilling my chest as my shirt dried.

"Wind Gap?" Sal asked.

"I don't know, but we need to get off this ridge. Get lower and out of this wind." The pig grunted in protest. So did Sal, who yelled over the wind.

"What's your assessment of distance to the shelter, Corman?"

"Shelter? No shelter. Need to stake the tent. Too windy here. All rock. Need to get lower, quiet side if we can. Let's keep..."

Sal wasn't hearing what I said. I motioned for him to follow. The knob continued. The wind grew. The pig balked, turning its back, sapping my patience by prolonging our exposure.

"I don't care if that pig is scared, we have to get off this ridge," I said.

"The President is not scared. He is assessing our options; that is all. Go ahead. We will follow when he is through."

In a quarter mile, the knob gave way to a soft dip and a bank of pines that offered some cover, but the wind whistled and peeled back boughs, shelling me with needles and cones. I put my light back on and scanned the data book. It offered no comfort, just a taunt: the town of Wind Gap lay a mile to the east. A man hiking alone or pig-free might on his own brave the ceaseless wind and seek the town's comforts: a bed, a shower, and some hot food. But I was neither, and I suddenly hated the pig more than ever.

When it became clear that the wind was going to stay in my face if I didn't change direction, I dropped my pack in the middle of the trail so Sal would not pass me and sidestepped down the mountain's shoulder. Wooden staff high and aimed at the dark, I counted my strides and drafted a mental map. I'd need to retrace my steps to find the trail again in the dark. "Not too far," I admonished at the count of thirty.

For sixty additional strides, I poked my way along the mountain's shoulder until stumbling on a makeshift fire ring. I swept the site with my light. Astride the ring were two tree trunks dragged to serve as backrests. Behind them, ten feet of old gray rope spanned two hemlocks. The bones of pine boughs littered the ground.

"We're not the first to retreat from this wind," I thought, running my hand along the rope. Old and fat, it broke as I pulled it taut. I kicked the pine bones away. "We'll camp here."

Through the wind, I thought I heard Sal calling. I called back but couldn't be sure there was a response. I called again, then began retracing my steps back to the trail. Sixty strides along the shoulder then thirty uphill, I reminded myself. I did the math aloud, counting off the strides into the wind like I was pacing off a treasure map. But an unfamiliar patch of thicket interrupted me on the shoulder. I spun down to avoid its thorns, adding to my disorientation. When I finally pushed my thirtieth stride uphill, I did not find the trail. I did not find it at thirty-five, or forty, or forty-five. I doubled back with no success.

"It's got to be here." But the Appalachian Trail figures it doesn't have to be anywhere it doesn't want to be. It's rarely straight, seldom broad, never the same elevation twice in a mile, and often indiscernible from a turkey run. The truth it, it has a shitty attitude.

My headlamp batteries were nearing death. In the dark, I retreated back to the shoulder, then up once again. The moon sparked between clouds and swirling treetops. Needles flew sharp, and one pierced the skin behind my ear. "If you're going to do it," I said to the sky, throwing the needle to the ground, "roll up and in." A few more steps and I called for Sal; not a brilliant move for someone being hunted, but I felt pretty sure that Smackspecter was riding this storm out somewhere. The wind answered my call with a new ferocity, deafening, whipping the forest as it would a wheat field. Beneath my feet, tree roots strained to hold their grip. No trail. The moon was gone and the temperature was in free fall. Thoughts of waiting until morning crossed my mind, and this became a serious debate until shut down by the thunderous crack of a fat pine crashing through the canopy like God's boot. I recoiled to see it land ten feet away. Lieut laughed. Only when my heart stopped pounding did I notice a white blaze painted on its trunk. I hadn't located the trail as much as it had stumbled on me, and it wasn't very happy about it, amplifying the wind and hiding the moon for good. I made my way up the mountain with the dim headlamp swinging to each incongruent sound, like the padding of paws I thought I heard, or the grunts, or the rustling alongside me. I kept reassuring myself, but it was getting harder with each noise.

Where the trail dropped off the ridge and fringed a jagged slab, I sat on a felled hemlock, gulping air and water. A shell-shocked moth braved the wind and trembled in the beam of my light. I felt the padding of paws/hooves/shoes again as if something ran around me. I gripped my staff and circled, eyes wide, stick poised, light swinging. What is it you said, Lieut, only boars charge like that? The brush beside me moved opposite the wind, parallel to the trail, uphill and away, looking for a point of entry for a downhill attack. A strange, hollow scratching rose, then faded, and the brush stood still until it turned and plunged toward me with a serrated rasp. I stumbled back, tripping, falling, pinned to the ground. I swung the stick wildly above my head, then rolled to my feet when through the briars squeezed a dog – a spaniel – chest heaving, teeth ripping at the burrs that covered its coat. I readied my staff and trained my lamp on it. An empty plastic jug was duct-taped to its back. I leaned in to be sure what I saw was what it was when behind me the brush moved again, and from it emerged a second spaniel: same teeth, taped jug and burred coat, but distinguished by four porcupine needles spiking from its festering snout. The dogs howled, circled, sniffed, then turned their noses up to the mountain as if they'd caught scent of the pig. They charged in Sal's direction, baying wildly. I thought to blow the whistle, to warn Sal, but if these were Smackspecter's dogs, I didn't need to confirm that they had found me. Let them lead him to Sal instead. I slid into the woods on the other side of the trail, but the dogs heard and returned, circled, sniffing, until a "Whoot!" from the woods set them howling again.

From the brush clawed a large figure in full government fatigues, hair like the spaniels', knotted in a fistful of burrs, filter of a dead cigarette dangling from cracked lips, blood beading along the dozen thicket scratches lining his arms. Nailed to his hiking stick dangled the severed paws of squirrels and chipmunks. His bedroll wrapped around the stocks of two rifles and the mechanical riser of a hunting bow. A long knife swung in a sheath from his belt. I sensed it had a fresh edge.

He kicked the dogs away from me. "Spilled the fuckin' water," he growled in a monotone. "Any ahead?"

"Few miles north," I said matching his tone, stepping on the trail and motioning back from where I'd come.

He stepped close, reeking of charred carcass, eyes perma-red from the smoke and twitching. "You been?" he asked, motioning to the east. "There."

I nodded.

"Rank!" he demanded.

"Grunt."

"No," he leaned in, sniffing. "You smell like a fuckin' lieutenant." His breath burned.

"Grunt," I assured him, tapping my chest, even as I named him the same.

Grunt's eyes locked. His breath flamed out. He walked around me as if my profile would reveal some truth. "S'there a shelter with the water?"

I nodded and flicked my eyes uphill. No sign of Sal.

He kicked at the spaniel with the quills. "Smell that rot? Remember that? Want to carry that back in your arms? Bag 'em and tag 'em, right, Lieutenant? Shoulda shot it yesterday, but this other one," he kicked at it too, "circles and circles."

Grunt stared up at the swirling trees, then down at my canteens. "Full?" he asked. I handed one over like lunch money. He spat a string of phlegm. The dogs fought over it. The stronger one lapped at it, then bayed to the north, uphill, in Sal's direction.

"There's no fucking water up there!" Grunt said, as if he and the dog had this conversation before. He sniffed a gust. "Rain." He thrust his hands at the sky; the festering dog cowered.

"How long you out?" I asked.

He leaned in close again. "Till I even it up."

He swirled the severed paws around his staff, and looked up through the trees. "Rain might spare that one a while; shitty draw to go out thirsty, but he spilt his fuckin' water and now it is, sir, what it is, sir. Dead. Just doesn't know it. Three minutes of rain, that's all, and the mud'll tell me everything." He drew a finger to his cracked lips. "Shhhh. I'm going know if it's you, Lieutenant." He whooted again and the dogs filed back into the woods. "Keep your eyes on your perimeter, sir."

Chapter 14

A stiff tailwind made quick work of the remaining climb, even as it made sixty-five degrees feel like forty. I took fresh batteries from my pack where I found it two hundred yards up trail, but Sal was nowhere. I didn't call for him, but I spun around each time I heard something, certain it was Grunt coming up behind me, only to disappear just as I turned. I found Sal on the knob, curled around the pig, motionless. I held for a moment of indecision, then rolled him over. He was shivering to the point of seizure. His eyes, fish-like, moved only slightly with my light. One of his mud-caked hands rested on the pig.

Was it my work, the double dose of smack? Hypothermia? Yes, I calculated, he's got smack-induced hypothermia – pharmothermia! I like to name things. It helps me stomach shit like this.

I held out my hand. The pig twitched. Sal did not.

"C'mon!"

He tried to speak, but only mumbled. I leaned in to hear, but he mumbled worse.

"Sal, you've got some kind of hypothermia," I said while ransacking his pack. "Here, help get this raingear on you; it'll block the wind, hold the heat. You need a fire. C'mon! Your arm, through there! Listen to me! Jesus! Give me your hand."

It's hard to be noble when the beneficiary tries your patience. I wrapped the raingear around Sal's shoulders and hooked my arm beneath his, pushing his pack off the trail with my foot, leaving it for his unlikely retrieval later. I was no medic, but Sal's odds were not good. And even in its stupor the pig should have known it, but it had this way of denying the facts, as if it could bend things to its own will. It was the same faculty that prompted it to eat its own shit; it literally could convince itself that the stench wasn't there.

Worse yet, the pig could make you question the facts too. I hated that about the pig.

Roused by our departure, the pig sniffed at the shallow body indentation Sal had scratched in the ground as if it were just another thing. I left it on its own to follow, and said to myself, "You can't get your pack on the first pass, but grab the matches and stove fuel on your way down. And hide your pack! This good deed won't go unpunished either; that pack's as good as gone by morning."

Sal mumbled something. I still didn't understand but said, "The pig's right behind us."

Maybe. Maybe not.

At my pack, I stuffed a box of matches in my shirt and tied a bottle of stove fuel around my neck using a bandana. Neither the wind nor Sal's shivering showed any inclination to stop. And I didn't have to do any math in my head to know which of the two was more unnerving. I don't like to press against anyone, and I hate anyone to press against me. Sal needed to serve some kind of function. I turned his headlamp on and rested his head on my shoulder for the sole purpose of aiming the light. And in that way, we headed down to the shoulder of the mountain, counting until I found the fire ring. I propped Sal up against one of the logs. He stared and blinked while I piled kindling, stared and blinked as I doused it with stove fuel, stared and blinked at the flames shooting into the air. The fire lit the mountain with the intensity and longevity of a flare. (No one could find us now!)

In its brief light, I assessed our camp. Fifteen feet from where Sal sat, the shoulder fell off into an abyss. One of us had gotten lucky, I thought, not splatter with someone pressing against me. But what of that pig? It could be in any ravine between here and the knob.

Soon the flames dwindled to embers, quickly taking the heat with them. I found a downed limb too long and too thick to snap, but doused the middle with fuel, then dragged it across the coals. In its light I filled my arms with shorter wood, and in ten minutes stoked a sustained fire that needed backing away from. When I smelled the singe of rubber, I pulled Sal and his crinkling raingear to the far side of the log and sat down beside him. His trembling weight fell against me again. In a moment of zero clarity, I put one arm around him, then the other, and I held him until all was quiet. It was an involuntary response, I reasoned. Like pulling my hand from a hot stove, there was nothing I could do to fight it. This reasoning picked up speed and I soon understood that the whole incident was involuntary, and more importantly would pass as soon as the stimulus did. From his breathing, that would not be long. And so I held him until down-mountain, a pig charged through the brush. Held him until he lifted a shaking hand to its snout.

I gathered my last armload of wood well beyond midnight, long after finishing my debate on how the pig ever found us. By then, Sal was warm and sleeping calmly in a flickering light, the pig too. Circling the fire, I pushed tent stakes into the ground to judge the depth of the soil. They clinked and tumbled and confirmed that just below the thin carpet of needles was a slab of rock; no tent tonight. I used a bootlace to suture the old gray broken-between-the-hemlocks rope and draped the tent over it, pinning its ends to the ground with gathered rocks to form a triangle of tarp above Sal. The pig stirred and circled beneath the tarp, standing over Sal, staring down, ears twitching independently, reaching for some note in the air, bending something to its will.

As the pig lay down, Sal arched his back to welcome it, not in the signature way one lover welcomes another, nothing like that, but more in the way pups swarm, coiling inside and around each other to create a familiar mass, something larger, safer and more reminiscent of a hopeful past than their current lives.

And there, on this night when involuntary responses were having their way with me, I turned lonesome. I stabbed the fire with Excalibur and imagined wedging the charred tip between Sal and the pig, heaving Archimedes (Greek!) style, fulcruming the moment, fulcruming the world, creating space for my multitudes and me so that we too could curl up into something larger, safer, and more reminiscent than ourselves.

Lieut laughed.

Yes, I heard you, Lieut! I heard you! We've been through this so many fucking times. I know I took my eyes up. I remember. I know I owned the ground on your behalf. But I did as you asked, Lieut. I did what you should never have asked me to do: I fed the cure. I stopped your screams. I leaned up and I leaned in, even when you looked back as the light went out as if to ask, what the fuck did I do? And then it was quiet, but the pigs came anyway—you never told me they would come anyway—and I fought them off to bring more of you back to you. But this isn't enough for you, Lieut. It's never enough that I did what you should never have asked me to do. Or that I fought the pigs until the others came to take what was left of you and what was left of me away, me, with my knife still in you.

At that moment, as at the cliff with my arms out, I saw myself from afar, Excalibur in my hands, fulcruming myself, projecting myself over the shoulder for the addition of my own subtraction, splattering. Clear my head, right, Lieut? Shake that shit from my head, right, Lieut? Kill the voice in my head, right, Lieut? Anything else? Anything fucking else?

I slid my back down the log and sat, sweat dripping off the tip of my nose. I was alone, yes.

I held a mouthful of water then spit it into the coals. The glowing limb hissed. Its firelight weakened. I slid closer, tilting my head to understand as the light dimmed. I felt as if I'd just killed something. The temperature fell. I felt as if everyone shivered.

I crawled closer and stuffed the fire with chips of sap-frosted bark until the flames spit the sap back, dancing higher. I was so tired. There was room for me beneath the tarp, but there would be pressing.

Close: Sal and the pig.

Distant: me.

Close: Smackspecter, Grunt.

Distant: sleep.

Rustling through my pack for the map of the trail, I leaned further into the fire's light. The fifteen miles we'd covered barely registered along the red line, yet every one of the promises made resounded. Like a bum shaking coins in a cup for a better result, I ran through those promises again.

My first promise was to me, not to die. Yet I kept looking for cliffs, fulcrums, and loopholes, so that was bullshit.

Second: *Against all enemies, foreign and domestic*. Let's face it, any guy looking for loopholes in promises to himself probably shouldn't be held to the high expectations of military oaths. Not to mention the fact that I had every right at the time of my oath to expect there'd be only one enemy at a time, and that he'd identify himself as such and not leave it for me to figure out.

Third: *True faith and allegiance.* To ghosts? To you, Lieut? Isn't it funny how because I didn't carry you out *then*, all I do is carry you *now*? Isn't it hilarious that because I quieted your screams, you now create mine? If I could put you down again, Lieut, I would. If I could roll up and in again I would, because it's like I missed the most important spot and left too much of you to remain.

And my fourth: *Without mental reservation or purpose of evasion.* I was being hunted! See promise number one! I had legions to evade: Smackspecter, Grunt, cliffs, multitudes, loneliness, a pig that would be President!

So what oath *could* I keep? Now is the time for all good men to come to the aid of their country? Did nothing matter to me? (God, I hate introspection!) Was nothing bigger than me? Worth more than me?

I did math in my head.

No.

What about the truth?

No.

The pig curling with Sal at the fire?

No.

Sal, who would walk through fire for me without even being dosed?

Nice play, but no.

Ohio? Red-haired girls?

No, and no.

My introspection peaked with the flames, leaving me to conclude that I would hunt me too. Shit, between the fulcrums and the cliffs, I probably already was.

Disgusted by my regrets, I stomped along the mountain's shoulder, stripping withered leaves from dead branches before dragging them back in bundles to the fire. I studied Sal and the pig as they slept and wondered if could they make it to safety without me, without smack? Because the truth was if no sign of a deal came, I would be scraping them off my boots when Smackspecter got close anyway. So maybe the best thing I could do was set them up, point them south and jump off the trail, pulling my scent (and Smackspecter) away with me. Freeing them and freeing me! That would allow me to be noble *and* serve me best! The long fabled win-win! As if to confirm, the roar of the wind above us stopped. The storm was over.

The trail guide noted a two-lane road and grocery store in the town of Palmerton, about twenty miles down trail, another full day's hike, but I could hide Sal and the pig near that road and go into town, buy them enough food and dose it so they had a chance for a while. Then I could hitch out; the state swarmed with long-haul guys. I spread the road map. Sure, PA33 ran to I-80W as I expected, which dropped down I-81. To where, I didn't know. Could it get me to the Keys? Mexico?

Sal and the pig would be okay, I thought, stealing the fact-denying trick from the pig. I could deliver them plenty of food from Palmerton, dose it, and slip out before dawn. Then, I began to envision, as long as they stayed out of sight and didn't get killed, they'd be okay, and my probability of getting a deal was improved! Smackspecter could only chase half of us, and I was sure it would be me and the smack he thought I still had, not Sal and the pig. Meanwhile, I would let him know through the logs that Sal and the original Pigasus with the telltale New Jersey were awaiting word from me to go public with the government's fraud. Yes, I simply had to let Smackspecter know the safeguards I'd taken around my evidence, and my deal would go down as conceived.

Comforted by my brilliance but still lonesome, I poked at the fire then squirmed beneath the tarp with Sal and the pig. When breath condensed on the plastic eight inches from my face and dripped on my hair, I comforted myself that it was my own unmingled breath. I turned to stare through the gap between the tent-tarp and earth at a narrow band of fading stars. I ran through my plan again and laughed. It's not *always* appalling to be aware of your madness. It can keep you company. It can curl around you. It can create a bigger whole.

***

The sun lit the eastern slope far too soon, lighting the wet of a nighttime shower. (Had I not just gone to sleep?) Sal scrambled from beneath the tarp as though he'd been waiting. I heard the rip of a pack zipper, his pad flip, then the scratching, scratching, scratching of a pencil, like a rat gnawing on bamboo. He was sketching his girl. I rolled over to watch. But Sal heard and quit until I stiffened.

At first his strokes were long and ambiguous. I imagined they were locks of brown hair bouncing off a shoulder. When his stokes accelerated, I pictured him refining the sinuous nape of a freckle-free neck. At times, his pencil moved in wild sweeps then stopped in mid-air, it seemed, like he was awaiting clarity before rubbing the charcoal with a slick thumb and scratching again. And when the sun broke and his strokes grew short and furious, I imagined the lines of a chin, perhaps, or the arch of a feathery brow.

But just that quickly, like a windstorm through the gap, it was over. Sal sighed, said something unintelligible to the pig, and buried the pad again in his pack.

"Thank you, Corman," he said, stirring the coals. "Last night was a time for all good men. And the President is safe."

Most things between men need not be discussed, but my probing skills were taking on a life of their own. "Sal, who's Geneva?" I asked, not caring at all who Geneva was.

"That's on a need-to-know basis only. The only thing you have a need to know, Corman, is that some things…" he shook his pack, "…can only be kept safe by keeping them away." He pushed the pad down in his pack. "Even when they want to run to you, it's the only way. But if I were to disclose her to anyone, Corman, it would be you, except no one can know her but me. It's how it has to be. I have to keep her safe. I made a promise." He paused for a moment, prompting me to celebrate prematurely. "But we're even in that regard, Corman, because I don't know your secret either."

"So it works, right, Sal? I mean, each of us has enough to worry about without the other adding to it. Besides, what are we going to do, right?"

"I made a promise to myself that I would never let anything happen to her, Corman. Yet the only reason she's safe is because of you. I don't know if that even counts."

"You took a pretty good beating for her, Sal."

"But she's still safe because of you. Just like the President and me last night. We're only safe because you got us safe. You are a great talisman."

"Last night was involuntary," I said more to myself than Sal, which was meaningless because Sal misunderstood it.

"Yes. These are the promises we make. But they do get heavy sometimes."

When Sal turned from his pack, he was snapping an envelope of instant oatmeal against the side of a saucepan with his left hand while pressing his right arm to his side. I spun out from beneath the tarp. "I'll do that," I blurted, taking the oatmeal. "Why don't you scout around for water?"

I was double dosing their oatmeal when Sal called out.

"Corman! I need you to see this!"

Thirty or so yards from our camp, Sal stood over the skinned carcass of a squirrel splayed on a rock. Needing to know, I pressed my index finger to a spot just above its amputated foot. It was cool but not cold.

"I don't know," I said, heading off Sal's question and leading him back to the fire ring. "Any water?"

"There's nothing here but rock and a little mud, Corman." He pressed his ribs then stopped in his tracks. "It looks like we had company last night." Sal waved me to the ground near his feet. Paw prints and Grunt prints in the mud around the fire ring.

"Shit," I said. "Eat up. Let's go, and keep your pig close."

"Who is it?"

"It's somebody. So let's go."

I headed up to the first blaze, but Sal sat back on the log, releasing the straps of his pack.

"I draw her each morning," he began.

"I don't need your secret, Sal. Let's go!"

But he would not be deterred. "It started over there, once upon a time. On the nights when I got to sleep, I would wake up at dawn with a girl in my head."

"Sal, I really, really shouldn't have asked."

Sal just kept talking as I walked away.

"Not a whole face, but parts. Her chin one morning, her cheeks the next, eyes, lips when I got lucky. She was always being unveiled, Corman, just the way women like, as a mystery to be solved."

I dragged a toe along the ground; drawing a knife.

"At first, I tried to just remember, to keep her in my head. She'd be safer there. I was sure of that; she'd be safer in my head. And it worked until we came under fire and I counted coup, not in the way of a Sioux brave, but in the way of our teachers. Then I'd have a dream that she was coming towards me, running for me, but she never made it. She never once made it, Corman, not once. And I wanted her to. I wanted to know what would happen if she did. Would she kiss me? I wanted to know. I wanted the kiss. I wanted to touch the color of her hair. But she never made it, and the memory faded.

"And then, when the fire died down, a new face would begin. After a while, I started sketching her, waking up at dawn while the vision of her was still fresh in my head. That way, no matter what, she'd be there the next day. And I'd hold her piece-by-piece, day-by-day, just one piece adding to the next. But never hair. She never made it long enough to reveal her hair, Corman. But… maybe this time."

"Good."

"The platoon knew and, around our coffee, I shared her. They called her Dawn, and they tried to look after her. But then the fire would come and I'd have the dream again, of her running toward me but not making it, and the next dawn there'd be nothing to add to her. I never completed her once. Just started all over again with a new face, Corman, trying harder and harder not to fire, not to lose her. I counted coup twenty times that I know of, once for every year of my life, and she died twenty times right alongside me. Each time I killed, I killed her. I was being punished through her. And I knew something wasn't right, Corman, because that's not how it's supposed to be. The Convention must have protected a man from doing that, from being made to kill the girl running to him. No man should be made to kill the girl running to him, Corman. And so I stopped firing. I stopped counting coup. And when I did, the others, they just stopped helping me keep my promise."

"Let's go, Sal!"

"I got the 'fatigue', Corman, and they swapped me home for a year at Reed. I'm never going back there. Even today, I don't know what she looks like, Corman, not fully, not complete, not yet. So now you know my secret."

"Yes, now I finally know. Let's go!"

He cinched his pack. "What's the plan?"

"It's twenty to the next road. Let's get that far first, then we'll figure out the rest."

"How long will that take?"

"Ten hours, maybe."

"Then remember the secret exposed to us by Excalibur and hike like a knight!"

"Will the pig make it?"

"The President will not be the issue, Corman."

Chapter 15

The pig was not the issue, I was. My pack seemed heavier. Not because of my decision to part ways with Sal and the pig, but because now Grunt was out there armed for an insurrection and sniffing around.

He'd come back to find me for a reason. What was it? What did he make of the pig? Of it curled around Sal? What did he make of the three of us beneath the same small tarp? He could have killed us in our sleep if that's what he'd wanted. Why didn't he? Look at me, asking big questions. Who did I think I was? Once again, I had no time to think about that, not that I wanted to.

But this much I did think about: I could draw Smackspecter away, but not Grunt too, not and find a steady gait to Palmerton.

The morning was cool. On rare stretches of flat ground, the pig made up distance between itself and Sal with an unpolished shrill and a wobbling distracted canter, like maybe it was hiding something and stumbling under its weight. Perhaps it awakened in the night and saw Grunt with his dogs in our campsite. Perhaps it had cut a deal of its own, seeking a return to political glory.

We hiked through Hahn's Lookout without even pausing to look out, and pulled up to the blue-blaze leading to the Leroy Smith Shelter a little before ten o'clock, logging five miles in two hours.

The shelter, an open-faced weave of logs stacked on a square of fieldstone, sat vacant. A tree arched over the full span of the corrugated roof, close enough to grab, thick enough to shimmy.

"You don't see a tree like that every day." I said.

"Because it's outwitted its enemies," Sal said, dropping his pack while I chugged water. "Grow straight in this shade and die. Grow sideways and grab the sun."

A breeze kicked up, swinging a shelter log in its bag against the siding. It thumped like an unbuttoned shutter. I took it down and, with one eye peeled, shuffled through its insipid musings. Missing was anything recorded in the past two days. I thumbed through the pages again, to be sure. Nothing. How far north had Smackspecter gone?

"Remember, Corman," Sal said as I stared at the missing entry, "the enemy cannot outwit us."

"Smackspecter is no simple enemy," I said, licking my thumb.

"Smack?"

"Smackspecter, the Fed trying to kill us."

"Is that his name?"

"I don't know his name, Sal, but that's the trail-name I gave him when I imagined him running from the stall covered in white powder, ghostlike. I told you about that. I like to name things. Anyway, I don't even know his face. All I know are those black high-top sneakers."

"He'd make a great archenemy with that name, Corman: Smackspecter. And all you see are his feet… in sneakers." Sal played with the name, placing the emphasis on different syllables. *Smack*specter. Smack*spec*ter. Smackspec*ter*. "The best one is Smack*spec*ter," he concluded.

"No. I've already named him. Emphasis on Smack."

"But this is when our training pays off, Corman. All those drills were not meant to prepare us to outwit our *enemy*, Corman, they were to prepare us to outwit our *arch*enemy! Smack*spec*ter the archenemy! All one word: Smackspecter. And we should capitalize both S's! Capital S, Smack. Capital S, Specter. Smack*Spec*ter. Having an archenemy is a whole different engagement, Corman. We had best be on our game."

"I don't care how you spell it, but I named him with the emphasis on Smack and that's where it stays. And he'll have all the tools of the FBI at his disposal."

"Yes, but they're not aware of our secret weapon; they cannot think like we do, Corman. They can only think in straight lines! And only deploy in straight lines. And that is what foils all archenemies: straight lines! But we can think in a helix, Corman. You've seen them, Corman, archenemies always erect those complicated mousetraps, but in their hearts, those traps, those works, the guts, are always in a straight line, so the superhero always escapes. The trapped superhero sees the mechanics of the huge mousetrap arranged in a straight line, and using his helix powers, knows… if… he… can… only… twist… his… legs around… and reach… that switch…with his…left foot… Bam! Free! But we can think in a helix, Corman. We can outwit."

"This is getting us nowhere," I hissed, unsure again where the smack ended and Sal's brokenness took over. I was inclined not to care, but it was getting harder to dismiss Sal entirely. The memory of successfully navigating Wolf Rocks hiking like knights was still fresh. I needed to tread lightly, to listen for something I could use.

"Now…" He was pacing again. "SmackSpecter does not know that we are up here."

"Two words, one cap, emphasis on smack and of course he does. He wrote in the log, remember?"

"No, he *assumed* we are up here, and *deduced* we are, but these are very different things from knowing. He expects to chase us on this trail. And why? Because this trail is essentially his straight line!

He must have a straight line to survive! And the only way he could surprise us on a straight line is if we didn't know he was coming, right?"

My head screamed for the far side of the Palmerton plan.

"So, Corman, in order to take his straight line away, we must let him know that *we* know!

The smack was affecting Sal in new ways. He saw himself as Socrates, without the annoying questions.

Taking the notebook log, he asked, "Will he recognize the name you made for him?"

"I think so."

"Then we could leave him clues, here, in these journals, like he's leaving for us, to let him know that we know."

"I was already thinking of that."

I was.

"Of course. He'd have to read them, right? That's what the straight-line part of you was afraid of, right? That if we wrote anything at all, he could figure us out and track us? Isn't that right, Corman?"

It wasn't right, but I let it be, allowing Sal to think he was way ahead of me by nodding mutely. But I knew I had to leave messages for the specter, just with a different motive than Sal's.

"Are you freezing up under fire? Think in a helix! Twist two truths together! Something must wrap around something else to be a helix. For us, it's truths! First truth: we are on the Appalachian Trail. Second truth: we know that he is on the trail too. Two truths, twisting around each other. That's life, Corman, is it not? Now what do we write?"

"What does the helix suggest?"

Sal stared me down to make clear that the helix didn't suggest things; it *was* a thing. "I suggest," he said, drawing out the I, 'Sorry we couldn't hang for the SmackSpecter'".

"I like it. Two words, one cap, emphasis on the smack. But don't date it. It's been three days since anyone signed that log. That gives him a window, but that's all. Let's find the spring and get back to the trail. We still have fifteen to go."

Sal handed the log to me to place back in its bag. I took the opportunity to scribble my own message: "A fool and his pig are soon parted."

Sal was watching.

"I just underlined 'hang'," I explained. Casting my eyes down the trail I added, somewhat unintentionally, "Speaking of the pig...."

Sal whirled around. "Where's the President?"

"How far could it go?"

"There's nothing but woods here, Corman. Distance is not the issue. Far is not the issue."

We circled behind the shelter; nothing but a downhill deer run and rocks.

"I'm going," Sal declared.

Holding briars from his skin, Sal sidestepped down the run while I watched and tried to imagine a deal without the pig. Outwardly I called the pig (lightly), while inside I saw it dead, glistening on a rock, skinned, foot missing. To be certain, I listened for rustling, but heard nothing except Sal's desperate cries.

When they stopped, he called me by name.

"Corman! The President is secure, Corman! He's okay! We're coming up now."

The pig emerged first.

"He was looking for the trail," Sal explained. "He 's never done that before. I've been worried that something like this might happen. What if he's hearing the call of the wild, Corman? Like that dog, Buck?"

"It's not. It eats Yodels and eggs. Let's just get some water and go already."

"What's our destination?"

"Lehigh Gap. But listen..." I choked on the next few words. "... the President needs rations, Sal. You can see its energy dropping.

That road at Lehigh Gap leads to Palmerton. There's a grocery store there. I can get there and back before nightfall, but I've got to hurry. I'm going to hike ahead, okay? You and the pig will be fine without me. Just stay out of sight. When you get to the road, just continue over it. Follow the white blazes. There's a spring about a half-mile past, right on the trail. Get to the spring, stay out of sight, and wait for me. If there's anyone there, just keep hiking. There's a shelter up another half-mile or so. Remember, stay out of sight. I should be there before dark. Okay?"

"Of course it's okay, Corman. The President and I are not children leaving for the bus stop. Make sure you get eggs."

"Yes, yes, and Yodels."

"Yes, and get something to kill the taste of water. The President has been complaining about the taste of water. Have you not noticed the way he drinks?"

I waved acknowledgement, but didn't look back. I didn't want to rethink anything. I just needed to feel muscles thump in my thighs as I sprang from one rock to the next, the simple and free straight-line mechanics of springing from one rock to the next.

The trail hung on the ridge and challenged me with a few elevation changes. In an hour, I crossed Smith's Gap. Math in my head put my pace at a blistering three-and-a-half-miles per hour, *over rocks*, deploying the chess knight advantage! I could feel it all hardening my body, beating something into and out of me. My balance grew, and even the swelling of my eye subsided. It turns out that some healing shows its cards.

My pack now was a natural appendage, disappearing into my weight, and I found myself wishing for the elevation to change. I wanted to test myself. Could I count fifty uphill paces before stopping? A hundred? Could I clock thirty miles a day, rather than the twenty we struggled for? At what pace might I outrun you, Lieut? Was I on it already?

Lieut laughed.

I pushed harder. By two o'clock, I'd crossed Delp's Trail and descended to Little Gap. I stopped to slake my thirst with a hurried gulp, but was inconvenienced by it, barely able to contain my drive. I tossed back a handful of nuts, pulled my weight up on my staff and set off again, strides longer, balanced, and arrogant. The buzz of gnats circling my sweat faded into a song in my head.

I know what you would have said, Lieut. I hear you yelling at me to turn it off. But it feels good now. Music never played there.

Now Jim Morrison spoke to me, keeping me company, advancing my pace. My hiking stick clicked in time.

Faces come out of the rain (click)

By five-thirty, I stood on the shoulder of PA 873, exhilarated by the descent. A brown trail sign pointed west: "Palmerton – 2 miles".

Chapter 16

The tip of my hiking stick charred in the softening blacktop for a quarter mile without a car in either direction. I drew a forearm across my forehead then angled back to the cool shade near the woodline, anxious to reread the data book. Obviously, in my haste, I'd overlooked some mention, some asterisk, to warn me that Route 873 was essentially discarded and irrelevant. I had not, and waited in the shade for another fifteen minutes before the first car appeared, a shiny Saab emerging from wavy heat. I thumbed with feigned nonchalance, the oldest hitchhiker trick in the book. The Saab slowed. I grew hopeful, then anxious again; SmackSpecter would fire through a window and leave me for dead. Instead, a middle-aged woman took a look at my bruised face, shook her head full of clean hair, shouted over the radio "Winners only," and accelerated. As if to confirm her assessment, a grasshopper helicoptered to my shoulder, only to move on with the same scorn.

How far Sal and the pig lagged behind me was anybody's guess, but by me standing they must be gaining on me. Route 873 was straight with a clear line of sight, and they could spot me on the horizon when they crossed. I did not want to revisit the separation. Less time together gave him less time to suspect.

I buckled my pack and started down the highway. In the unbearable heat, Morrison spoke to me again. But I don't really remember what he said.

Another half-mile and a second vehicle approached from behind, pistons clanging like hammers on an anvil. I did not turn. I did not thumb. I missed SOFA so much. The vehicle stopped anyway, a badly rusted pick-up. I yanked at the pitted door handle, but the driver waved me off, leaning over to open it from the inside. Wrappers swirled around his sneakers, but white, low and torn, not new, black and high. He scraped a few newspapers on the seat towards him.

"Sorry about that, man! Palmerton?" He pushed a faded Phillies cap back on his head. Oily stalks of hair draped across peeling sunburn. A quarter-sized fleck of liberated dermis quivered on the front of his black shirt.

"If you're going."

I threw my pack and staff in the back. The door wouldn't latch. "Pull it hard, man, and lift the handle at the same time. There, see?" The truck shuddered as it accelerated. He turned to look at me, sizing me up, nodding his head at the scabs over my eyes and creased lip. "I've got twenty says you're spending the night in a cell."

"You gonna have something to do with that?" I challenged, pulling at the door handle. Nothing. "Son of a…!"

"Chill, man! I'm not messing with you! Cops got everybody spooked around here or what? Don't you know about the station in Palmerton? If they got an open cell, you hikers can spend the night and clean up. I woulda thought you knew about that. It's world renowned, man."

"Yeah, yeah, I remember now," I lied. "No cell. Just groceries."

The clutch ground between gears. "*Jesus H Christ*!" He jammed the shift up the column three times before it held. "There she goes.

Whew, huh? She's a little stubborn, but she's got a right to be. Just took me fifteen hundred miles. 'Course, once you get her on the highway, she purrs."

I barely heard him over the siren song of pistons knocking. Was SOFA wilting in the summer sun? Tainting ground water beneath some sprawling scrap yard? Enduring daily ridicule? Who did I think I was to leave her that way, even if my choices were few? Choices are always few!

I found solace in knowing that under similar circumstances she would have left me too.

"Yep, these old Fords purr. Anyway, where was I? Oh yeah, can't say as I blame you about being a little spooked. I've seen enough cops these past few days to last me a lifetime, man."

I did some math in my head. Fifteen hundred miles was about right. "Chicago?" I asked.

"You?" He motioned again to my face.

"Nah."

"Well, I seen all of it, man. Check this out!" He lifted the Phillies cap, revealing a strip of shaved hair at the crown of his head. "Count them, man, twelve stitches! One for each apostle! Courtesy of the Windy City!"

"Cops?"

"Who knows? Shit flying everywhere. Coulda been cops. Coulda not been cops. Here, check *this* out too."

He unfolded one of the newspapers: front page, a picture of the melee outside the park. "You can't really see me but I'm… right… right there, behind that colored guy. Groovy, huh?"

We came to the crest of a hill and were stopped by an unapologetic flagman. Beyond him the road was blocked by a crew dragging ditches with shovels that they emptied over their shoulders onto a creeping flatbed. The creep of the men and the creep of the flatbed gave me reason to conclude we'd be there a while. I thought of finishing on foot, couldn't be more than a half-mile more, but the cover of the pickup truck gave me some comfort, until the driver droned on.

"And I only went for the music! Wasn't no music that day, I can tell you that! The whole damn city just lost its groove! And that mayor, what's his name? Yeah, Daley. Jesus H. Christ, what a renowned turd he is, man." He unfolded another paper. "Read this headline here."

Daley declares: "The policeman isn't there to create disorder; the policeman is there to preserve disorder."

"Turd, right?"

I read the brief article. Rubin, Hoffman, Seale, Dellinger, Davis, Hayden: all sighted in Daley's scope and cited for inciting riot. Great editing.

The pickup stuttered too. He pumped the accelerator, revving the engine, clanging the pistons. The flagman misunderstood and waved him through with his middle finger.

"You particular about your choice of grocery, or is that one there going to do?"

"I'm good," I said, yanking on the handle. "Peace."

"Wait. I was planning on taking you back to the trailhead, but I guess you *could* try to hitch another ride."

"I'll be quick," I predicted, underestimating the force against me: a price-check on aisle four. Thirty minutes later, having clearly overshot the mark with four bags of groceries, I was surprised to find the truck still there. Who has that amount of patience? I wondered. Who has this little to do? I nodded and loaded the haul into my pack. Twenty hotdogs, half-a-dozen cans of soup to kill the taste of water, frosted Pop-Tarts, Kool-Aid to kill the taste of water, Yodels and eggs (four dozen each), peanut butter, Tang to kill the taste of water, mix 'n eat Cream of Wheat, and instant coffee to kill the taste of water. More than enough to stress the pickup's springs. More than enough to hold Sal and the pig for a while.

"Whoa!" he shouted. "Guess you won't be stopping again in Wind Gap, huh?"

"Hiked through Wind Gap two days ago."

"You're not a through-hiker?"

"Just heading the other way."

"Well, if you're heading south, your next food run is Duncannon."

"Far?"

"Four days, but you bought enough to carry you twenty."

"You know a lot about hiking this thing," I said, teasing my probing skills.

"Oh, I did my time, got where I had to."

I slid back into the truck, fumbling with the door again. "You've got to lift the handle at the same time, remember? There. See? Ok, say, listen, I've been thinking. I don't know your story, none of my business, but since you don't seem to know a whole lot about this trail you probably don't know anything about Duncannon either – stuff that might, maybe, be important to you."

We missed the light. I was annoyed. Two lights and they couldn't time them? The truck was shuddering again. "What kind of stuff?"

"Relax, man. I'm just trying to help you with your own groovy cause, whatever you've got in store. Duncannon, well, let's just say there are a lot of guys hiking this trail for their own reasons. Some never even get off, just yo-yo back and forth, Georgia to Maine, Maine to Georgia. Others just got to get someplace. None of my business, man, just like I was none of theirs. But no matter why they're on this trail, every one of 'em stops in Duncannon. All I'm saying is, if you're looking to circle yourself with kindred spirits who can help you, get to the Royle." He sang, "You're gonna meet, some gentle people there…"

"Do I look like the Flower Power type?"

"It ain't Haight, man. I'm just saying you might find people who are thinking a lot like you… however that is. And they'll help you. Not that you need it, 'cause that's none of my business."

"Royle. What is that?"

"Truthfully? It's like a really bad hotel, but nowhere near as nice. But the thing is, it's renowned and there's kindred sprits there to help you, you know, if you should need it, which is none of my business, as I have said."

"Showers?"

"Sort of. But you can get your head under it if you try. Just be sure to let the water run for a while to let the rust out."

"Beds?"

"Sort of. But there's a bar *and* a grill and *every*one hiking through stops to fatten up. Of course, it's September and the through-hikers are all way north now." He paused to calculate. "Vermont, probably, if they're going to hit Maine before snow. But Jesus H. Christ, some just get to the Royle and stay! For whatever reason! None of my business! Just stay! Anyway, now you know. And if you do go, tell the girl behind the counter – name is Micki, a full-size girl, a little bite, a great laugh – tell her Bituminous said hello. It's been a while, but I hope she remembers."

The same flagman that stopped us on the way in waved us to a stop, flashing the same yawn and the same finger. The same crew had changed sides of the same road, now throwing the same dirt from the same flatbed into the opposite ditch with the same enthusiasm they'd excavated earlier. Bituminous took it in stride. I did not; the sun was setting. When the flatbed was emptied and we were waved on, Bituminous pushed his Phillies cap back on his head and urged the truck forward. Two gears up and the clutch screeched. He jammed the shift up the column like a rusted rifle bolt, towards him, back, towards him, back - three, four, five, ten times, his "Jesus H. Christ!" louder with each thrust. But something would not hold. Exhausted, Bituminous let go of the shift and put his head back.

"One stop too many for it, I guess. I'm afraid I'll need to leave you here." But I suspected it was my weight and that of my enormous food haul that brought it over the brink. I was getting good at making an impact.

We pushed it off the road and I cinched my pack, teetering under its tonnage.

Bituminous's voice cracked, and I understood why. "Remember the Royle. And Micki too," he said.

Something in my knee popped, reminding me that I too would pay dearly for this good deed.

The remaining stretch of road was relatively level, but that hardly mattered. Under my haul of food, the soft blacktop dented beneath me, softening, sliding out to the edges of my boots and sticking like black dogshit, and reminding me of the soft ground I'd come from, a fading but firming memory. I could look back down the road and see my path of dents: one-foot dents while I meandered, two when I pulled up under the weight. Strung together, the dents looked like links of sausage trailing into the past. I was getting nowhere fast. The late sun was in my face, then on my chest, then only on my shoes. It was setting on me, I thought. Who did I think I was? All I could do was push on and hunt for words to explain to Sal why I was leaving.

I would tell him I needed to move faster to outrun SmackSpecter. He would say faster is always a straight line, and straight lines never outwit anyone.

I would argue I came on the trail to save the pig, and now it is healed and I must go. He would argue that, yes, the pig is healed, but I could not know my motivation for leaving; I could only assume it, which is not the same. There are forces at play, he would say. No shit, I would agree: the rule of irony, the rule of no good deed going unpunished, the rule of price-check on aisle four certainty! But the President is healed, he would remind me. I would insist he is wrong; I never healed anything! He would say the evidence is to the contrary.

And so I found no words, but in the final moments of twilight I did find the trailhead behind a gravel parking lot hosting a clean and empty Buick sedan. It was flesh toned, and I wondered. But the plates told me she was from Massachusetts and I relaxed a bit. As I circled, a new plan evolved. Looking over my shoulder, I pushed her handle and the door opened. The smell of her dampness held me back a moment. She was no SOFA, that was a given, but soon I was running my fingers deep into her glove compartment, beneath her seat, and over her visors. She was a tease. I found no key. The plan faded, and I headed uphill.

The loss of twilight made footing treacherous. I lit my headlamp, catching in its light the crisping edge of hoofprints. A half-mile in, before the trail ascended steeply through a dark tunnel of pine, a campfire spit sparked over the rhododendrons. Like a contrite father wobbling home with Cracker Jacks, I lengthened my stride with misbegotten enthusiasm. Yes, I had a lot of explaining to do, but I had Yodels and I had eggs and wouldn't Sal be goddamn delighted?

But it wasn't Sal pacing before the fire.

He was tall, draped in a colorful concealing serape that swept the ground from the back to his feet. Upon my approach, he squatted near the fire, stirring a soup of celery and bullion. He spoke with a slightly British cadence, a pronounced air of indignation.

"Broth?" he asked.

I studied his camp. Candles lined a rock path to his bedroll, dimming in the breeze. Blue raingear swung like strange fruit from a swooping rope casting cartoon shadows. But most disturbing, the camp was pitted with dozens of freshly dug holes. He'd been there a while, a long while. Glaring up from the simmering pot, he took notice of my bemusement.

"If you must know, I'm searching for an original idea."

"I'm good," I said.

"Spare me your incredulity."

"I'm just looking for my friend."

"You heard right. I am staying out here until I foster an original idea."

"Foster?"

"Well, isn't this intellectually stimulating?" (This from a guy digging holes.)

"What's with the holes?"

"I thought I was onto something. That's all"

"I'm just looking for my friend."

"I've seen no one."

I nodded and started up the mountain.

"But I've heard… a lot. And it's a dire distraction! How can I seek an original idea while being haunted by a tired old pangram? What's to plague me next; the quick brown fox jumps over the lazy dog? Hush! Listen!"

From high above us, Sal called out a weeping refrain of "…for all good men to come to the aid of their country!"

I looked to the original idea guy as if he could offer something, and named him Plato in my head. I needed to name him something if I was going to stomach whatever Sal had in store. "Wait," he urged, signaling uphill with a tip of his head, like he'd heard something I didn't. Then rolled down the mountain Sal's long sad cry, sad enough to hold me at bay. This had tears written all over it.

At first I pictured the pig lost, but Sal's cry was so mournful I soon envisioned him holding the dead pig in his arms, rocking it. I took a step uphill, yet another involuntary response, but the weight of my other good deed, my food haul, brought me to a merciful halt.

But when Sal's cry shook the darkness again, I knew it was not the lost body of the pig he was calling for, but its lost double-dosed soul. I shrugged, lit my headlamp, and started uphill, scanning the mountainside for the sweep of Sal's light.

Just what I fucking needed.

Chapter 17

A snap of wood brought me to a halt.

"Sal?" I called in a whisper. I heard the snap again, placing it now as only Plato feeding his fire down below, where he talked faintly as I ascended. The air grew dank and loud with crickets. My feet slid on thin mud. The night webs of spiders sagged across the trail face-high, sticking to my bruises and scab. I chopped at the blackness ahead of me with my hiking staff, but not before pulling something off my neck and spiking it into the ferns that swallowed the trail.

"Sal?"

Nothing.

The climb was just too much for the pig, I would tell him. But he wouldn't hear it. He would tug my hands to the corpse as I recoiled; a dead pig held only slightly more charm for me than a live one.

"Sal?"

I side-winded through a hundred yards of scratchy brush before spotting a blue blaze and its discernible trail to the shelter. And I found Sal as I'd imagined, cross-legged in the lean-to, rocking, eyes filmed gray like those of a cod reeled up from the deep. But there was no pig on his lap. Without looking at me he said in a dead monotone, "The President has been killed, Corman. There is nothing you can do."

I let my mouth fly open for effect. "SmackSpecter?" I asked, steering the conclusion.

Sal continued staring forward. "Yes. Yes, he was here. This morning."

I got the sense he was answering a different question. He lifted his arm with a hiss of pain, pointing at the shelter's log lying in the dirt near the fire ring. I read the last entry: "You took an oath that doesn't end. You belong to me. I am here to take you back," it said. I rubbed my chest. Sal hissed in pain again. I could dose him, I thought, but his ensuing clarity of thought might just provoke him to wonder if the pig was all I had of SmackSpecter's, or worse yet, to wonder why SmackSpecter would kill what he purposefully came to retrieve. I withheld the dose for a less combustible time. My truth required Sal's misplaced faith.

"I have failed in my mission, Corman. I have failed to protect the President and I have failed to outwit our enemy."

"Maybe the climb was just too much for him," I recited as I'd practiced.

"It wasn't the climb, Corman; it was my miscalculation of how cruel our enemy is."

"Where is it?"

Sal motioned weakly to another narrow path that led to the spring. "He just wandered for a minute, Corman, just while I was wrapping my ribs." Sal lifted his shirt as if compelled to prove it. "I heard nothing, no one. Our enemy is stealth. Or enemy is cruel."

I left Sal to his miscalculating and aimed my lamp down the shoot, following it past the spring where a creek split into forks. There, the lifeless pig was strewn on the rocks, its orange head bobbing in the water like a buoy with ears.

Well, there's one less, Lieut. I'm about ready to call it even. How about you?

I took my headlamp off and waved it above the double-dosed carcass. The pig's panniers were missing, and it was bloating already, and its eye – Jesus, why do they always look back? I pulled the lamp down its knobby spine to its twisted tail where, in the strange light, the water appeared to run red. I drew my boot through it, but there would be no correction; my lamp made sure of that when it fell upon the rear leg of the pig and its sawn-off missing foot. It wasn't my double dose that killed the pig.

I stepped back over the wet rocks. I moved my lamp back up to the pig's blank eye before wedging my hiking staff to roll it over. And there, protruding from the center of its hideous New Jersey, was the broken shaft of an arrow.

Grunt.

I might have thought of more immediate things, like my own safety, but instead imagined Grunt's hiking stick collection of peeled squirrel feet augmented with the clunky hoof of a sow. Did he consider how the hoof would draw flies for a week before drying out? That it would swing with a greater force around his stick than the others? Did he think of that and how annoying that might be, untangling them all the time?

Who did I think I was? But I finally got to the task at hand, disposing of the carcass. Death by arrow or not, there would still be discovery. There would still be autopsy, and questions, and toxology and toxicology, and inquiries. We had to bury it. Besides, the woods were getting ready to feed. I rolled the pig back over, then returned to Sal, looking away from him as I approached. "We need a shovel," I said. "The guy below has one."

"...Just for a minute. While I was wrapping... I cared more about me than him... I was an unworthy bodyguard."

"Yeah, well, we all suck at something," I said. It didn't cheer him up, but then again, it wasn't meant to.

Plato was filling in holes when he spotted my light coming down the trail. It reflected off the steel of his spade and made him pause. He was no more original moving dirt for the sake of moving dirt than the ditch-balancing road crew earlier that evening. By the tone of his voice, he didn't need me telling him that.

"I will not discuss this with you," he said, tamping loose dirt with the shovel's back.

"I came to borrow that," I said. "Those cries you heard were from my friend up top. His pet died, and we need to bury it before anything comes to feed on it."

"You mean the pig?"

"I thought you saw no one."

He stabbed the shovel into the earth. "It got conspicuously quiet up there. How do I know you didn't just kill this friend of yours? I must see your friend alive and the pig dead before I can agree to lend you this spade."

"Sure, come on up. But the pig was murdered with a silent arrow. And its foot was amputated, you know, like a scalp. And it's bloating up with maggots in this jungle heat. Still, come on. I just can't swear we'll be alone. Whoever did it is still..."

Plato handed me the shovel. "I'll be needing that back." He waved at some of the open holes. "I'm not done here."

"Burying something of your own?" I asked.

"Clearly."

As was my habit when listening for the *fffft* of an arrow, I climbed slowly. When I arrived back at the shelter, Sal was much as I left him, legs folded, glassed eyes locked on the same point on the horizon. Now, however, his sketchpad was open on his lap.

"Now, because of me, she will be gone in the morning, just like all the others," he said with zero encouragement. "And so this is how it will continue, Corman. Until now, I did not know *how* it would, only *that* it would. I have failed to protect the President, and he is therefore dead at my hands. So I will be punished in the morning as if I'd counted coup again. I have outwitted nothing, and I will now lose her as I have lost the President... and nothing has changed, Corman, nothing. This is my life, to be relived over and over; my once upon a time that will not let me go. Why is it always the eyes, Corman?"

Eyes? What did I know? Had I not just asked myself the same thing?

"Why is it, Corman," he clarified in my silence, "that just as the eyes appear, the end occurs?"

Did I stutter? Did I speak? Who did Sal think I was? What did he think I knew? I only knew that the pig was about to be a banquet, and what was left would be discovered in the morning. I held up the shovel. "This needs to be done."

"I can't."

"Last wishes?" I asked, pausing in front.

"He didn't say. He didn't know he would be killed. He did not foresee the cruelty either."

"I mean *you,* Sal. Any wishes?" I stopped him before he annoyed me by answering the wrong question again. "I mean, do you have any last wishes for the pig?"

"Full honors. He was to be Presiden–"

Sal's eyes did not move when a throat cleared in the dark, nor did they follow my blind swing of the shovel. But the throat's words sent Sal scrambling, not to the back of the lean-to for protection, but forward, with Excalibur poised to cave in a skull.

"You have something that belongs to me," the throat said, stepping into the light.

I halted Sal mid-arc. "This is Plato," I said, "from down below. Shovel's his."

Plato came into the moonlight with a certain swagger, with a certain flourish and pride that comes with just getting a nickname.

"Plato?" he asked, trying it on.

"I name things."

"That's been done," Plato assessed.

"Not all of it."

"Well then, *this* 'Plato'", he ran his hands dramatically down his arms and legs, "has come to assist. I need the shovel back. I need to get on with my work."

I waved Plato to the narrow run leading to the dead pig. Sal resumed his lotus position and catatonic stare.

Down at the fork where the pig head bobbed, I plunged the shovel into the rocky ground.

"And yet I wonder…" Plato said.

I was careful not to show the slightest interest in what he was going to say next, but that was not enough to head it off.

"…I wonder if I have the guts to see it all through, what it takes. The mettle, as it were."

"Wedge that hiking stick beneath this rock," I said, adding, "and listen to the woods for any movement."

With the shovel, I rocked it forward. Plato answered with a push of the staff. He pushed. I pushed. The dirt surrounding the rock cascaded beneath it, slowly raising it free. With a push of my boot, I sent it tumbling into the abyss. I listened for a lucky yelp, but heard none. In this way, we had half a grave dug in half an hour. We might have stopped there, placed the pig there, and piled the rocks there.

But the woods were alive now with the instincts of organic recycling, with scampering and stalking and the flash in the brush of a passing eye. Plato pulled up stiff.

"Keep digging," I said. But he couldn't, snapping his head, his hearing, in the direction of every wind-blown pinecone or scraping branch or – and I thought I heard it too – the frantic clopping of paws, spaniel paws. The beasts were circling.

Plato doubled his pace. We promptly dragged the pig to the hole, where its rapidly bloating body needed some unfortunate coaxing to fit. Plato gagged at the shovel wound, holding his breath and looking away. He'd never been in-country, that much was clear. I covered the pig with excavated dirt, then covered the bulge with rocks, leaves, and twigs to make the ground appear undisturbed, even as the mound gave the truth away.

"We don't want anyone wondering what's here, but that's the best we can do on this giant slab of rock," I said, throwing the shovel back over my shoulder.

I found Sal kneeling near the fire ring. He didn't look up.

"Have you prepared the President's body for full honors, Corman?"

"It's buried."

"Then we must march to his grave under the full honors protocol; first you, Corman, his healer; then you, Plato, his Chief Burial Assistant; then me, the one who failed to protect and serve."

When neither Plato nor I moved, Sal ushered us forward, imploring us to march, not walk. "Like this!" We circled the fresh grave. Sal stopped to do math in his head. "We will salute together seven times."

I did my own math; we were performing a twenty-one salute, salute.

Holding the seventh for a protracted moment of silence, the wood noises quelled and Sal fought with his emotions. When Sal's protocols had all been met, Plato walked him back to the shelter where, between sobs, Sal managed, "I am concerned that the end of the President signals the end of the SmackSpecter too."

Plato looked to me for explanation. I offered none.

Sal took up his lotus position again. "I am concerned that now that he's had his revenge on us, SmackSpecter and his cruelty are long on their way. But I am not done with him, Corman. Yes, done outwitting, but his great cruelty and his archenemy black sneakers have put new rules in play."

"Sneakers?" Plato asked.

"It doesn't matter anymore," I said. "Right, Sal? He's long gone now."

"No, he's not," Plato said. "He barged into my retreat just after you and my shovel left, demanding to know if anyone had hiked through, two guys, one with a beat-up face."

Sal unwound his lotus. I rubbed my lip. "So that's really what brought you up here, isn't it?" I asked.

"Admittedly, it's not very original, but who am I to argue against strength found in numbers? I told him two guys came down an hour before to hike into Palmerton. He stepped real close. Didn't dress the part of a killer. Very shaved. Brylcreem. That's when I saw the sneakers."

"Did he hike on?" Sal asked.

"No. He drove in, and he'll drive out. But as we speak, he is stationary," Plato said. "Down below, parked on the shoulder, hood oriented toward Palmerton, awaiting your return."

"*Right* below us?" Sal asked.

Sal was doing math in his head, but I pushed him his pack, listening to the woods for sounds of Grunt. "Now's our chance to put some distance between us," I said.

"It is not distance from him I seek anymore, Corman."

I nudged his pack again. He wanted nothing to do with it. Plato wanted nothing to do with the conversation and wandered out of earshot. Why he was still hanging around I didn't know, but I sensed he had something else he needed to share.

"Vengeance is the quickest way," Sal said. "And she will be gone in the morning anyway, for what I have done to the President."

I knew where his argument was going. More importantly, I knew enough to stand back and let it happen. That kind of training I *did* have, though I had not counted on this. I did not see this coming. It did not appear in my math. How could it? God was never one to waste a blessing on me. But here one was, ripe for the picking: a chance to get SmackSpecter taken out while I stayed clean. If Sal felt compelled, who did I think I was to stop him? That's right, who did I think I was? Yes, it was Grunt who killed the pig, Grunt that was still out there with his dogs and knives and bow, just beyond the trees maybe, collecting the feet of other killed things. But if Sal saw it otherwise… *That's* who I thought I was. But I needed to cover my tracks. "Vengeance is the quickest way," I repeated. "It is a straight line."

"No," Sal admonished. "*Ego* is the straight line, Corman. Ego. Vengeance is just its messenger." Sal paused to digest this revelation. "And now, I am its, chosen by the trail when it revealed its knight steps. Chosen by Excalibur."

"These *are* the forces of legend," I admitted.

Plato was back and Sal was pacing. "The SmackSpecter would not have killed the President and circled back without a reason. He must hear voices, Corman, and he must feed them."

Plato grew spooked. "I must return to my camp now. But as I was saying, the next road down is Ashfield Road, six miles, near Lehigh Furnace. Someone in a situation might catch a ride there. As an alternative, I guess I could…"

"Our archenemy is here," Sal said stoically.

Plato held up his palm and stepped back. "I came out here to mine an original idea, not to be complicit. But here's some reality: this yellow brick road you are skipping down gets really rough south of Ashfield where enormous rocks will bring you to your knees. You're charging into a section that scares more hikers off the trail than any other. An objector came through last week, confronted those rocks, then whimpered home to enlist. He figured a year in your Vietnam would be wiser."

"So we're trapped," Sal said.

"What I'm trying to articulate is: if there's an original idea buried on this part of the trail, it's too deep for any excavation of mine. In other words, the place has been picked clean. Additionally, I have it on good authority that the water below will cease to be potable any minute now. I must pack up and seek my idea elsewhere! That Buick down below is titled to me. Assuming it starts, which it would rather not do, I am relocating my quest. And against all logic, I am willing to help you down the road a bit. Should nothing regrettable occur between now and then."

"South?" I asked.

Sal waved Plato away. "Our archenemy is here, not down the road!" Sal urged.

If I didn't misplay it, I had a clear shot at a daily double: Sal taking out SmackSpecter, and Plato taking me seventy miles from the deed. I just needed to play the two hands at once and quit mixing metaphors. "Yes, Sal, he is here, and you know what you must do. She'll be gone in the morning anyway."

I called to Plato. "How far south?"

"Port Clinton. There are rides to be had there."

"What about Duncannon?" I asked, recalling Bituminous' advice. "What do you know about Duncannon?"

"I know everything, but that's not much when talking of Duncannon." He put the accent on cannon. That was annoying. Did I really want to share a long car ride with him? "Seventy miles down trail; big hiker rendezvous; and the only thing that ever stopped there for long, is time."

"Seventy miles of trail is a lot of trail," I said. "I'll take that ride to Duncannon."

Sal stood erect, gritted his teeth, and said under his breath, "The time to outwit is past, Corman. Our enemy is cruel. Our enemy is here."

"We are called to different things, Sal. You know what you must do, but this is where we part."

Sal sat, turned, turned again, then nodded. "Yes."

Plato stepped back. "There's six miles to Ashfield Road, that's three hours' hike. I'll drive by there at 8:45. If you're there, I'll stop.

If you're not, I'll be on my way." He yawned and threw the shovel into the darkness, heading down the mountain. "8:45!"

I was hungry. I suppose Sal was too. I tossed aside the first white Yodel sleeve from my pack to keep it from Sal's view. I didn't need any more weeping about the pig. Hotdogs followed, then the six cans of soup. The clanging urged Sal close. He pushed me back to calculate what the outsized food cache meant.

"We've got bigger things to worry about right now," I said.

Sal grabbed my pack and dragged it to the shelter, tipping it over with a confirming moan, spilling its stores naked on the worn plank floor: the nine remaining sleeves of pig Yodels, fifty hotdogs, four-dozen eggs, Kool-Aid. He grew more agitated with each item until he slapped the thirtieth envelope of Cream of Wheat. "I do believe you made your own plans, Corman."

"Got a little carried away, that's all. Jesus, I was buying for a pig."

Sal was not listening, not to me, anyway. "No, sir," he said, "I do not know what his plans may be, sir, but a few week's of rations would certainly, you are correct, sir, indicate a change in his plans. Surely he must have realized we cannot carry such weight and still be fleet of foot."

"The enemy is below, Sal."

"You were leaving us, Corman."

"Yes, and the man who killed the President is parked below, waiting, a man, I might remind you, whom only two days ago we left behind in Chicago."

"You couldn't know that this afternoon. You were abandoning this unit."

"We were talking about provisions. They'll serve you well. Remember, the enemy is below, and you were chosen."

Sal leaned back on his hands, eyes to the side, thinking. Smack or no smack, he was zeroing in on the gaps in my story.

"Do you know what else runs in a straight line, Corman?" he asked. "Secrets."

"It's nothing like that."

"It's everything like that, Corman! We weren't leaving with these rations, were we? These aren't marching rations; they're too heavy. They're not reconnoitering rations; they require fuel. No, these are digging-in rations. Was that your secret, Corman? Was that your plan, that the President and I dig in here while you moved on, even as the President's assassin drew near?"

"Sal…" He was not listening. I paused to question why I was arguing, since I was leaving, but I did it anyway. Who did I think I was? "Sal! You said yourself, how could I know SmackSpecter came through; I was in Palmerton, remember?"

"We drew our plans together, Corman! We drew our plans as a platoon! But it doesn't matter anymore."

"No, it doesn't."

"Because in the morning she will be gone and, as you move out to meet Plato, I will head down the mountain to the road to count my final coup. I will avenge her loss, and I will avenge the President's death, and you will be free, and I will be free from everything but my once-upon-a-time. It is my gift to you, Corman, despite your deception."

Against my better judgment, I let Sal's words sink in, inviting voices in my cerebral hinterland to rise up.

But they did not come.

I did not ask twice.

Who did I think I was?

In the flicker of the fire, Sal punched his sleeping bag flat. Beyond the fire ring, beneath the cover of old fallen leaves, a battalion of mice advanced, breaching first the charred trunk of a felled maple, then flanking deep ridges of dried mud and sentinels of gray stone. After regrouping among the warm rocks behind the fire, when the moon slid behind clouds a scouting party darted to the foot of the shelter, nosing the cache of food thrown upon its floor as if it had found the fabled city of El Dorado. It had not, and I slapped the planking to be sure they knew it. The scouts retreated.

“Better get that food up,” I said. “They’ll be coming again.”

“Everything comes again. We cannot guard against it all.”

I skipped a rock through the fire, splintering embers into the air. The battalion fled toward the trail that led to the spring that led to the pig.

Chapter 18

The early morning was not so much a dawn as an afterbirth of the night before: gray, pink, moist, something to be cast aside for the greater good as soon as possible. The wind groaned every once in a while when the clouds collided into a roll of thunder somewhere dark over the ridge. My eyes tired of the sky. I prepared to leave my sleeping bag when in that tweed light came the irritating sound of a pencil scratching.

At first I failed to recognize its significance, but as his carbon point rounded against the paper in frantic and revealing arcs, the meaning emerged: Sal's dawn girl was not gone, not yet, and Sal wielded his pencil with a desperate inspiration, as if his Giverny was fading, his pencil seeking an essence of a passing thing. I read it as a wake, a fugue, a wake to celebrate a life clung to without the chattering of obligated family around the bed. I might have read it as a beautiful thing, but I had no training in that either.

And it dawned on me that perhaps the wake was equally for the pig, but it really didn't matter because if Sal were about to die in his faceoff with SmackSpecter, this was the morning (sans brewing storm) he must have prayed for: one final detail of the girl, one final hour to mourn the pig, one final move against an enemy. And while it was all too cumbersome for me, who was I to deny him that, as long as he just got on with it?

These were heavy thoughts for a man who had to pee, and I replaced them with a heavier one: I felt as I imagined Lieut felt when the math in his head told him we only live at the end of the day, the week, or the tour because some other grunt didn't; that the number who would make it out was already cast; that the toll was going to be extracted no matter what. Isn't that right, Lieut? It's the eyes, right, Sal? It's the eyes, right, Lieut? I get it now, all right. The eyes of the dead pass on their debts.

I might have continued my Lieut-loathing slide, but the task at hand thumped my head. I needed to be sure Sal didn't mistake any dream from the night before as a sign to abandon his vengeance now. He had my enemy to kill.

The hands of my watch were clear. 6:00AM. Fifteen minutes before the hidden sun crested the ridge, before SmackSpecter leaned forward in the front seat of his car, bleary-eyed, wiping drool from his chin, and growing anxious that he had missed us during the night. He'd head back to Plato's camp again and find him gone, but in the daylight he'd see the prints of the pig heading uphill from the day before and know we were here.

I rolled.

Sal sketched.

Thunder rolled.

Sal sketched.

I stood, stretched, yawned, and with a deep groan rolled out my sleeping bag.

Sal sketched.

I slid down the blue-blaze to fill my canteen. Part of the pig's grave was excavated. An odor wafted. I pushed the dirt back in place with my boot and swallowed three handfuls of Gorp.

Sal was still sketching.

"The enemy is below, Sal," I gritted through my teeth.

He licked his thumb to smudge something. "Not anymore, Corman."

"Sal, he killed the pig! He killed the President!"

Sal's pencil moved in swirls. His head seemed to follow. "I have finally been blessed, Corman. It is right that I am last, but finally it has happened. She's alive, Corman and I have been chosen to add to her. It is not as we feared. My once upon a time is over if I want it."

"But it's not over, Sal. The enemy is down there! There! Yes, there! Remember what you said about the oath to defend the President? It's true! You *are* responsible. And you need to avenge, and your dawn girl will be fine. You know that now. If the breach of your oath to defend didn't make her go away, then neither will doing the right thing by avenging the President's death. The SmackSpecter was cruel, Sal. I saw the missing foot. I know what he did. And so do you. The President is dead."

"Yes, he is." Sal closed the sketchpad and held it up to the east. "But she is not, and that's the thing, she is not. Corman, can I tell you? Her eyes have revealed themselves to me. Her eyes, Corman!"

I like stuff that reveals. It helps me lose my patience.

"Sal! All along you thought you were chosen to defend the President, but it's clear now you were chosen to *avenge* him. Right now the enemy is below, but not for long."

"No. Can it be, Corman, that in each loss there is gain?"

"What? No! The math stays the same. The same number will be taken, it's just a question of whether it's you and me or not. That's the law of war numbers!"

"My once upon a time is over if I want it, Corman. And I want it. We will mourn the President, but it's time to move on. You are the healer, Corman, enlightened and trusted, and if your path is to

Duncannon, then so is ours." He patted the sketchpad to validate the plural before stowing it in his pack. "To everything there is a season."

I hated the Byrds as much as pigs for the obvious reason. Plus, the thunder grew louder. I didn't need the rain slowing me down, so I convinced myself the storm was moving away.

"Just because you walk away doesn't mean these things stop hunting you," I said. "Do you think SmackSpecter is going away? Do you think he's okay with loose ends?"

Sal stirred the ashes with Excalibur. "Even over there, I looked for a sign that one day I might be okay, that I might get to move on some day." He belted his pack and winced. I let him. Smacking him (I like to name things) would do me no good now. Especially if it was going to play out this way, where I could no longer outrun everything, but still must outrun him. As it was time to part, I'd let his pain do the rest… after one more try at pointing him downhill to SmackSpecter.

"But this isn't it, Sal. This is no sign! There's no moving on from this until it's all cleaned up."

"This is it, Corman. She didn't leave, and, while her eyes hint at something I do not understand, I believe they are forgiving. And they belong only to me. She has reminded me, Corman, that a thing cannot end until someone stops. And so I am stopping."

"What?"

"I am hiking on. How far to the road?"

"Six miles, and it's hard, and you'll be carrying the weight of the President's murder, and I can't wait for you down below."

Again he wasn't listening, his attention uphill. "I am no healer," he said, "but could it be that it's what we leave behind that heals us the most?"

"Where are you getting this shit from?"

"One day, Corman…"

One day? When is that?

Okay, so the point he was making was that it was all beginning to pass by. But so what? Did I care about the passing of time? I cared about getting to Duncannon before SmackSpecter crawled up my ass.

I held up an envelope of dry oatmeal and imagined someone choking on it as it coagulated in his throat. "Eat quick," I urged Sal, tossing it his way. "Swallow this, and chase it with a little water."

Sal stepped uphill. "I will not consume the stuff of your deception."

"It's not like that," I said. (But of course it was like that). "What else do you want from me? Here's the real oath, Sal, here's the thing we both should understand: we pledge to just leave each other to it! To the things we've seen. To the things we've done. That is what we do. That is what I do. I leave you to it. And you leave me to it. We understand that we leave each other to it!"

Sal stabbed Excalibur into the gap between rocks he was standing on. "We were in this together!"

The sky was not getting any lighter.

"No, we were not!" I shouted, holding each syllable longer than intended, as if time was not my enemy, but I had to kill this notion now. "What I've seen, *I've* seen. What I've done, *I've* done. And what I've got to do, *I've* got to do. Don't say we're in this together. It's not true."

"What healer allows himself to bleed, Corman?"

"The kind that never was!" I said, dismissing him and any further discussion with a flick of my hand. He nodded then stuttered toward the spring and the grave while I read the guidebook silently. The trail ascended over very rocky terrain for three-point-two miles to a ridge of dense conifer and challenging outcropping. Afterwards, climb to twelve-fifty (cross over a tunnel for the PA Turnpike, where you'll hear traffic but not see it) before descending steeply to Ashfield Road and Lehigh Furnace Gap.

Sal returned with wet eyes and sloshing canteens, disturbed to find me still in camp. He brushed past and started immediately up the trail. There was nothing more to be said, no reason to call him back. I'd be damned if I was going to dose him now. He earned his pain, besides, I needed to leave him behind. I emptied my pack onto the floor of the shelter, shedding the remainder of Palmerton provisions and any other unnecessary weight. There'd be no need for weight anymore. I downed a canteen of water and spun to shoulder my hollow pack, to run over to Sal, to get to the road, to get to Duncannon light and free when, in the far corner of the shelter, I saw the log lying open, face down. Sal must have scribbled in it when I was getting water.

"When is a straight line not straight?" he scratched next to a pair of lashless eyes drawn with three curved lines each.

"Who the fuck cares?" I screamed. All I knew was that I was behind, and Sal was ahead, and that would not work. Play it one move at a time, I snarled. First, shake Sal. Next, get to Duncannon. If Bituminous was right, Duncannon was a town prone to misplacing its trust, and I needed a fix of that right away. I could fill up there and figure it out.

The trail again ascended steeply again. With my nearly empty pack, I anticipated catching Sal and his painful broken ribs in about a mile. I did not. What secret chess-move trail passage got revealed to him this time? I was nearly flying at a pace of three miles per, uphill, and he was nowhere to be found! What the hell was he doing? I was flying!

Flying, that is, until a series of S-turns sent me looping around myself, winding me like a fisherman's knot around the visible straight-line ascent up the mountain. At one S I burped the oatmeal, and two S's later smelled it. Why wouldn't the world straighten out for me, just once?

So, when is a straight line not a straight line, Sal? Now! Now Sal! I get it! But who cares, anyway? Pick up your pace. Drink while you walk. Fucking rocks, keep your eyes down when you drink. What could he have meant with his inscription? Doesn't matter. Everyone wrote stupid shit in those books; he just added to it. Did it have something to do with eyes? How he finally dreamed of her eyes, and wait, maybe that wasn't a sketch of the eyes of his girl at all. Maybe they were a warning to SmackSpecter that he was being watched. He'd recognize Sal's writing, wouldn't he? That's it! Sal wasn't done counting coup, he was just jigging SmackSpecter forward, luring him forward into some kind of giant helix mousetrap, in Duncannon maybe! SmackSpecter would be killed yet.

I pulled up. I gulped water. I rallied around my rebounding faith. I hummed the 1812 Overture! I faked the Lord's Prayer! I sang some unconnected words of an Ave, all preparing for a long burst to close the remaining gap to Sal, when right then the image of Grunt and his festering spaniels intercepting Sal on the trail projected in my 8mm head. I hated 8mm, hated how my thoughts jerked and chattered that way, hated when they jammed and flamed out as if against the white-hot bulb. Who did I think I was?

It took another half-hour of now-frantic rock hopping to catch him, but I found Sal sitting in the middle of the trail where a wash crossed, stacking small stones into little cairns. Thunder rumbled from the north. I pulled up. He looked up. We did not speak. I checked my watch. I checked the sky. Time and space were conspiring. Thunder rolled from the south. The storm was surrounding us. I looked at my watch again. Nothing had changed. I looked over his shoulder to study his series of cairns. Together, whether he meant to or not, they formed the semblance of an arrow aimed south along the trail. Just an arbitrary wandering of his mind? A directional message for SmackSpecter? A sign that he knew about the arrow in the pig, and therefore my deception as to who killed it?

The first splat of rain hit my neck, the second a speckled stone atop the cairn that marked the point of the arrow, knocking it down, darkening it. When a boom nearby shook the mountain, I plunged to the ground to avoid shrapnel. Pinecones dropped and rolled at my feet.

The air smelled of ozone or something about to explode. Sheets of rain slapped the mountain. I scrambled over rocks and surfed the muddy ridge for shelter. Where runoff veered through a carved rut above me, I held my pack to divert the cascade from hitting my head. Rain sliced. Rain blinded. With each flash of lightning, I expected Grunt to appear, bow or rifle or knife drawn to add to his collection. Was he still unsure of me? Worse, was he sure?

Lightning lit the valley below. No Grunt. Upwind, green wood smoldered. I yelled to Sal through the wind, then felt my way behind the crag, searching for a cave or deep ledge. Now was no time for Sal's penchant for pharmathermia, not with him still on task, anyway. What I needed was Sal alert and focused on SmackSpecter. And what I needed was for the rain to end so I could get to Duncannon.

But as often is the case, nothing gave a shit about what I needed. Out to the west, across the ridge, the sky mocked me in its clearing even as the storm stalled above us. Bolts flashed over the wet granite. I slapped my hands low along the rock wall and found a deep indentation about two feet high, big enough for one of us without pressing, two with. Rain dripped from the moss, making it more grotto than cave. Which was right, because wedging in, we were more mermaids than men. Wedging in, we were unbearably close.

Any port in a storm never contemplated this.

The sky tore, and why not?

Chapter 19

Flat on my stomach in flashes of lightning with the ceiling of the grotto an inch above my head and Sal an inch from my face, and every single thing closed within an inch of me, rain coursed along the underbelly of rock, letting go in a drumbeat against my back. My back was the only thing keeping my chest and the smack dry. I didn't know how long that could be sustained and could have spit at the irony that would have me carry the smack this far, only to lose it to the water here.

"What a mess," I said.

Silence never lies; at least not the kind poised to address something unfinished, or the kind that shrinks already tight spaces.

Sal searched for my hand, which was tucked along my side, which was awkwardly along his side, awkwardly near his hand. He dragged it across the thin slice of rock exposed between us until it stretched outside the cave, predictably getting wet when the rain hit it like thumping fingertips.

"You are a healer, Corman. You cannot deny it. Your hands heal and yet you…"

Not this again. I pulled my hand free. Sal grasped it again, his fingers intertwining, firming.

"...and yet you collaborate with the enemies inside you, choosing to fester when you could choose to heal yourself. You cannot deny it, Corman."

I pulled again, but his elbow was locked and his grip was strong, and I acquiesced until a clear, unassailable, obvious answer hit me. I hung onto it for a moment, but it seemed right.

"It's not true." I said, smiling. "I never healed anything. And I never wished I had."

I paused here, not for dramatic effect, not to signal conclusion, but to search for words that would not crawl up my ass. "But I see it now for what it is. I'm not the healer – you are! Think back. Each time you thought my hands healed the pig, *your* hands were on top, just like they are now." I tightened mine beneath his to illustrate, but I didn't like it. "Don't you see? You are the shaman. Not me, not the mud—you, Sal. You!"

Sal eased his grip, releasing my hand to examine his fingers slowly, studiously, like he'd never seen them before.

"Remember?" I asked, "In the culvert? The pig's ear sliced in half? I had the mud on my hands, but nothing changed until you put your hands on top. Remember?"

I think Sal's face softened, but he was too damn close to come into focus.

"And the day after," I continued, "in the park, when the cops beat on the pig, remember? Bruises and swelling everywhere. It couldn't even walk, splintered! And remember? Remember? I'm doing everything you're asking me to, Sal, against all common sense because you think I'm the healer. But think back! See? It was you, Sal, putting your hand above mine, moving it in circles. Yours on top of mine as you counted Mississippis. Remember? Your hands, Sal. Yours! Only then did the pig revive, not before! I didn't heal it, hell, I didn't even want to! Why? Because I. Am. Not. the healer. You are, Sal. You fix broken things. You fix things that aren't as they should be. You were chosen."

Sal studied the grotto's moss as if the answers clung there. And I, feeling forever liberated from the weight of shamanhood, left him to it, just left him to it, silent, silent, ten-Mississippi… until he shook his head. "Could it be, Corman?"

"That's what I'm saying, Sal. That's what I've *been* saying. It's not me! I never even liked the thought of it! Me? Healer? No, it's you! You are the fixer of things that are not as they should be, things like maybe SmackSpecter being alive after killing the President."

It was worth a shot to bring him back there, but he just studied his palms a la (French!) Macbeth (Scottish!) and mumbled, "You're right."

Yes, I was.

"It's been clear all along, Corman, hasn't it?"

"It has."

"We don't often see the things that are right in front of us, do we? In the sky or on the ground, doesn't matter. We don't see them."

"No. No."

"And one of those things is that – I see it now - you are not the healer."

"True. Only you can make things as they should be, Sal."

"Yes. I see it now. It was never you healing, because it was *us.* Together!" He grabbed my hand again.

"What?"

I twitched. He turned, inadvertently flicking his nose against mine. I froze. There can be no end until someone stops.

"Isn't it possible, Corman, that the same force that put us over there could put us *here,* too? We were halved by our once-upon-a-times, Corman. I know that. But is it not possible that the force that halved us has brought you and me together to make a whole?"

"No. The Law of War Numbers…"

"And now on this mission with you, Geneva's eyes have been revealed. It is as it should be. Yes. You, me, a whole, leaving our once upon a times behind."

No damn room to squirm into the slap of the teeming rain. I'd known rain like this before. You learn in a hurry to listen through it. And when I did, I heard a *whoot.*

"Shhh!" I warned.

Sal slid back a few inches I didn't know he had. As he did, the rain began to puddle. I pinned my back to the rock above me, dangling the smack just above the water, breathing with my stomach sucked in and my chest still. I craned my neck toward the grotto's opening, then cocked my head as if to confirm a frequency. Outside, the torrent continued; the blackness upon the mountain continued; the thunder, sparks and discomfort continued, each compromising what little ability I had to discern the voices in my head from any actually approaching me. Right, Lieut? What is it you said? What is it I heard?

There came another *whoot,* closer. I fumbled for a rock for weapon and slid back a half-inch of my own, questioning the frivolous thrust I would exert upon the enemy laying on my stomach with eleven inches between the floor and ceiling.

It came again right above us. Sal heard it now and scraped at the moss to wrest a rock of his own, but too late, claws raked a foot from our eyes, splashing, frenzied, scoring the granite and inching closer in their madness. Hot breath spattered my face along with the smell of pus and rotting flesh. Lightning flashed, then a pair of frothing snout, then four eyes, then a *whoot.* Sal held, as if he had a choice. Lightning. Eyes, teeth, froth, *whoot,* then a swinging boot, a familiar wail, and the voice of Grunt.

"Goddamn it, that hole ain't big enough. Nothin' in there but skunk." His hand clutched the mane of the healthy dog and yanked it back. "You get that stink on you and I'll kill you right here." But the dogs were sure of what they knew and charged again. As Grunt reached for a mane the second time, the festering spaniel bit his hand. Grunt spit, "You fuck!" A second boot swiped, and a whimper faded down the trail, ending with the *ffff t* of an arrow.

"I done you a favor," Grunt said. "Half a you was dead already." His boots moved away and I was in the middle of finally exhaling when the top end of his hiking stick came stabbing out of the dark into the grotto. It rapped from floor to ceiling in the inches between Sal and me, tassels of trophy feet pinging our heads: squirrel, rabbit, chipmunk and pig. Somehow, Sal held his silence. "Like I fucking said," Grunt growled, "too small. Now move south, before he hits that road."

In the chill of my pissed clothes, I held still and silent in the grotto until the sun fully emerged some ten minutes later. In that light, a number of things grew perfectly clear:

1. The smack was saved.
2. Grunt was a good shot. He split the spaniel sixty feet down trail.
3. Grunt was psychotic. He took one of its feet.
4. Grunt was hunting whoever he thought had come on the trail to take him back.
5. Grunt thought that was me.
6. His arrow into the spaniel didn't make a noise. The next one wouldn't either.
7. Lieut's "Law of War Numbers" was asserting itself again, here on the mountain.
8. The sun was setting on Sal's usefulness to me, but not just yet.

He crept from the grotto, wearing the same catatonic stare as when the pig was killed, but there was no wet in his eyes this time. I read it as resolve. I read it wrong.

"It was not the SmackSpecter, Corman. The President's assassin did not wear sneakers. His assassin wore boots. I might have counted coup on a non-combatant, Corman. I might have killed an innocent, except that Geneva saved me. That is why she showed me her eyes this morning, Corman, to save me from killing the wrong man."

Sal's power of belief was exhausting me.

"True, Sal, but now you know who the real assassin was. There will be no mistake. Now is your chance, Sal, to keep your oath, to come to the aid of your country, to make things as they should be. Here, take my knife. Just lean in and up between the ribs. Just up and in."

Sal paced. Time passed. "She saved me, Corman. Am I now to dishonor that? Those boots, Corman, *his* boots, were our boots in our once-upon-a-time. There can be no end until someone stops."

"You can't wish this stuff away with that greeting card shit. This is about duty!"

Sal shook his head emphatically. "So much has been revealed."

"What's been revealed is that Grunt killed the President and he's is going to kill you and me if SmackSpecter doesn't kill us first."

Sal's eyes blinked with clear thought. His growing clarity was getting exhausting too. "Grunt?" he asked.

"I name things."

Sal's head was still shaking. "Even as so much is revealed, Corman, you choose to conceal."

Two can play this stupid circle-logic game.

"Has it never occurred to you Sal, that what I conceal from you, I conceal *for* you?"

Check.

"That I concealed from you only so your full energy could be dedicated to keeping the President safe? That I was the one who carried the burden? For you?"

Checkmate. But why stop?

"Yes, I knew Grunt was out here. I had the pleasure of bumping into him and his mutts yesterday. And yes, something told me – maybe the crossbow, maybe the rifles sticking out of his pack – that he could be dangerous, very dangerous, but I kept that away from you anyway, took it upon myself to watch for him rather than have you distracted from your oath."

"But you pointed me to the SmackSpecter."

"You said yourself that he's our archenemy, remember? So of course I thought that's who did it! Anyway, it doesn't matter now. You heard Grunt yourself: 'Move south before he hits the road.' For all we know, he's waiting for you or me down there. We just don't know which."

I kneeled to pick up my stick. "You know what? Fuck it. I need a straight line right now, and that's me to the road. I won't wait for you."

Sal was still a paragraph behind. "We know which one, Corman; it's you. And I would think you would want me manning point, manning the whistle for you. I think we still share a mission, to be whole again."

I screamed inside, *Not that half–to-whole thing again*! Unless my missing half was quieter than my remaining half, why the hell would I want it? I didn't know. But what I did know was I needed just a little daylight downfield to make Duncannon, so any block Sal threw for me would be better than none at all. I would descend at my top speed, and when I passed Sal with his broken ribs and annoying propensity to stop and think every hundred feet, when I left him behind, I would be making an honest trade.

I tossed him the whistle. Sal sped down the trail. "Keep your eyes on the ground," I called. "Bent grass tells you everything."

Right, Lieut?

Even as the sun burned off the mist, rain caught in tipping leaves Pachinkoed through the canopy, deepening the black mud and echoing the storm as I hiked, drowning all sounds in the distance.

Rocks on the trail eased for a while, and the downhill slope aided my descent to a pace of about three miles an hour despite the mud, fast enough to make up lost time and meet Plato at eight forty-five.

Shockingly, Sal achieved the same speed, remaining a hundred feet or so in front of me, but loudly, like he was mostly falling, like it was just a matter of time until he could no longer keep up his pace. Of course, that would be moot if Grunt's dog heard him. Then an arrow would find us in no time. Still, that Sal could push this hard without a dose made me wonder.

Soon the boulders returned in large numbers, as if herding up to dry in the firming sun. But they gave me no pause. My confidence was high, so high in fact that if I didn't have Lieut's voice screaming to keep my eyes on the ground, I might have fatefully lifted them and missed where Sal's fresh prints mingled with the spaniel's.

Shot from a turkey run, the dog prints blurred through the downhill mud for twenty feet before fading back into the brush. I stopped and listened and heard nothing but the dripping canopy. I poked the top of a paw print with my hiking staff where the mud was thinnest. It bent wet and fresh. I mapped the ground for Grunt prints. None. Would the dog have crossed without him?

My pace slowed with the question. My confidence faded. Every boulder climbed came with the expectation of *ffffft* and searing pain. I thought I heard him, but it was just wind. I thought I smelled him, but it was just forest decay. And, where the trail turned right and into a dark stand of white pine, I thought I saw him at the break, crossbow pinned to his shoulder, last dog dead at his feet. But no, just trees and rocks. I smacked myself in the chest. "C'mon," I urged. A small puff of smack swirled from my collar.

Sal had paused around the bend. I closed in behind him.

"They're ahead of you," I said, rushing by him.

Sal ran to catch up and passed me, leaving a large amount of phlegm at my feet.

Behind us, on the other side of the mountain, in an idling white Ford Falcon, SmackSpecter was peeling his eyes down the Palmerton road, wondering where we were and if this would be his day.

Ahead, like water in a drain, Grunt was closing inexorably in.

Chapter 20

I advanced quickly to where the green canopy surrendered to a moonscape maze of blaring sun and rock. When I paused on its edge to pee, Sal flew by without a word. As I jiggled, I watched him navigate. Within the stretch of his elongated shadow, only a single white fading blaze was visible on the face of a pallid boulder. Sal leaped to it, but I could tell by his hapless spinning that the blazes vanished from there. He scoped the horizon, hopping from rock to rock, shielding his eyes against glare, swinging Excalibur in frustrated *whooshes* until he found the next blaze swiped on the dark side of an elevated tor with a commanding profile, like a patriot of something. The tor's brow appeared furled, and coupled with its jutting metamorphic chin gave it the look of a cartoon rock monster, one pissed off at a hapless intrusion. I felt a strong kinship to it, feeling that way most of the time myself. Sal climbed the head and spotted the next blaze splashed twenty yards away. Six chess knight moves later, he stood on top of it. He was proud of himself, and I watched him pat his ribs in appreciation of their effort. I thought to pass him and leave him to his celebration to ensure I made the road in time, but thought it better to let him clear the open field of arrows first.

Forty yards beyond, at the edge of a new stand of trees, Sal found a wooden sign on a rusting rod, waved it back to me and moved on. I coursed toward it. "Ashfield Road, 1.2 miles", the sign said. My watch read 8:20.

The trail straightened, and where the woods resumed, the mud resumed. But the canopy had finally dropped all its rain, and in the quiet I could hear the distance. "Shhh," I said to no one. "Car." I read my watch again. It couldn't be Plato, I hoped, not twenty minutes early. I did math in my head. With twenty minutes to rendezvous and Sal keeping pace, there would be little chance of shedding him now. That would have to wait until Duncannon. Besides, perhaps there were other open fields for him to clear. The Law of War Numbers might not be done with us yet.

I lifted one of my boots, only to create an unwanted and discouraging sucking sound. The mud grew deep in rushing rainwater, gathering along the footpath in wide colliding flows, forcing me to freestyle through thorns to higher ground. I accepted their sharp scraping as a simple price to pay. I'd been through worse loss of blood than that. The thorns only raked; they did not attach and drink.

My pace quickened, and with one final bound I burst onto the edge of a gravel road where Sal and his miracle ribs studied the ground. Once again, the fresh tracks of a spaniel cut across the trail. This time boots accompanied them, pacing parallel to the road, thirty or more yards up from the trail, thirty or more yards down from it, as if seeking a safe crossing of a river swelled by a monsoon.

I swung my head up and down the road (no Plato) and turned back to the prints in the mud.

"This is a man possessed," I said. "He's moving three times our pace, and we were moving. He could make Duncannon tomorrow on foot."

"He's not going into Duncannon, Corman. Look." Sal's attention was on the indecisive footprints. "Roads are his Kryptonite. That is why he paced here. Up and down. See it? If he fought so much against a dirt road like this, how could he prevail against pavement?"

I pointed to the trail registry on the other side of the road. "Did he cross?"

Sal slid back into the woods. "I do not know, Corman. I give you the lead now." He threw me the whistle.

With my hiking staff at the ready, as if I could swat arrows, I spun my way across the dirt road. There, in the ascending mud, fresh lines of spaniel and boot print pooled up, none more so than those at the registry.

I opened the cabinet slowly, navigating the squeak of rusting hinges. There were three new registrations: one by someone called Mountain Monk, and another by someone hiking under the name of Dousing Dancer. It did not escape me that I was getting off the trail just in time, but as if I needed further reason, the third registration offered it in spades:

Name: SS
Address: Behind you (or not)
Length of hike: Until I take you back or finish it here.

I wondered how long SmackSpecter spent contriving this little ditty, trying to spook me, to prove his cleverness against the superior word play of Sal. And while I hate the obvious answer, the simplemindedness of his post made the answer clear: not long. But it refreshed my conviction that if I could just get a little running room, I could create enough daylight to spring all the way to the Keys, if Grunt didn't trump me. I looked down at his deep boot prints and wondered what he made of SmackSpecter's words. And then the obvious answer hit me again: Grunt was reading SmackSpecter's posts, his registrations, his log entries, as addressed to him! I ran them back through my head. There was no other way for Grunt to read them!

"Until I take you back!"

"You belong to me!"

"You took the oath that has no end!"

Ergo (Latin again!) Grunt wasn't hunting me, he was hunting SmackSpecter; he just hadn't identified him yet! And while Grunt was clearly closing in, maybe he just needed a little nudge in the proper direction. I took the pencil nub from the cabinet and added to SmackSpecter's entry: "I will "sneak" up behind you in the silence of my hightops."

I was proud of my cunning, but not enough to dampen my urge to run. I was still in the line of fire, and no one outruns an arrow in a three-legged race. I needed to be free of Sal with his shoelace of conscience. Then I could outrun SmackSpecter and leave Grunt to it. And I would have to, because pavement or not, Duncannon or beyond, SmackSpecter was still coming for me. There was no confusion on his end, no Kryptonite for him. I assumed he'd interrogated Mountain Monk and Dousing Dancer and learned they knew nothing of us, therefore assessing we were behind him, explaining his doubling back the previous night to stake us out. But SmackSpecter wouldn't wait long, if he was waiting still.

"Grunt crossed," I said to Sal, who crouched in the undergrowth beyond the drainage. "Fresh tracks on the other side. He can't be that far ahead, if he stayed ahead."

"He crossed and so he stayed crossed, Corman. Look at the torment in these prints. Back and forth, toeing this imaginary line, like a third rail. He may come back to this road, but he will not cross back over. If Plato comes in time, we will not see Grunt again. These roads will hold him here. Whatever happens to him happens down trail."

"Are you sad about that?"

"We were all halved. I had the President and you, or at least I did. And now I have Geneva. Who will make him whole?"

I kicked my free leg at a few of the prints. Sal didn't appreciate the silence as much as I did. He was annoying that way.

"Where is Plato, Corman? It's 8:55! The code of rendezvous requires you to be on time! Were you sure Plato understood that?"

Now it was Sal who grew reflective and quiet, for a moment. "It will be good to be off this trail," he said, more to himself than me. "The ground is hard and mud is thick. The enemy grows, and we cannot hold a hill. And my memories here are bad."

I began to tell Sal about SmackSpecter's message in the registry across the road, but in an hour or two we'd be in Duncannon, and Sal's utility would be over, so what was the purpose? This wasn't softness, or some compunction to free Sal from weight and worry, now that her damn eyes had been revealed; I was just tired, and that was the point.

My aggravation was interrupted by the popping of gravel beneath the tires of Plato's Buick. Plato was annoyed too.

"That took longer than anticipated," he spat, popping the trunk. "Stow your packs here. Just move my goods if you need to." His goods consisted of a pair of jumping cables, his shovel, a kite, a ring full of keys, and a half-case of clinking red wine. Eyes darting, I quickly flattened my empty pack, jammed it on top of the wine and slid up front. Sal squeezed his to the other side before wedging in among Plato's gear in the back seat, sketchpad securely on his lap. Everything smelled of mold when the doors closed.

"Was his car still there?" I asked as Plato pulled away.

"Yes." Plato said. "And the windows fogged. I do believe we caught the cat napping!"

"Have we abandoned the creeping meatball?" Sal asked. "Have we escaped the giant mousetrap, even though we're not superheroes?"

Plato sat up behind the wheel, turning his head slightly toward Sal so his voice could be heard. "Among the original ideas I pursued was indeed a mousetrap."

I filled in a gap for Sal. "Plato here is on a mission to find an original idea. Something to do with digging holes."

"An unfortunate dead end, as was the better mousetrap," Plato continued. "You know what they say about the world beating a path? I suppose you want to know how it worked?"

I slumped my head when Sal said yes.

"My trap employed the ageless continuum of cheese, spring, slam!" Plato clapped his hands together on the wheel. "Except, well, let me ask you, what is it you find most revolting about trapping mice?"

"The eyes," I mumbled into my window, hoping no one heard.

Everyone heard.

"Yes, Corman," Sal said. "It's always the eyes."

"Precisely!" Plato continued, "Staring up at you, like they were asking 'why'! Glossy, forlorn, desperate eyes staring up, as if God himself were assessing you! But not with my trap! No, sir. Mine took the God out of the killing."

Plato paused for effect, to let that sink in. I let it linger the length of a slow swallow, then said, "I know a certain government that would pay for that."

"Precisely," Plato said. "The trap was perfectly conceived, designed to send a small current through the dead body immediately after the slam. Not much, no need to cook it, just enough ohms to cause a reflex, closing its eyelids at the moment of expiry, simulating peace. Dead mouse, no glossy eyes, no God. Peace. Guaranteed!"

I looked down to find the armrest denting in my grasp. Maybe this was the missing piece, right, Lieut? If The Law of War Numbers couldn't be stopped; the least it could do was jolt your eyes shut.

The silence grew, but Sal's throat-clearing told me how short-lived that would be.

"All the makings of a winner," Sal said.

"A winner? Would I have told you about it if it met the litmus? Would I still be seeking an original idea if I'd already found one? I couldn't even secure a patent on that trap! It had all been tried before! As it turns out, the adage is a myth! There have been scores of better traps created all through history, and the world has never rushed to anyone's door. Not only was my idea unoriginal, it was sixty-three years old! Three times older than me! Now you see the quixotic chains that bind me," he said. "Yet I remain committed."

While I pondered the multiple definitions of "committed", Sal rocked in the back. As we passed through a valley toward Fredericksburg and onto the highway, he said with no provocation, "No. Too long a journey with too many roads." Plato assumed Sal was talking about him and postured to defend himself when Sal said, again with no provocation, "Grunt will never get this far."

While I appreciated Sal's confidence about Grunt, I didn't appreciate his consistent dismissal of my golden rule, which was: speak only when spoken to. The math in my head told me: If everyone followed it, there would be far less talking, potentially none, and life would be sweeter for it, only who was I kidding? Who did I think I was? Sooner or later, some idiot hearing voices would just start it all up again.

And right on cue, here Sal went, back to Plato's search for an original idea, clearing his throat first to alert me. "Perhaps inventing isn't the answer," he said. "Perhaps wrapping two thoughts around each other like a helix to create a new one would offer you a better result."

Plato tilted the rear view mirror, as Rubin had. Sal did not acknowledge him, staring out the window instead, but Plato was intent. "I have experimented with that. By juxtaposing the principles of displacement, I sought to answer what I anticipated was a never-before-asked question. If you drop a coin into a glass of water, the level of water rises. Conversely, if you extract the coin from the glass, the level of water will fall. If you apply the same principle to the oceans through the inexorable extraction of sea life, then it becomes possible to predict..."

"How far seas will retreat when all fish are caught?" Sal guessed correctly, pissing Plato off.

I didn't help when I said, "And where the next beachfront property will be."

"And *that,* gentlemen, is the problem with discussing a potential original idea. They cease to be original halfway through the act of being spoken. I do worry sometimes how this quest will end. Some things are better left unsaid."

"Everything is better left unsaid," I offered, successfully snuffing the discussion. I welcomed the many miles of silence that followed and used them to commit to stealing Plato's Buick as soon as the opportunity presented itself in Duncannon. It was no SOFA, but I could take comfort in her. The highway shot around Hawk Mountain, Port Clinton, and Shubert's Gap, past Pine Grove and a fraying towrope of river towns. Signs for Harrisburg counted down forty miles.

"What else do you know about Duncannon?" Sal asked.

"Duncannon? Let us just say that in the pantheon of original ideas, it doesn't appear as anything other than discarded. It retains, I'm afraid, the requisite caught-by-surprise generation hanging on, wondering why. Brewery town once, until everything flushed upstream killed the water. Now it plays the role of Hamlet with nothing to lose, fighting this war. Wars get fought by towns like this, gentlemen."

"I knew a town like that once," I said.

"The only thing still drawing breath in that town is the hoards of hikers passing through, some dodging, some not. I guess some stay."

"Looking for original ideas?" I asked.

Plato scoffed. "Original ideas aren't panned from ruins."

"Let's hope lunch isn't either," I said. "A guy in Palmerton asked me to try the Royle Hotel. Something about a full-sized girl and a renowned burger."

Chapter 21

Where the Juniata River died in the arms of the Susquehanna, the valley stretched in rectangles of green and brown. A pair of concrete bridges spanned the churning water. Crossing hikers paused to acknowledge the faint peace signs bleeding through fresh paint on the abutments. Turkey vultures rode thermals westward. Beneath them, in full view, Duncannon tilted.

Along Market Street, people rocked on porches of peeling houses. One man waved, gold star hanging in his window. I tapped Plato to stop and walked up, asking for directions.

"Royle is just down the road here a bit. If you hit the Methodist Church, you've gone too far, but isn't that always the way?" he laughed. "Don't know your plans, son, but you don't want to be staying at the Royle. Only hikers like that place. Smells a bit. Gets loud at night too. They're like cowboys at the end of a three-month drive. Crazy."

"I like them," his wife said.

"Well, I like them too, but they're smelly and loud, aren't they? Am I lying?"

"And I like that Duncannon is midway in their journey," she added.

"No, we're not."

"Spiritually, we are. Yes. we are! And that sort of makes us something, don't it?"

"Anyway," he rolled his eyes, "they get a day of beer in them and by midnight we gotta sit a cop there for a few hours just to hold it down. But lucky for you, there's a nice new motor court down off Highway 'Leven. Six miles maybe. That's where I'd stay if I was you."

"Actually, I'm a hiker too. So are my friends." I motioned back at the car.

"Well, don't I feel the fool then! Sorry about that. We don't get too many hikers in cars."

"Oh, who cares?" the woman said. "Would you like a cold tea?"

"No, thanks." I pointed at the gold star.

"Oldest," the man said, pursing his lips for a moment. "But we still got one. Just have to get him home. Thanksgiving, we hope."

"Loved his creamed cauliflower," the woman said.

I nodded. "Down this road before the church, right?"

"Less than half a mile," he said. I started down the porch steps. "But listen, they got no air conditioning there. Hell, they barely got plumbing! Gonna be ninety today!"

"Hot already." His wife mimed, fanning herself. "You sure you boys wouldn't like a cold tea?"

I walked away, wondering if Lieut got a gold star someplace.

What's that you screamed, Lieut, get home whole or don't? 'Cause nothing short of whole matters? 'Cause nothing short of four matters, get it, new guy? You want your daddy doing your fighting? Your mama wiping your ass? You want your folks sitting on a porch with that look in their eye that says, 'Death ain't the worst thing sometimes'? Is that want you want? 'Cause that's what less than whole means. You married, new guy? Well, mine's twenty. You think she's gonna wait around for me to open her door 'cause I'm in a chair? Unsnap her bra with hooks? Think she won't look away? Plus, I got a boy, Boot. I got a boy and I don't want him wheeling his stump of an old man around. That's why you gotta take me out. If this shit takes part of me, you gotta swear to me you'll take the rest. Swear it, Boot. Put it right here and lean up and in, right here and just lean in. You gotta swear. We ain't diggin' till you do.

***

Plato steered the Buick down Market where the Royle's four-story brick façade flaked mortar to the sidewalk, a crumbling monolith among Salk-like cubes of white aluminum siding.

"Pull down Maple here," I said, "Now turn up there on Apple, there, by that U-Haul lot."

"My God," Plato snarled. "Market Street to Maple to Apple? This is worse than I remember! My walkabout for an original idea just took a giant cliché to the head. I must leave here quickly!"

"Pull in over here," I said. "And stay out of sight until I get something arranged."

A moth's carcass dangled in a web below the transom window where the "H" in Hotel curled away from the glass. The door stuttered on bent hinges. Pinned snapshots fluttered on corkboards in the vestibule. Rows of empty Formica tables held rows of ketchup bottles next to rows of saltshakers in front of a row of cigarette machines that lined the wall. An air conditioner strained. At a bar of knotty pine sitting on the end, pack at his feet, a hunched man slurped cereal. To his right, a long-braided full-sized woman scraped the grill.

"Give me five," she exhaled without turning.

In an adjoining room, fluorescent lights hummed above a troubled pool table: beer-stained felt, Marlboro-burned rails, back wall dotted with holes from the butts of cue sticks. As I entered, two hikers stopped arguing.

"Huck," one introduced himself. "And that's Jim."

"Huck and Jim?"

"Shit, yeah! Jim here got himself married and I,,," he lifted his glass as if to toast himself, "am going to free him! But my damn beer is empty. How'm I going to free him with an empty beer? Can't be done. Micki! Micki!! Yeah, the idiot got married and now I'm running him to freedom. Micki!"

"Don't pay this drunk any attention," Jim said. "Yes, my real name *is* Jim, but hikers call me Otterface." He stroked his long black beard, pulling it taut from his chin until his lower lip fell. "Guess I'm a little scraggly. Anyway, welcome to the world- famous Royle Hotel, where you cannot possibly lower your expectations enough! Been upstairs?"

"Not staying," I said.

"Not what?" the braided woman snapped.

"Yep, that's Micki. She owns the joint. Micki!" Jim called out, waving his glass. "What the hell?"

Micki swiped a towel across her forehead and turned. She was a full-sized woman and broad at the shoulder, like she'd swum her share of laps. Her face was softer than her voice, and her braids coursed halfway down her back, pulled tight against her head, exposing ears of a good size. Behind one ear, her fingers had left a streak of grease in the shape of a fingered peace sign. I named it Peace Grease because that made me laugh, and because I had to name things to stomach them. The braids seemed to smack more of want than convenience. I got the sense that in this way she was hiding her beauty, that maybe her hair was actually voluptuous and shiny and sufficiently concealed her ears when it was all combed out, but I also sensed that was a bother to her and would lead nowhere good anyway. Look at me! Who did I think I was? Except I was pretty sure I was right.

"Listen, you fucking new guys," she started.

Fucking new guys?

"It's ninety degrees and I'm working this grill! You're lucky I'm even open, could have closed, gone way up north where it's cool, maybe Lake Placid or Saranac. Let someone cook for me once, mmm, a nice chicken parm from the Belvedere! But no, I'm here, making sure you fucking new guys get a breakfast, a bed, and a buzz. We're the only B&B&B in the country, and you want to hassle me?"

"No, Ma'am!" Huck said, then turned to me and groaned, "Every beer comes with a speech."

"I'll give you a fucking speech!" Micki warned. "I'm tired of trying to save the world, done planting flowers in guns, done raising consciousness, done thinking Dylan is Christ too! Done with all of that. Done! I only got one thing that keeps me here talking to you outcasts, and that's a six percent mortgage! Not love, not some fight against tyranny, not some sick motherhood thing with smelly hikers, just a godawful mortgage. Now," she stepped toward me, "What do you mean, you're not staying?"

There was a delay in my response, and her arched eyebrow told me she read it as stupidity. But it was less that than I was sure I'd seen her before. I leaned in, trying to place her. Ohio? Saigon? McDonald's on the Thruway? As I debated, she drew near, eye-to-eye, nearly lash-to-lash. "Looks like someone had their way with your face. Why're you here?" she demanded.

I lowered my voice. "Bituminous sent me."

"Bituminous?"

"Shared a ride to Palmerton."

I meant it only as a fact, a truth, but she read it otherwise as negotiation on the room rate. Her eyebrow arched again. (That was getting tiresome.) "Damn it! Okay. Six dollars1" she barked.

"Six?!?" Huck screamed. "You charged me eight!"

"And I'm gonna charge you twelve if you don't shut up!"

She turned back to me. "Six dollars, and there's no room service here. Make your own bed, too. The grill stays open until midnight, then closes until five for breakfast. No tabs, pay as you go. What a dream I'm living, huh? Four hours sleep and a six percent mortgage."

"I don't need a room. I'm heading on. But a guy out back does."

"You'll take a room," she decreed, holding her hand out. "Six dollars."

I ripped a ten from my pocket.

"Good. Now, whether the bed ever sees your ass is none of my concern. And your buddy's paying for a room too."

"Bituminous told me you could help me."

"You dodging?"

"What kind of news do you get here?"

"Most of it within a week or two."

"From Chicago?"

"My God, were you there?"

"The guy Sal I'm with was."

She shot her eyes to the poolroom.

"No, not them," I said. "Out back. And Bituminous said you would help."

She smiled. "He went, didn't he?" She strutted behind the bar. "He's okay?"

"Took a few stitches, but he's okay." I led her out of sight. "Micki, can you help this guy Sal?"

Seized by a spontaneous need to overreact, she threw the ten back at me. "Goddamn it! I want out of this! The world doesn't want to be saved."

"But this guy Sal does," I said.

"It's all a damn joke, right? Is the revolution anything more than a joke? A dream? More than just something I wake up seeing each morning?"

Where had I heard that before?

"No," I said.

"Does it have any chance?"

"Zip." (I could have spent a few more syllables maybe, but who did I think I was?)

"Of course not," she said. "So… Jerry? Abbie? The SDS? What do you know?"

"What do you need to know?"

"Are we really going to dance cute like this? I hate cute."

Apparently you didn't need to order a beer to get a speech, because here it came, and with volume.

"You know, I was in Washington when they thought we could levitate the damn Pentagon. Rubin, Hoffman, they kept swearing, 'It moved! It moved! Did you feel it? It moved!' The hell it did. Nothing moved. That's when I got the brilliant idea to fight the war with something more than their illusions. What an idiot I was, huh? That's when I bought this shack about a year ago, to help the guys heading to the border, a safe house, you know, underground, to stop feeding the machine. 'Don't worry,' they said. 'Karma is always repaid,' they said. Karma, my ass. You know how many hundreds of kids we fed coming through here? How many we patched up? How many letters home we drove over to Ohio so they could be mailed and not traced back? And do you know how many of my dodgers sent Canadian dollars back to help the cause? Zero. Let me tell you, delusion is no better than illusion; it just costs more. The day they actually *do* levitate the Pentagon will come a lot sooner than the day this place breaks even. Anyway… Jerry? Abbie?"

"It got ugly."

"Right," she challenged. "So to lay low, they did the only logical thing and ran that pig for President? Brilliant! Saw that on Cronkite, for Christ's sake. That's what I am now, a Cronkite…"

She was heading into another one of her manifestoes. I cut her off. "Micki, can I tell you something? Can I trust you?"

"Just don't be dragging me back in, is all."

"I need your help, Micki. That pig? The one they ran for President? Pigasus? He's dead."

She waved at the newspapers on the counter. "Um, I know."

"I don't think you do know." I held up my hand, then started a story from the beginning, a story that rolled so easily off my tongue I wondered where such skill had been hiding, a story that started off true enough, but morphed into one with a huge bleating (or was it bleeding?) heart. More uncomfortable with each sensitive syllable, I told it all with the end in mind: I needed to dump Sal here, in Duncannon, on Micki, so when SmackSpecter came sniffing around he'd find enough to slow him down. I was heading to the Keys and the other pirates, and I needed Sal to throw one final block to free me.

As I stated, the story started out true enough: The pig in the paper, imposter. The real Pigasus smuggled out of Chicago by Sal, and the FBI knew it. FBI chasing him to get the real pig back because they can't afford bad press when the real pig shows up, don't want a martyr, they don't want a messiah. I helped Sal get to the Appalachian Trail for the good of the cause, but I was afraid to leave him there alone, so I hiked with him because I'm a vet too, and no man left behind is our sacred oath. That's how Sal felt about the pig, no man left behind, only that pig was slowing him down, so when the Fed closed in, Sal killed it to make his getaway. Sal's been broken by 'Nam, and he doesn't remember killing the pig. That's how 'Nam goes. It's best you don't remember. Instead, Sal believes that a man called Grunt killed the pig and get this, took one of its feet. But none of this matters.

"What do you mean 'None of this matters'?" Micki demanded, backing away. "We don't need the FBI around here, shutting us down! I'm this close to broke now! And I can't babysit any tripwires!"

"Sal's not much of a tripwire. The truth is, it broke his heart to kill the pig, loved it like a boy loves a dog, but thought it was a better way than what the pigs, I mean the Fed, would do to it. And as far as the FBI, look, I never did a noble thing in my life, and I don't know why I'm starting now, but I like Sal and I want to help him, so on the trail I left a lot of clues to make the FBI think it was me that took the pig, and they bought it. They're not chasing Sal anymore;

they're chasing me. They think I still have the pig. All I need to do is leave a little note to them at the first trail registry south of here and they'll pass right over you, Sal and this town. It's me they want now, and that's how I want it. He'd never stand a chance against them. I guess those oaths we take stick more than we know. Now is the time for all good men…"

Micki shook her head. "No. See? You're dragging me back in! Enough! Now leave me alone! Look, I'm all backed up here." She waved at the hikers waiting to order, then swiped a dime tip off the counter. "Yep, I'm raking it in! That guy here just wants toast. Sergeant Peppers over there, just one scrambled egg, and the one abusing my jon right now just wants hash browns, no onions, like anybody puts onions in hash browns. Meantime, I guess I've got windfalls like this." She picked my ten-dollar bill up off the floor and stuffed it into her apron. "And fugitive pig-killing tripwires."

I pointed at my money in her apron. "I'll take three cheeseburgers for the cause," I said. "To go. Then you can keep the change."

"In that case, you're in room eight, two flights up through that door there."

"I don't need…"

The cereal slurper choked.

"No. What you 'don't need' is a damn key. Just stay to your own stuff and they'll stay to theirs. Nobody bothers anybody here! What kind of place do you think I'm running? Key! These burgers will take fifteen." She banged a cylinder of frozen beef on the counter. "Make that twenty."

I waved surrender and made my way to the door upstairs, doing math in my head as I went. The next six to eight hours should be free of threats, I calculated. It should be that long before SmackSpecter realized we slipped by, circled his car back to the Ashfield Road to catch our scent again, chased the spaniel-pig prints down the trail until they disappeared, and then aimed his car south to cut us off elsewhere, likely here.

Getting Sal set to throw his block couldn't come soon enough, and neither could my commandeering of Plato's car. The chances of sustained freedom hinged on my using these hours to burn off my scent, and that would take miles, hundreds of miles.

Behind the door leading upstairs was an ornate staircase. Three stories of dizzying balusters rose from a chipping checkered linoleum floor to a patch of rain-stained ceiling forty feet above. As I circled, a door above slammed and the floor creaked with deliberate steps, as if a brewery ghost were leaving a barmaid's chamber.

Huck and Otterface laughed over the rail.

"You coming up for the first time?"

I wobbled the newel post. "Will it hold?"

"Not sure about that, but we've got to see this, don't we, Jim? We've got to see the look on this man's face when he beholds the opulence of the Royle for the first time."

"Sure is nothing like the first time," Otterface concurred. "C'mon up. We'll wait for you."

The temperature rose as each step sagged. Schoolboy snickers grew.

"Now, whatever you do," Huck snorted as I hit the landing. "Do not judge this resort by its beautiful staircase."

The sweltering hallway held seven mismatched doors, some chipped brown, revealing white, others chipped white, revealing brown. Some had no paint at all. The doors shared only the styling of their numbers, hand-drawn in a lefty slant in green marker.

At the end of the hall, breezes wheezed through a crack, nudging the dangling lightbulb. Mated to its socket, heavy orange extension cords raced to each room to power clanging hassock fans and shadeless floor lamps.

"I think Micki assigned me this one," I yelled over the clanging, pointing to the number eight, entering the room and adding under my breath at seeing its condition, "As if I needed another reason to head out."

"Now, I know what you're thinking," Huck said, "you're thinking, there's no way you can run this fan *and* read by those lights at the same time without tripping the circuit. Well, I wouldn't worry about that." He opened a small metal door in the hall to reveal a carriage bolt substituting for a fuse.

"Oh, sure, it ain't to code," Otterface acknowledged, "but it keeps the juice flowing. We know. We had your suite last night. Stole some more fans from one empty, a few more lights from another to clean some gear, had cords going every which way, and the fuse bolt *still* held! Oh, and in case you couldn't tell, this is a bed. Check it out!"

The headboard was thick with many coats of the same paint flaking from the doors and sealing the lone window. Springless, the thin mattress folded like an upholstered taco shell. "Relax," he said, depressing its two inches of foam. "At least she can't sag, right? And look," he spread the mattress, then let it recoil. "When you're done with her, she folds herself up automatically! Now that's convenient! But before you repose, check out the bath."

The slippery tub was of another century, its rust ring circling halfway up the enamel like the stain of an Old Testament tide. Locking pliers substituted for a broken faucet handle, and a brick stood in for a missing clawfoot. I thought of Grunt and wondered how he would react to learn someone beat him to it. From the tub's spout snaked a five-foot length of garden hose, strengthened in spots with knobs of electrician's tape.

"I see why you changed floors," I groaned.

"Oh, this ain't why. *That* is." Otterface looked up at the ceiling where a plastic bag swelled with dripping water. "She fills up about every two hours, depending on how many times we flush up there. You have to empty it like a colostomy. Stand back!" He pushed me playfully. "But it's not *all* bad," he continued. "You can get to the porch from this floor." Huck waved me to the end of the hall through a door where the tang of fresh blacktop rolled by on waves of heat. Picking decaying wood from the railing, I said, "I think it's safer out here."

"Yes, and if it's as warm as last night, you'll have plenty of company," Huck replied.

"I'm not staying."

From the corner of the veranda, I surveyed the length of Market Street and pinned the smell of blacktop to an orange-vested crew five blocks up wind. Down Market, plastic signs above the papered storefronts yellowed like old blisters. A pawnshop/check-cashing/currency exchange lit up the corner with hope for anyone wanting out. A banner in its window read, "Open 365 days a year, or by appointment." I did math in my head, but chose not to figure that out. Next to it was a post office in case anyone reached back. While I was never so inclined, my attention went back to Sal.

"Appreciate the tour, but I need to get with Micki on something."

I returned to Plato's car with the burgers to find our gear on the grass and Plato revving the Buick's engine, anxious to leave. Sal ignored him, as if it had been going on a while.

"Where the hell are you going?" I asked.

Plato stripped the burger from my hand and put the car in drive. "Birnam Wood hath come to Dunsinane!"

"Duncannon," Sal corrected.

Plato wore the look of an original joke fallen flat. "Yes, and I must leave before the cliché of Duncannon stains me in perpetuity! Adios, gentlemen!"

And before I could yell, "Wait!" Before I could rethink my plan to the Keys. Before I could smash the Buick's windshield with a thrown rock, Plato squealed out of sight.

"Have you won the heart and minds of the locals, Corman?" Sal asked.

"Chipping away, sir!"

I threw his burger as hard as I could. He pinned it against his ribs.

Chapter 22

The Royle was dotted with hikers now. They sat with legs extended and shoulders stretched against chair backs in modest comfort, sipping, waiting for something sizzling on the grill.

I followed the sizzle. Micki slung a dollop of Crisco and without looking up said, "You know, I wasn't always caked with grease."

She turned to face me, cheeks glistening. All I saw was the "after" and Peace Grease.

"Bituminous didn't seem to mind," I said, averting my eyes.

"Yeah, like I needed one more boy to look after. Throw me that towel." She scrubbed at her cheeks. The sheen remained. "That fool said if I ever changed my mind, he was heading to the Rockies and I could meet him there. Imagine! And then he only gets as far as Palmerton! Scratch off one more option for me, huh?"

"Can we talk about Sal?"

"You were over there together? 'Nam?"

"Not together. Met in Chicago. Anyway, I need to help him."

"Is he…?" Micki tapped her finger to her temple.

"It's more like he's on the other side of the mirror or something. And he has this problem with trust."

"Great, 'cause what I need is more paranoia around here."

"No, he has way too much of it. Wears it all over his sleeve. It's unshakable. It's exhausting. Maybe you two are alike, huh?"

Micki shook her braids. "Don't you dare!"

"No? Look around, this whole place is built on too much trust. Those Canadian dollars are coming any day now, right? Right? Well, Sal's the same way."

"I know they're not coming."

"No, you don't. And you can't, otherwise how could you get up in the morning and do this again? But that's why I know Sal can count on you."

She said nothing.

"I need to get out of here today," I said. "Without Sal. Time is everything."

"Look who's got misplaced faith now! It's Labor Day. The truckers are all home. Nobody's heading out today."

"But you'll take him?"

She led me to the back door. I sensed a speech coming and again tried to head it off, this time with something called empathy. Not my best suit.

"I know," I said, hinting I understood her.

"You know nothing! Listen, you're a vet, pledged some shit in your high school gym you wish you hadn't, I get it. But you wouldn't be here seeking *my* help without some acknowledgement of what needs to happen now, right? We've got to stop feeding the machine, right? What if somebody threw a war and nobody came, right? That's what we do here, we starve the machine. We're like a hub on the Underground Railroad, for Christ's sake. You know that? You do? And yet you draw the 'masta' here without thinking that maybe what this place does is slightly more important than you outrunning your boogeyman? Yes,

yes, we have friends here in town, a lot of folks looking out for us, but there's a never-ending lynch mob storming these barracks, which, in case you forgot, has a goddamn six-percent mortgage!"

I tried again. "Micki, I know it's sticky."

"Sticky? That's the best you've got, *sticky*? What are we, at Makeout Point or something? The things we do here require constant defending, you damn fool. Did you think about what happens if they shut this place down? Did you? Sixty kids a month and my six-percent mortgage get spooned right into that machine. That's what! And while I might occasionally dream about it all washing into the river, I can't take that chance."

I squinted. She threw her head in disgust.

I summoned empathy again, like a guy who keeps pulling the trigger on an empty gun. "Micki, we're both in this."

"There's no we!"

She jammed a plastic pitcher into a cupboard stuffed with other plastic pitchers, took an audible breath, and turned. "See that shed on the back line? The guy you're dumping on me can stay there until I'm sure he's not a tripwire and no one's chasing him. But he's got to stay out of sight, and quiet. It'll be hot in there, no electricity, no plumbing. I'll leave him food and water on the step when I can. That's the best I can do."

I expected the credits to roll on her speech and stepped out the back. But when she continued, it occurred to me that she was preaching to the choir, and I laughed. Every once in a while, something strikes me.

"I'm not God!" she said, like God. "I can't help you all! I have to choose. And I can't take a hit for everyone. If the government comes sniffing around here, I'll turn your Sal in as a stowaway without so much as blinking. I've got to save this place."

Sal was standing in the shade of a large tree, leaning against its bark, finger coiled to flick an ant off his leg.

"Hotel's full," I announced. "But I got Micki to offer you private quarters for the time being. You'll be staying there," I motioned to the shed, "until a room opens up. " I held my pointing arm up through his long empty pause. "Okay?"

"You book me in a jungle box and ask if everything is okay? Let's see, Corman, which is it? Fatally hot or blindingly dark?"

And it was both.

Warped on its hinges, the plywood door closed at a slight angle to the opening, allowing an obtuse triangle of light to enter at the top. Inside, the heated smells of damp earth and plastic tarp shaded the musk of accumulating mouse shit and moldering houseplants. The floor, elevated a foot off the ground by hollow cinderblock, promised a highway for any number of nighttime vermin. Butting up to the back of the shed and giving the vermin cover was a field of waist-high weeds that ran clear to the back road. Field of High Weeds, I named it. (Sioux!)

"Do these quarters befit the guardian of the President, Corman?"

I reminded him the pig was dead.

Sal cowered at my honesty, wedging his back into the shed's darkest corner and leaving only the glisten of his eyes to speak to.

But he did not slump in the corner long. Soon, an uppercut of his emerging clarity sent me reeling, even if it was off-subject.

"You insist on concealing your once-upon-a-time, Corman, but it is surfacing whether you want it to. Your decision to leave the President and me after Palmerton came too easy, with none of the torment you should have felt because you've done it before, have you not? Yes, I just felt your flinch, Corman, even here in the dark."

I shoved the door open and, though resolved to run, wobbled on ground suddenly soft. If this was how we parted, so be it. I tried. I tried with you too, Lieut! I did! But you can only lean up and in so far before the eyes are too close. We've been through this so many goddamn times. Aren't you tired of me saying it? Aren't you tired of asking me to?

Micki was standing between the Royle and the shed, watching me stagger. She snapped a newspaper in her hand as I steadied up near her. The headline was one word: "Subpoena!"

"You?" I asked.

"No, Abbie, Jerry, some of the others, Chicago, next week. Here." She tried to hand me the paper, but I wasn't interested. I waved it off in silence because words just beget more words. "You don't care? Well, for your information, it seems Daley is intent on making his charge of 'inciting riot' stick. Abbie's paranoia is playing out after all. He was *always* being followed, set up, something; just ask him. Couldn't sit without his back to the wall. But now it turns out to be true! Ever hear of COINTELPRO?"

"What-?" I took the paper from her and started to read.

"Co-in-tel-pro," she said, "and there's nothing in *there* about it. Completely covert. Then last year, one of their operatives jumped ship and spilled his guts to the college paper in Ann Arbor, wanted to atone, he said, for being played twice by the government."

I shrugged, but I didn't mean it. The atoner from Ann Arbor's subsequent disappearance underscored the Bureau's omerta (Italian!) code: Like the mob, you talk, you disappear. Everyone understood that. That's why SmackSpecter couldn't look away, and why I couldn't stop moving.

"Atone," she continued, "for being played to go to war against Vietnam, and then by the same government, to go to war against the kids here."

No time was a good time for reflection, now in particular.

"You really don't care, do you?" Micki said.

"I care about getting a ride. Any chance…"

"Zero. I'm taking too big a chance already. Your best bet might be after 3:00 when the bar fills."

It was a little before 1:00.

"Two more hours? I guess it's a good thing I'm not being chased or anything. I'm going upstairs to hose myself off, catch some of that tropical box fan breeze, and put my head down for an hour."

"Do yourself a favor before you start counting palm trees. There's a bag in the ceiling."

I sprawled on the taco bed to keep the edges flat, hair wet from the hose. The fan threw a breeze where I couldn't feel it, low across the floor. In the heat, I wrestled with an insistent fly and a gnawing urge to think back through things. I hated to reflect. Who did I think I was?

Okay, I got played for a fool like the Fed in Ann Arbor, but my only sins were this poor choice of hotel and a need to, what, take a stand in the guts of something bigger than me, while it swallowed?

Who did I think I was? But that's how I saw it: I was Gepetto screaming from the inside, "Shoot the whale!"

See, you can't make sense of stuff like this, because there's no sense in it. This is what reflection brings. I learned years ago not to seek my own motivation. What is it you said, Lieut? I'm not here to think, I'm here to do, so don't think another thought?

All I needed was to stop tossing. All I needed was clarity of thought. I rolled onto my stomach in annoyance and was reminded by the lump there that clarity remained taped to my chest. I flipped onto my back and brought my hand to the envelope of smack, but even with all my voices screaming, I knew there might still be need for a quick, painless way out, and I couldn't take the chance of falling a dose short.

Chapter 23

Awakening to brain fuzz and the clanging of the indignant fan, I bolted from the bed, the mattress snapping closed behind me. What time? What day? Chased! Rides missed? Sal. Damn! Not what you think; I just needed to know Sal didn't run off, didn't leave me as the sole scent behind.

I raced down the stairs, balusters clicking, treads squeaking, full boisterous bar staring back at my clamor. I found Sal in the shed where I'd left him, propped in the corner like a casualty awaiting angels. His miner's lamp was on and lit, and he held the open sketchpad before his face, staring. I followed the light as he turned his head.

"Do you recall, Corman, what it was like for the ground to dissolve? Remember what happened to the ones who fought against it?"

"The same that happens if you don't."

"Yes. It was a thing you couldn't get out of alone. That was how I felt all the time, without her; the ground gone beneath me, and alone." Sal flipped the pages and I saw for the first time the evolution of his sketch, the way he captured what got revealed the night before in available space between other sketches. Get it down before it was gone. On one page in one corner, the general outline of lips, smudged.

Near it but alone, the lobe of an outsized ear, and strands of hair that stopped abruptly as if the ends were split into a separate dream.

Turns the page to a "U" or a "V", which I took to be a chin, and aside it the shading of a nose below the circles of cheeks.

Turns the page to the rise of the cheeks, a study of the philtrum (Greek!) the cleft in the upper lip, and a tight, almost Mona Lisa squeeze to the mouth, as if it were built more for sarcasm than kisses. I wondered how Sal reacted as he drew it. I'd had terse kisses. They always came as a surprise. Was it like that for him? Did I care about it?

Turns the page, and the brow curved beside a frantic sketch of a sinewy neck, as if the owner were yelling and the artist pressed for time. I wondered if it were drawn that morning in Chicago, when time Sal's time was compressed as he sought the whereabouts of the pig. I imagined him tormented but called to duty.

Turns the page, and alone, with detail not captured in her other elements, are the eyes I'd seen at the dawn of their founding, but I am really seeing them for the first time, and they are not soft eyes, they are doubting eyes as if she desires another spin of the bottle. But they are honest eyes, and they are eyes I've seen unsketched before.

Sal pauses his page-flipping and moves his lamp to a dark corner.

"Why are you showing me this?"

"Because you kept us safe. And I want you to know something of her before you leave."

I let the fact that I stuffed him with heroin dissolve within me. But it was nice to have his misplaced faith to work with again.

"I cannot see the future, Corman, but I believe tomorrow will be the end. She will be whole then, and I'm scared that I won't wake up to know her anymore, and that my dreams will then be of other things, Corman, bad things maybe. It seems that I'm always losing her, and this will just be another way."

I felt compelled to tell him that this was the way of the world, that lovers always get revealed over time to everyone, whether dawn girls or real: first her laugh, then her tits, then her dreams, then her meatloaf, and then her intolerance for your growing dispassion. Until one day it's all been revealed and it snaps back and she begins to leave, maybe because you were too red together. But why tell him? Who did I think I was?

"But she's beautiful, Corman, is she not?"

"Remarkable," I said, pointing at the pages of disembodied parts. "When…?"

"She's back here." Sal motioned to the back of the pad where he'd assembled the pieces. "And tomorrow I may see the all of her, Corman. And I would share that with you, so that you may know her too." He grew sullen. "But it's clear your plans are otherwise."

And with a nod, I left him to it.

The bar was full of locals blaspheming Nixon and his campaign promises to end the war.

"Party's just getting started," Micki called over the chatter.

"Interesting crowd," I said.

"Small town, we gotta pretend to get along here." Behind the bar was a small stool. Micki dragged it with her foot, then stood to violently clang a bell jutting from the top shelf. The floor went silent. "This is a tip bell," she snarled. "I ring it whenever I get a tip. I better be ringing the shit out of this bell tonight or I'll pass the phone every time your wives call. Now, while I have your attention, a friend of mine here's looking for a ride south. Kind of an emergency. Who can help him?"

The argument about Nixon resumed with greater volume.

Micki shrugged. "This is what they do, squabble. Pullman over there, yep, the really loud one with his chest out, he's certain Humphrey will drop the bomb."

"Great."

"No, no. He thinks that's a good thing! He's voting for him because of it! What, you don't believe me? Go ahead, whisper 'peace-with-honor' to him and watch what happens. And Brooks in the Tabasco cap over there shaking the cigarette machine, he's got a seventeen-year-old kid, you'd think if anyone here wanted us out, but I wouldn't whisper 'peace' to him either. He's petrified McCarthy's going to win and just pull the plug on the whole damn war! Make us a laughingstock! Promises to kill himself twice a night 'cause this country's gone soft and it ain't his anymore. Of course he's quick to point out, he would have killed himself if Bobby made it, too. And then we got Pinto over there on the last stool, smoking, our local 'pharmaceutical entrepreneur', hash mostly. Whatever it is, he's against it. Just screams 'bullshit' every once in a while and goes back to his beer. Welcome to my sideshow."

"And yet a guy like me can't get a ride?"

"Trust me, by the time their wives drag them out of here, you wouldn't want to be in a car with them anyway. Truckers should start moving tomorrow, after the parade. Meantime, what can I get you?"

"I'll take a couple of beers up to the veranda. I can watch the streets from there."

"See that? What other hotel gives you a tree stand for six bucks a night?"

"I'll need something for Sal, too."

I took a grilled cheese and root beer out to the shed. Sal was still thumbing his sketchpad. We didn't say a word.

On the veranda, Otterface and Huck sat in the sun with a half depleted bottle of whiskey giggling like schoolboys, which they practically were. I started to leave, pissed off at how crowded the place was getting already when my attention was drawn to a weathered box of abandoned gear: a latrine shovel, K-rations, canteen, tent stakes, jungle juice, a nest of bug netting and for some reason a government pamphlet on VD.

"Hiker's exchange," Huck explained, struggling to his feet. "Take what you need, deposit what you don't. Ham salad?" He offered me one of his K-Rations.

"I've had my fill," I said without thinking, pushing his hand away. "Know anyone with a car here? Got a bit of an emergency back home."

"You've been over there?" Otterface asked.

Damn it.

"Is it as bad as they say? Women? Kids?"

"What?"

"Sorry, man. I didn't, it's just, well…I'm going to be nineteen. That's all."

"You're dodging?" I asked.

Huck stepped between us, chest inflated. "No, he ain't dodging. He hasn't even been called yet! It's just this fool got married."

"Yeah, you told me this already."

"But I didn't tell you he up and married our local talent. Married her because he thought that would keep him out of the draft, get a deferment, only as everybody else knows, Uncle Sam doesn't play that game anymore. Married or not, your number still goes in the hat."

"You better not have touched her!" Otterface screamed.

"Everyone touched her, you idiot! Except you, maybe! And now I'm marching you north to freedom, aren't I?"

Otterface pushed Huck away. "Some guys survive being over there, right?" He studied the latrine shovel. "I mean, you did, right?"

"Survive?"

"Well, you're here!"

"This is surviving?" I waved my hands at the crumbling façade and the tumbling town. But in the distance where the blacktop crew was calling it a day, and the shadows of the houses stretched, I could see the three traffic lights running up Market. They turned green at the same time. It was beautiful, as if to say not everything was spinning out of control, and I found some comfort in it until a Duncannon

Police car split the yellows, sirens on, rushing toward the Royle, and instinct pushed me back into the shadows.

"But you're back," Otterface continued over the sirens as they faded down toward the highway.

What could I tell him, that no one comes back? That nobody comes out who they were? That who I was when I went in and who I am now wouldn't recognize each other at a wake?

"Look," I said, pinching the bottle from his hand. "You'll settle in. It gets a little easier once you learn the Law of War Numbers."

The light dimmed in Otterface's eyes. "But I'm no good at math."

"Yeah, well, you get good in a hurry," I said. "Because as long as you can still count, it was the other guy whose number was up."

Their wide and dilated eyes told me I'd killed their buzz. I thought I could get it back. I put my finger in Otterface's chest and cleared my throat for a Lieut accent, but it was mine that made it through. "And *no* songs, new guy! Keep the girl out of your head! You need to be watching the ground for wires, fucking new guy! You can't allow some hairspray memory to ambush you, not when you married the local talent, even if she has red hair! Not when you're up to your waist in shit water. Not when the ground is sliding. Not when you can smell Charlie hiding in the reeds. Not ever. All it takes to waste you or the guy next to you is misting-the-fuck-up or lifting your eyes for one second! You know how many legs danced their last time 'cause of memories of prom songs? That's when Betty blows and the guy who was beside you –."

"Hey—Hey, you okay?"

Twisting my feet to firm my footing, I scanned the street and focused. With a chuckle, I slapped my hand on Otterface's shoulder and nodded. "Keep your eyes on the damn ground!"

He forced a smile.

"And you've got an even chance."

Back in my room the clanging of the fan was good company. I unfolded the mattress to wait out the hours. Above the toilet, the bag dripped.

Chapter 24

Up the stairs and through the hall came the mad scraping and tumbling of barstools and the buzz of many voices. I sat up with what I'm sure was a dumbass look on my face and imagined all the wives having arrived to chase their drunken men home. A second later, Otterface fell through my door.

"Cops," he wheezed, leaning back into the hall. "Got everyone up against the wall. It's like a raid or something. Not sure who they're looking for. They cleared me, but Jesus."

From the base of the stairs came a command. "This is the Pennsylvania State Police. You are ordered to remain in your rooms!"

"Clear?" I whispered, pointing to the hall. Otterface barely had time to nod when I blew by him, pack in tow, out to the veranda. Below, lights swirled as they did that night behind the line of Chicago Snapjaw. One, two, seven cop cars! State cops, county cops, village cops, mall cops! Each car empty, each with their doors open, running, not even a sentry! If only the Fed was this stupid. The village car caught my eye, but I knew the beating that would bring. I shook the railing for a firm section, flipped over, dangling, feet aimed between two cop cars a story above the ground. I felt the top railing sag and shimmied my hands down to the bottom one, closing the distance between me and concussion by three feet, which was critical since I hit the ground as if my parachute failed to open, crashing on my pack but missing the cars. My ankles rang from the fall, but nothing splintered.

My first step was toward the back of the Royle and the shed, but I caught myself. "No. It's time you threw me that block, Sal," I said aloud for some reason, then redirected beyond the streetlamps, past the blocks of cube houses, to the unlit U-Haul lot where a fleet of trucks nosed against the curb. The tailgates to the cargo hulls were never locked on those things and I slid beneath one in the middle, careful not to let it latch from the outside, fearful its light would leak and give me away. I lit my miner's lamp just long enough to make sure I was alone, then slid to the back corner.

There in the dark, the cargo hull was hot and as empty as my stomach. I wished I'd kept some of the Palmerton rations. I wished I'd taken the ham salad MRE from Huck. I wished I'd helped myself to part of Sal's damn grilled cheese before delivering it. But I found the crumbs of my Gorp in my pack pocket and savored them off the tip of my wet finger.

My pack made a lousy pillow, but I decided to keep my bedroll secure in case I needed to fly in a hurry. There was a long and beautiful silence, broken only by the occasional hum of tires. But the rain came again, slowly at first, just a ping on the metal roof, then another, soft and soothing, then a shower, then a deluge that wet the roads and made the tires loud. There was no wind, so the rain held its drum roll tempo, orderly like the traffic lights down Market and comforting in an unwanted way. But the rain always makes you miss something, as if its sole purpose is to remind you of the empty distance between things. I always hated that about the rain.

Before long, the rain was winning and got me yearning, for what I didn't know. Was it SOFA and the way she and her blue streak committed so fully to me with a set of keys of my own? I wondered again what had become of her. Was she waiting for me at the diner, the way a sailor's wife awaits a spot on the horizon? Had she been violated there, on blocks, tires missing? Had she been rounded up by the Fed and impounded like a Hooverville hooker?

Or perhaps I yearned for pizza and its orange grease because I was starving and Gorp crumbs only get you so far. I could taste it. I could imagine its glow on my fingers, which was good because I didn't want to overcomplicate this yearning thing or overthink it or even succumb to it. But that damn rhythm of the rain and its unrelenting current toward reflection swirled me into a hole, fighting for air. And when I came up, I was reflecting on whether it was it the other half of me I missed.

I wanted to sleep and escape it that way, but feared it would only rise in my dreams, like lips or eyes, and I would be trapped again by it, commanded by it. It was a living thing now, a thing needing to be fed like some Roger (no relation) Corman carnivorous plant, sucking out my life to preserve its own. And it would surely eat me. Right, Lieut? Kind of funny? All we can hope when the end comes is not to get eaten, yet look at you, and now look at me.

But feed this thing *what*?

Was it not enough that I was shaking, or that I was on the run, curling up in the corner of a U-Haul in darkness? What else could it possibly want from me? Contrition? For what, taking you out, Lieut? I wasn't sorry and I couldn't fake it, not any more than I could fake a love of kittens.

So, if not contrition, then what? I had nothing to feed it, nothing to offer. Should I heal something? I never healed anything in my life. Should I do something noble? Like what, walk an old lady across the street? Tuck in a homeless guy? As if any of that would change anything. And if this night was to be the long-avoided comforting of you while you died, then count me out. What was I to do? Hold up your head? Hold back your hair like a drunken prom date, only to hear we were just too red together? See your eyes ask, "What did you do?"

I reached over to shake him for an answer, but recoiled. I didn't want to see those glossy eyes again. Instead, I lit the miner's lamp and, holding it in my hand, illuminated the right side of my face. I clicked the lamp off, then on, then off and on, creating a fleeting fuzzy silhouette on the ribbed wall of the truck. The irony occurred to me that I was in a way exposing myself to myself for those seconds at a time, and just how fucked up that was. I retreated back to my options.

I could expose the Fed, but that wouldn't change anything either. Grunt screwed that up. The untimely death of the pig (and its hideous but telling New Jersey) killed my evidence of the FBI pig-switch. All I had now was a half-empty envelope of heroin that, let's face it, did nothing but indict me. I could see it now: "Hey, *New York Times*! Here's your scoop! See this plain white envelope with $30,000 worth of heroin in it? The FBI gave it to me, no, COINTELPRO gave it to me, to plant on Rubin and Hoffman in order to send them away for life and fatally disrupt the hippies' antiwar movement. And this is only half of it! Run *that* above the fold! What's that? The other half? Did I use the rest? No, but I did apply it. See, there was this guy and pig and they were pretty broken up inside on account of cop beatings, but I needed them to hike mountains with their shattered ribs to help me set up a deal with the Fed, so I applied the smack to their food as a sort of field homeopathy to kill the pain. Hell? Yeah, I know, but I was going there long before this. What is it Lieut said: "On the road to redemption, I'm nothing but a pelt, just one less squirrel in Swellsville."

Right, Lieut?

I knew when you made me pledge that night (laying on me that you had a boy) that it had nothing to do with the Law of War Numbers getting me. You just wanted to break me and make me one of you, who saw it all in numbers, not in flesh. You were either going to break me, or put me in the numerator, Lieut. Isn't that right? So I pledged, the way I always pledge, to get away from something. And even that wasn't enough to take you out. You made me swear to carry your parts out so the pigs didn't get you. And none of it was anything but you trying to break me like everybody else. When that Betty blew and I wore the pulp of your legs fifty feet in front of you, splattered like a fleshy Rorschach, I didn't stop to wonder what I saw. I heard only ringing and the pledge you made me take, 'cause you had a boy, remember? And that was on me.

I kept my pledge, but didn't know the limits. I didn't know yours, and I didn't know mine. And as I leaned in and your eyes rolled so glassy with that look that says, "What did you do?" I again did not stop to wonder what I saw. I did not stop, and as we know, nothing ends until someone stops, right, Sal?

I don't reflect, Lieut, you knew that, but I do remember, so when your eyes asked "Why?" I wasn't inclined to find out. I ran east, leaving the knife and you behind. I don't pray, you knew that too, but I do sometimes, in moments of weakness and hope, and sometimes I hope the others found you, knife up and in before the pigs, before your second greatest fear came to be. They showed me otherwise, but I've got to figure they tricked up that picture just to break me too, like you, to get me to agree to a fucking jam like the one I'm in now back here, Lieut. They had me, they had the knife, but they always think they have to break you too. It's what you all do. And look at me now. You broke me, all right. I'm not sorry. I was following orders. And it was a boar, Lieut, and you knew it, but you were gonna pop my cherry one way or another. Yes, I was just following orders.

It was a long night and a lot of time to spend with a dead guy. But after a while, when the rain finally stopped, Lieut turned away. "I am still here with you, Boot," he whispered in reassurance.

"Not any more," I said.

I let the hours pass as they were always meant to, in silence. But it was his lingering words that kept me there in the truck, kept me from using the night the way I was always meant to, dodging the rain, dodging the lights, snaking south toward the Keys.

And so I fought sleep by thumbing the corner of the envelope strapped to my chest, watching the motionless Lieut, staring into the back of his head as I waited for the cargo hull to warm in the sun, a sure sign the night was ending, allowing us to move on or, more to the point, me.

But like so many things I fought, I lost. How long I slept I do not know, but not long. My brain was fuzzed again and my ankles hummed. My sleep had been brief and interrupted. Still, as I rolled over, Lieut was gone. I reached to where he'd lain and felt along the metal floor. It was cool, and I fought the need to draw a conclusion from coolness or reflect on coolness because the rest of the hull was warming and my watch read 5:30 and when I eased the tailgate up the dawn was breaking and my stomach was growling. I briefly wondered about the Royle and how it had fared through the raid, but mostly wondered if Micki was busy firing up the grill.

Yes, it was hunger and *not* a need to know about Sal that drew me back to the Royle. If he had successfully thrown his block and if he pushed SmackSpecter off my trail, Sal was in a cell someplace if he wasn't dead, sketching and completing Geneva if he kept possession of his pad.

I did some math in my head. That was a lot of ifs, but none more unsettling than the idea that Sal might have lost his pad to SmackSpecter, and might have lost his only chance to finish his girl. But who could dwell on that on an empty stomach? I charted a course through the village toward the Royle and its wafting bacon smell, zagging for cover, trashcan-to-trashcan, spooking raccoons at their feasts.

I dropped my pack in the Field of High Weeds and swung around the back of the Royle where little residue from the armies of the night remained. I went first to the shed for confirmation that Sal took the fall. A tray of dry eggs on the step seemed to confirm that he had. With a lift in my step, I stepped over the eggs to be sure. Peering through the door's wide gap, I found him sitting in the middle of the floor, miner's lamp on but dimmed by a weakened battery.

I stifled the word *Fuck*.

Sal was sketching, flipping from pages of parts to the page of the whole. He was building her, tuning her piece by piece.

I thought of just leaving him to it, writing off my faith in him as a short-term loss. Who was the one of misplaced trust now? But with my eye pressed against the opening and a sweating palm pressed to my chest, I pushed against the door. It was locked. I growled his name.

"Softer," he said, I was sure, to himself. "Softer."

"Sal."

Nothing.

Micki watched me as I moved toward the empty counter. Her braids snaked out of a dishtowel kerchief.

"Word must be out on your eggs," I joked, waving at the empty room.

"It'll fill for the parade," she said. But there was something else on her mind, and she was clearly readying a speech she'd been preparing on the outside chance she saw me again. I scrambled to head it off.

"That was something last night, huh?"

"Don't even think about it," she said, pushing me back to the door. "I *told* you not to bring your shit on me! I *told* you that what we're doing here matters much more than you, and what do you do? You not only bring it, but you run when it comes! Leaving me hanging!"

"Run? I was here," I swore. "They got me upstairs, asked me a few questions and told me to get out. So I did. What would you have me do? Jesus, I spent the night in the back of a U-Haul!"

"What did you tell them?"

"What could I tell them? There's nothing to tell!"

"Well, let's see. I guess you could have told them what you told me, that the guy collecting feet was only a figment of your friend's imagination, or guilt or something. That's what you told me, just a figment. Only it turns out to be true! Your figment is armed to the teeth, and he's out to kill somebody!"

Wait, I thought, were they looking for Grunt, not me?

"So now they're going to shut down the trail, flush out as many boys as they can, run checks on every one, and feed them back into the machine. Every cop for three counties will be posted, and they're running a real dragnet! Stuff cops around here haven't done since moonshine. Sending three troopers up the trail from here, and another three down from Delaware Water Gap to corner this guy if they don't catch him on the road. This will be great for business, all right! No hikers, no dodgers. The blessings just keep rolling my way, don't they? You included! What else aren't you telling me?"

"I was as surprised as you. You have to admit, it's kind of hard to believe, a guy collecting feet, don't you think?"

Micki shook her head, but not at the question. Her speech was about to get back on track, replete with more of those verbal ellipses she loved so much.

"Last night was just the kind of night that gets me shut down and you just keep playing these games, telling me half the truth. You're telling me halves, half the story, half the truth! Well, half the damn truth will trip us up! Thank *God* we didn't have any dodgers in here last night. Two weeks ago they'd of rounded up twenty. As it was they took those two kids Huck and Jim through a ringer, kept them interrogated until the draft registry cleared them early this morning. But it could have been otherwise. It could have been the end for twenty or more, and the end of me! Now, I want the truth. *All* of it! But just the relevant stuff. I'm not a shrink. I don't deal in feelings."

Me neither.

"And I don't want to know you piss the bed, even if it was mine in number eight!"

Wait.

"Just the whole pertinent truth!"

I took a breath, more to stall then to begin, but it didn't matter. I had misjudged her; she still wasn't done. She had a rousing dismount planned and she was intent on sticking it. "And I'm not God," she continued. "I am not God! Quit thinking I'm God, all of you!" She paused awkwardly to acknowledge I was the only one there, but the line was written. "I can't help you all! I have to choose, and I choose truth!"

She pushed me to the door again. I took it as a sign she was finally finished.

"Micki, last night, when the cops broke into my room, my first thought was of Sal and that they were here to collect him and the pig, the evidence, Micki, which I already told you about. Remember? And that was the whole truth, or at least I thought it was. Look, when Sal told me about this tripwire that killed his pig, at the same time Sal is trying to outrun the feds, and I never saw him, and we were together all the time, well, you know what? Forget it. I only came back for some eggs."

"Back? No one comes back."

"Well, I did. I told you I spent the night in the back of a U-Haul! I could have kept going, *should* have kept going, but all I could think about was you making me some of those famous eggs I read so much about in the trail logs."

"Bullshit."

"You know, when the government sticks you eight thousand miles from home just so they can watch you die, all you think about is eggs, bacon, and a little rye toast if you have it."

"Eggs'll cost you twenty. I want you out of the hotel. You can have the shed with your friend, but that's all. And I want you both out of here by this time tomorrow."

I started to object, then questioned why, since I was leaving after eggs anyway. A hiker stumbled in, dropping a hollow pack. He was fit, as if he'd just logged a thousand trail miles, and irritatingly polite with his ma'am's and sir's.

"Pitcher?" Micki asked.

He groaned, rubbing the notch of his stomach. "Water's good, ma'am."

"Breakfast?"

"Maybe just chips right now, ma'am. Something salty." He pressed his stomach again.

"And I suppose you want a window seat for the parade for that?" Micki groaned.

He caught her sarcasm. "I know, been dreaming of this all the way down, ma'am, saved my first real off-the-trail meal for here. But I'm still looking forward to a sizzling shower to boil seven hundred miles of dirt off me."

Micki saw my eyes roll and scowled back.

"I know it's Labor Day and all and that I didn't reserve a room, but if you've got one for me then it's all good, as perfect as they wrote it was." He waved at the dining room. "Lots of chatter about your place in the logs. And you too. It's Micki, right?"

"That's me, 'chips no breakfast' Micki!"

Again, he pressed his stomach, this time like he was trying to move it from one side to the other. It rumbled. "Sorry about that, ma'am, I don't know if I caught some kind of bug…"

"This just gets better by the minute," Micki interrupted.

"…or if this murder's just got me all in knots, but I don't think I could hold anything down right now."

"Murder?" Micki exclaimed before I could.

"Yes, ma'am. You didn't hear? Sometime after midnight, I guess, based on the questions the police were asking me. Up near Pine Grove."

Micki gasped.

"How far is that?" I asked.

"Fifty, sir."

I did math in my head. If it was Grunt's work (and of course it was), he covered sixty miles in a single day, a pace that would have been unfathomable if I'd not seen him do it near Ashfield Road. And that would put him in Duncannon by nightfall. So much for Kryptonite. Clearly the roads weren't slowing him down, let alone stopping him, not the small ones anyway.

Micki peppered the irritating hiker with questions, keeping him talking about how he didn't know who it was that got killed, and no, he had no guesses either. I could see Micki doing math too, accounting for her dodgers, their hour of departure, their pace, and their calculated proximity to the scene. There was an unscripted fear on her face that hardened her tempered lines a bit.

"All they told me, ma'am, sir, was to hitch around to Duncannon and pick up the trail here. So I did. Suppose they'll be some more rockhoppers behind me soon."

I looked at my watch. 7:15.

On cue, the metallic slap of pack frame on tile spun our heads toward the door. The hiker trudged to the bar.

"A pitcher."

"Coming from the north?" Micki asked.

"I've answered those questions already. All I want right now is beer and not to be bothered. That's what bars are for, right? Beer and no bother?" Micki arched an eyebrow. He picked two tens from his wallet. "This one's for the beer. This one for 'No bother.'" Micki's eyebrow relaxed to a flutter.

Car doors slammed and the Royle's squeaked open, setting off the air conditioner before it was really ready. Two more displaced hikers took seats, faces firm. Micki waved empty mugs. They nodded.

Before long, the bar grew congested with odors and speculation. It was the government asserting control. It was the mafia asserting control. It was the world spinning out of control.

But most agreed they'd heard some "facts" from the cops. The victim was male.

The victim was shot. The victim was shot in a parked car at the trailhead. Wait: *The victim was shot in a parked car at the trailhead?*

"With an arrow?" I asked.

"Yeah," the hiker who wanted no bother said, "with an arrow, and through a windshield. Because that happens a lot."

OK, so it wasn't an arrow, but the math still gave me hope. I backed into a stool, sending it wobbling into another. Could it be? Could the casualty be SmackSpecter? Had forces finally tilted my way in a sort of glorious anti-karma? My smile was met with collective derision. My drum roll on the bar fared no better.

"Don't you see," I said to Micki, thinking quickly, "this means the victim's not one of your kids." Micki allowed her arms to fall to her sides, relaxing the bar as she did. She ran a few private calculations. I did some of my own. Grunt had taken my clue from the registry and run with it. Ha! "Sneak." "Hightops." Ha! It was brilliant, and he got it all! But more remarkable was that he found, identified, and eliminated SmackSpecter all within a day's time. You had to marvel at his efficiency.

"This is good news," I declared.

"You're still leaving," Micki directed with a pointed finger. "I don't know how you're responsible for this, but I know it didn't happen without you. Something tells me shit like this has been following you for awhile, and just you being here is putting my place in jeopardy."

She clunked down a tray of scrambled eggs, their deep unnatural yellow hinting of an origin earlier in the week. "This is for all the liars out back. Your last meal," she said.

I grabbed two glasses of water off an abandoned table and made my way to the door with a lightness the eggs did not share. With Grunt about to be cornered and SmackSpecter dead, I was, for the moment, free. Of course, the Bureau would send others. I was still their mess to clean up, but my run to the Keys was now wide open.

Chapter 25

I carried the tray to the shed, eyes bobbing on the clinking water glasses in the creasing middle. Sal heard them.

"Leave!" he ordered.

I kicked the door open anyway. Water splashed onto the eggs. It didn't help.

On his back, Sal breathed heavily, the palm of his hand shielding his eyes from the daylight, sketchpad unfolded face down on the floor an arm's length away. He showed no interest in the floating eggs or in me.

"Is she done?" I asked, closing the door and darkening the shed again. I bent to pick up the sketchpad. Sal threw his hand on top.

"I think SmackSpecter is dead," I said.

Nothing.

"And Grunt did it."

Nothing.

I swallowed slowly to gain time, but Sal stole it.

"I searched for you last night," he said.

"I was detained."

"Just to know if you were gone. And you were."

What was his point? "If I'm right," I said, "and SmackSpecter is dead, it wont be long before they flush Grunt out too. They're squeezing him as we speak from the north and the south. In a few hours it'll be over, Sal. You're free."

"Nothing ends until someone stops, Corman. Grunt will not be taken back. And if they come for me, to take me back, I will not be taken either. And so you see, it continues."

At this thought, I faked a bleak moment of silence. Sal stole that too.

"And you *were* gone, Corman."

Now it was Sal missing the point! Yes, gone, but back! Back to tell him about SmackSpecter. Back to tell him about Grunt. Back to bring him semi-reconstituted eggs. Back to tell him he was free! I could have kept away and left Sal to stay in the shed until somehow, someone told him what had happened. Weeks, maybe! But I didn't. I came back.

He was unmoved (he didn't even blink), so I built a stronger argument, listing the ways he was free. Free to raise political pigs. Free to be alone with his paper doll. Free to let me be free!

But this argument collided with his same indifference. Somehow, like a stammering pitchman hawking fruit dehydrators, I just couldn't get it to add up for him. This is precisely why I made it a rule never to do math for others, or aloud.

That said, I accept that maybe my argument failed because my sincerity lacked a certain sincerity, because I knew Sal had always been free and because, if_I reflected, I'd know that I was trying to make these events about him when they were really about me, how I just wanted to buy a little bit of peace as I walked away. But I don't reflect, so instead I motioned to the pad and changed the narrative.

"I came back, Sal, because you promised to introduce us."

This, Sal registered. With pronounced hesitation, his hand slid to the edge of the pad and I couldn't be sure if the look on his face was one of fear or one of hope. Did he fear that she wouldn't meet my expectations? Did he hope I too would think her beautiful? Weren't these essentially the same? This was the problem with Sal; no matter how you read him, it was the same thing! He riffled the pages like the shuffling of a deck of cards, stalling, maybe wishing I would just reach down and grab the pad to take the onus from him. I did reach down, but only as far as his shoulder. I let my hand sit there still for a moment, much longer than I intended, but when I felt his breath steady beneath it, it was just as easy to leave it there than move it. That is, until Micki burst in unannounced, filling the room with blinding daylight and condescension, her Peace Grease gleaming where the light bounced off it.

"Come see your handiwork," she barked, nodding to recognize Sal squinting on the floor. "You too. They've got it all on TV. They're taking out the dead body and are closing in on your 'figment'."

Sal spoke from behind a shielding hand again, one eye closed, the other squinting. He couldn't see her in the bright light. "Grunt will never let them take him, and I'm not going either."

(Jesus, Sal, she's going to break into a speech! See!)

"I don't care where you go," Micki snapped, "or what rock you end up living under, you're just not staying here and screwing this up. Look, you don't know me from Eve and I'm sorry about everything that ever happened over there, but one thing I know is the war gets us all, just in different ways."

(I told you, Sal!)

"You and he got broken. Okay, I get it. But I'm going broke. There, we all have broke in common. So if you'll excuse me, I still have a little work to do here because they keep throwing boys into this grinder, and I got a mortgage."

As Micki stepped close to punctuate her position, she blocked the blinding light from the door. Sal lowered his hand and stood slowly, eyes locked on her face as if he were trying to understand a cloud. Micki slid back, spooked, but Sal slid with her and pressed his fingers on her face, swept his thumb across her cheek as if softening a charcoal line. Micki slapped it away, then poised herself to slap the rest of him. As Sal backed off, she backed out of the door, yelling, "I said, no tripwires! I want both of you out of here!"

The door slammed behind her but then eased open a few inches, throwing the shed into dusk. Sal was still in the corner, but had turned to face it.

"Sal."

His reflex of silence was getting old. I came up behind him and tried to turn him with my hands on his shoulders for the second time in an hour, but I left them there.

"Can it be, Corman?" Sal finally said into the corner. "I've never thought it. I've never dared wish it or think it or pray it. Even in our once-upon-a-time, who could allow himself that?" Sal's shoulders relaxed, an invite to try to turn him again. I did and found tears coursing. He stepped to the pad and stood over it, staring down. "I've never thought it." He flipped the pad's pages to the back and pushed the completed portrait of his long-dreamt dawn girl toward me, a portrait of Micki!

What does a guy say except, "Holy shit!"

"Yes, Corman." Sal was crying with delight. "Yes, it confirms what you have refused to accept: you are a healer, Corman. You have brought me to Duncannon so that I might find her here. I never even prayed it, but here she is and you brought me."

Sal tilted the portrait toward the light, illuminating all its detail. The braids of his dawn girl pulled tight against a worried forehead before falling over value-sized ears. Her eyes seemed to be preparing her lips to parse words, but more yours than hers. I was no judge of these things, but it seemed to me Sal had not sketched Micki as much as captured her. "She is beautiful, is she not?" he asked.

"Yes, Sal," I said, shaking my head.

Then Sal's mood changed quickly. He exercised it by pacing. "But what does this mean, Corman? What happens now? Do I have to share her? Have I already?"

I shrugged. What did I know? Who did I think I was? Besides, the sliding of Sal's shoe soles across the unplaned planks of the floor was monumentally distracting, and I couldn't really focus.

"Does she know me, Corman, the way I know her? She didn't seem to. But the light is not good here. Have I come to her in dreams as she came to me, a ghost, a passing memory? I don't think I can share her, Corman. I don't know how to share. I never planned to. I just never, because who would? Who could? Yet I don't know, Corman, what if, I mean, what if she refuses me because I was broken? What woman wants a broken man? I just never thought it, that Gen-, Gen-, Gen–"

"Micki," I advised, dropping his needle past the scratch.

"That she would have to approve of me. But she is beautiful, Corman, isn't she? Beautiful here," he pointed to the pad. "And beautiful there." He waved at the Royle.

I nodded. Sal stood still, his damn enthusiasm waning once more.

"I did wonder what she might be like, Corman, not look like, *be* like. Once I allowed myself to wonder what was inside her, if she sang, how she laughed, would she like to hold hands, could she love a broken man? And it was so good." His mood flipped again. "But she's not what I imagined. I imagined her soft and kind and," he rubbed his cheek with the back of his hand. "I don't know, less shiny."

I snorted, but Sal didn't hear it. He was too busy swinging his mood back to euphoric.

"But perhaps she's a little broken, too, Corman. Perhaps like you and I did, together, she and I make a whole!" His mood fell. "But what do I do now?"

Seriously? Sal wanted me to play Cupid? Grunt was a better pick for that, plus he had a bow. Yet without dismissing the astronomical odds against Micki and the dawn girl being one and the same, I had to recognize that unfathomable shit like this happens. Once, back in Ohio before I was too red, I cut a Christmas ornament out of construction paper, folding it and nipping it with a confidence that hid the truth, the truth that I had no idea what I was doing or what would become of it. I just nipped away, and as red paper flakes snowed to the floor, I found the eyes of classmates settling upon me to witness whatever sordid creation my scissors and I gave birth to. (I had a certain reputation of crossing the line.) Anticipation built, and with great drama I unfolded to everyone's amazement, my own included, a perfect replica of Saturn, rings and all. Yes, it had nothing to do with Christmas, and it's true that Saturn is a stupid planet, but there it was, and I had no idea how. The thing is, unexplained shit happens all the time. What it means, I don't know.

Sal was back at it. "Should I talk to her? Maybe show her? But what if she doesn't like it? What if she gets mean again?"

"Sal!"

"I know, Corman, I'm acting like an insufferable schoolboy."

"Insufferable is a big word," I smirked, but I was only half-listening. I was calculating whether this development was narrowing my path to the Keys, but I couldn't see it. If anything there should be less gravity now to hold me. Unless, that is, Micki acted like Micki and threw Sal and his pad to the curb while I was still in Duncannon. My urgency to leave awakened.

Sal resumed his pacing, swinging his moods around circular arguments. I was more interested in the news of SmackSpecter and Grunt and in finding a ride out.

"I'm going back," I said. Somehow Sal read this as an invitation.

"I'm not ready, Corman. I'm not ready to see her. "

I recognized many of the locals throwing elbows at hikers beneath the flickering black-and-white TV. Micki stood back, watching from a distance. Her eyes slid to the side when she sensed me staring at her. It was uncomfortable for both of us, but mostly me, knowing what

I knew. I was mentally able to place Sal's portrait of her next to the real face; the resemblance was eerie, right down to the Peace Grease behind her ear. Micki ended my study with a flick of her middle finger before receding to the kitchen. I moved my attention to the TV. The locals focused their debates not on the war, but on the likely impact of the murder on their town.

"This will change everything," Pullman raged. "Everything about Duncannon."

"Everything that ain't changed already, you mean!" someone said, maybe Brooks.

"Bullll-shit," Pinto challenged, holding the two l's for one beat too many. "Nothing ever changes here!"

"We'll get changed by it," Pullman declared. "And it didn't even happen here!"

"You gonna lock your doors now? Huh? No, you ain't!"

"Shut up! Look! They're pulling the body out!"

Two EMTs rolled a gurney from the back of an ambulance. I pushed forward, squinting for any clue. And then I got one.

"It's a hiker!" another hiker gasped.

Micki came out of the kitchen. "Are you sure?"

My question exactly, but my darting eyes answered it for themselves. Dangling from the bottom of the coroner's sheet were two feet, and the heavy lugs on their soles told me everything I needed to know: That my faith in anti-karma had been misplaced, that my day was about to get worse, that my path to the Keys was closing, and that SmackSpecter was still alive.

"Shut up and listen! Looks like they got the guy who did it pinned down near Table Rock!"

The TV news cut to a woman reporter. She stood too close to the camera and spoke into a heavy microphone that obscured a good amount of her face. The word "live" pulsed across her chest, then disappeared. The camera backed up. She gestured to the ridge behind her. Dog teams yowled on leashes. Cops tilted their hats forward. Someone in the bar offered that it was like a scene from "The Fugitive", and it was.

"Ev-er-y-thing gonna change!"

"Shut up! Listen!" Brooks yelled.

But I'd heard all I needed to. Sal knew how this would end for Grunt, and so did I. Grunt was coming off that ridge in a bag.

The TV news switched back to the morgue, where an official announced they had not yet identified the victim, a white guy with out-of-state plates, thirty to thirty-five. I wondered why Grunt would kill a random guy sleeping in his car. Did he mistake him for SmackSpecter? Did he miss my clues? Did he misread the out-of-state plates? Or was his urge to "even it up some" so strong he just needed to feed it someone, like that flesh-eating plant?

I looked at my watch. Eleven-thirty. The morning was disappearing, and I had loose ends to tie up before I could head out, things I'd been thinking about lately and now decided to do.

But once again, the world didn't give a shit what I decided to do. The paradiddle of a single snare drum was all it took to yank everyone away from the TV and send them scrambling for position on the sidewalk. A murder was one thing, but a parade was something else.

With neckerchiefs cinched in studious knots and merit badges sewn with precision, Webelo Troop Forty-Four led the parade down Market Street in a formation of circling cardboard tanks. Behind them, fire engines blared like they were clearing the way. Young Republicans skipped Nixon buttons through the stilts of a balloon-tying Uncle Sam. Bagpipes screeched like they knew how I felt. A bedsheet painted with 'P.O.W.' flapped from a second story lintel while below it, as if on cue, the Women's Auxiliary snap-leveled a banner announcing the county's Oldest Living Vet. He rode shotgun in an open-topped jeep and never moved his head from forward. Men on the sidewalk removed their hats anyway.

Sponsored by the steel mill, a reluctant River Queen waved from her castle of chickenwire and tissue. The crowd jostled to see her, bumping me. I spun to confront someone breathing on me. It was Sal. He was clapping to the piper band. He was scanning the crowd.

"She's inside," I said, speaking of Micki.

Sal's head drooped, but popped back up to clap for the middle school's marching band playing a Rolling Stones song in nothing but sharp whole notes. They marched in a strange sequence, tapping one foot four times to the ground before lifting the other, potentially delaying the back half of the parade through Thanksgiving, until mercifully the base drums of the IBEW shoved them along. The crowd roared and roared again when the Teamsters appeared balancing on a fleet of flatbed trucks. When the flatbeds crawled to absorb the adoration, two hippies darted from an alley and taped "WDWYFW!" signs to their bumpers. "We Don't Want Your Fucking War," someone advised. Corralled by Local 492, the hippies were never seen again.

And then the parade was over. Sal stayed as the others left.

"I don't think Shriners do encores," I said, heading back.

Sal was in deep thought and, while he knew what he needed to do, that didn't make it any easier.

"Go on!" I said, nudging him back to the bar and Micki.

"But what if..." he started again.

"I don't know," I growled, "But what if?"

That's the point we'd gotten to: finishing each other's sentences. If I needed another solid reason to leave Sal and Duncannon behind, this would do.

Sal followed. The bar sagged again with locals gluing their eyes to the TV.

"Write it down!" someone said. "Here's my prediction! This killer will turn out to be some vet! Sure, hiss all you want, but I keep telling you these kids coming back are fucked up. They just can't handle it the way we did."

"He's only broken," Sal said.

"Ain't nobody I know broken by Korea! Nobody in the parade sayin' 'Look at me, I got broke by Guadalcanal'".

The bar laughed. Micki appeared from the kitchen to see what the joke was about. Sal didn't see her.

"Right? Was the ol' man in the jeep broken? Ninety? Broken? I don't think so, son! 'Broken'? What shit is that?"

"Broken!" Sal said again.

I caught Micki's eyeroll. She threw a towel across her shoulder and stomped over.

"I told you I want you gone, both of you! You've had your last meal here."

Sal turned to her and stared. Micki raised the back of her hand.

"We're not doing this again, Tripwire! Stop staring."

While Sal pretended to read the menu board above her head, I offered an explanation to her by way of, "He thinks he knows you."

"Like hell he does," she said.

"Tell her, Sal."

Sal's lips quivered. There were words there and I gave him room to get them out. As his eyes slowly fell back upon Micki, he steadied his lips and tapped the menu board and asked, "Is the spaghetti here from a can?"

"Are you staring at me?" Micki snapped. "Knock it off!"

Sal dropped his eyes to the bar's old brass footrail.

Without him seeing, I put fifty dollars on the bar.

Micki softened, picked it up, spread the bills into a fan, then threw them at my face. "Everything here is from a can," she sort of growled.

"Then I'll have that." Sal said.

Micki softened again and seemed to stay there. "That's good," she said to Sal before holding up a can and announcing to the bar, "Loves his canned spaghetti! Now this is a man after my own heart!"

Sensing his own path clear, Sal smiled, leaned in, and said, "That I am."

Micki pushed him back and waved a fist toward me as if to repeat, "No tripwire shit!" She spun the can of spaghetti on the metal counter until getting the opener to hold, twice looking back at Sal to assess. Who could blame her as she moved quickly to kill the whole awkward moment, stabbing the opened can at the air repeatedly as if air were flesh, stabbing until a reluctant cylinder of pasty orange *fflumped* into the pot? She shook her braids as she stirred it. Sal had something to say, but waited for the headshaking to end before easing toward her. I couldn't see Sal's face, but I could read Micki's lips. I did some math in my head. The sum wasn't good.

"You want to show me something? In the shed? Just you and me?" Micki wrapped a cloth around the hot pot handle and wristed the spaghetti into the garbage. "What am I, in sixth grade, going to fall for that? Get out!"

Sal looked to me for answers, but the math in my head said this was his own "too red together" moment. What did I know about fixing that? Who did I think I was? All I knew was I needed to keep my path to the Keys open. My clock was ticking, SmackSpecter's footsteps were gaining, and I had all those loose ends to tie up, which I could not do until I knew Sal was staying in Duncannon. Against my better judgment, I approached Micki as she banged the pot and her words against the trash pail.

"Suppose, you, want, me, in, the, shed, to, show, me, some, thing, too?" she metered. It was actually more annoying than that toe-tapping whole note marching band.

"No. But I've seen what Sal has to share with you. And who do I think I am, but maybe you should go. Maybe it means something."

Micki threw her head back at my dimness. "So then… does it mean anything to you?"

Poor Sal, I thought. Did he calculate the length and peril of this "till death do we part" tour of duty? Did he adequately multiply the time he'd lose being hung up in ellipses? Did he subtract what must be extracted from him to endure a lifetime of speeches and well-schooled probing questions? And had he calculated the addition of her subtraction, which I was rapidly leaning towards? In other words, did he do the damn math?

"No," I said, "but do you want me to come with you?"

Micki pulled her apron off with a spousal sense of affront. "I can handle myself." She turned to Sal. "This better not be a fucking trick. And I'm only going because I haven't seen anything new since I bought this place, so don't be thinking its otherwise! What are you grimacing about?"

Sal's face scrunched with fear and resignation. He looked at me as if to say, She was supposed to be sweeter, but he voiced, "You coming, Corman?"

"No," I said. "It's all you from here, Sal. Besides, I need to see a horse about the horse." I smirked at my own inside joke and clever play on words. It was like naming things, which I liked to do.

"That's not how that saying goes," Micki mocked.

I rubbed my chest. "Yes, it is."

***

I returned to the bar an hour later with a pack on my back and a ride to the Virginia line, bought and paid for in a series of transactions behind the 365-day (or by appointment!) pawn shop/check cashing/currency exchange. Pinto was alone and waiting and pulling himself a draft in Micki's absence.

"Let's go now," I said.

I pulled from my wallet the curling strip of pig pictures I'd taken at the rest area what seemed like weeks ago when my plans still rang clever. I tucked them beneath a coaster on the bar and looked around. I could have waited for Sal, or I guess I could have banged on the shed to tell him, but Micki's absence from the bar told me his personal loose end was likely being tied at that moment and he'd be staying in Duncannon for a while.

Besides, who did I think I was?

Aftermath

And so now you know, Sal, as you requested, the "whole truth" as I remember it, though I can't imagine it matters. With so many questions, I have to wonder if the smack I fed you reset your clarity for good.

As for the wad of Canadian dollars mailed to Micki, well, there are several million Canadians, Sal, so who can be sure who sent it all, but yes, some came from me. But Jesus, don't do what you always do and misread this as a healing thing! It was not. I just couldn't carry the smack anymore where I was going, not without flinching every time I got hassled for hitchhiking. And yes, Pinto was happy to broker the deal, for a cut of course.

So it's clear now, right? I never healed anything. Even when I sent those Canadian dollars to Micki to pay off her mortgage, courtesy of "Your most thankful dodger" I didn't do it to confirm for her that her faith was well placed. I did it to break the money trail because greenbacks can be traced, Canadian Loonies cannot, not with so many getting caught in American vending machines and all.

Sure, I guess I expected the money to help you too, but who'd have guessed that Micki would use it to pack up, leave you, and move to Saskatchewan? Who moves to Canada unless they have to, Sal? Their flag is so deciduous! And so red! What nation chooses a symbol that falls blood-red to the ground every year by the billions? We are the Eagle, Sal. They are the Leaf. Count your blessings.

And to be clear, there was nothing weak like kindness involved when I sent those dollars. And I guess that's the point, because I don't love much, Sal, but I do love irony, I do love the things that are never supposed to happen but do. Think of it: I sold the Bureau's heroin/smack/horse, which they meant to use to cleanse the world of hippies, sold it to pay off the mortgage for a woman who *harbored* hippie draft dodgers, only for her to use it to close shop and move to Canada, leaving a loving American vet alone with his sketchpad again. I trust your dreams have resumed.

Am I making a speech? Well, there's one for you, Sal.

As for me, I can't come out there with you yet. I've got to keep this going until I don't have to anymore. Besides, your Rockies are cold and the fish there are small.

The End

Continue reading!

Want to know more of what becomes of Sal and Corman? Treat yourself to the hilarious and poignant coming of age novel, *Last Stop, Ronkonkoma.*

Last Stop, Ronkonkoma is available in hardcover and paperback from your favorite local independent bookstore, Amazon, or direct from the author's website, www.fredjschneider.com.

eBook available on Amazon, Apple, and Smashwords.

For readings and updates, or to yell at the author:
www.fredjschneider.com

Media inquiries, or to *really* yell at the author:
Email info@glimmerglasspublishing.com

Acknowledgements

All the girls in my life: my wife Robin and daughters Summer and Casey, for their years of support.

All the folks at Colgate University Writers Conference for their work-shopping and guidance, especially Brock Clarke, who shook me pretty hard to get this ready, when I thought it already was.

Loren Shoemaker for pushing me forward for thirty years.

To my beta readers: Thank you.

To the late Abbie Hoffman and Jerry Rubin, without whom none of this could have been inspired.

Sam Wildman and that ghost ship, *Congo Lust*

About the author:

A retired humor essayist on Public Radio and author of *Last Stop Ronkonkoma* Fred J Schneider makes his home in New York with his wife Robin. During the horrific age of disco, when its insipid mirrored ball spellbound half the country, he raged against the machine, quixotically paying homage to the, alas, all-too-mortal, Jerry Rubin and Abbie Hoffman. It was useless, it was expensive, and it disappointed his parents, yet even today, embers burn.

Follow Fred at www.glimmerglasspublishing.com, www.fredjschneider.com, or on Facebook @fredjschneider.com

CPSIA information can be obtained
at www.ICGtesting.com
Printed in the USA
BVHW031514180419
545862BV00001B/1/P

9 781732 951815